JOURNEY'S END

Also by Josephine Cox

QUEENIE'S STORY
Her Father's Sins
Let Loose the Tigers

THE EMMA GRADY TRILOGY
Outcast
Alley Urchin
Vagabonds

Angels Cry Sometimes
Take This Woman
Whistledown Woman
Don't Cry Alone
Jessica's Girl
Nobody's Darling
Born to Serve
More than Riches
A Little Badness
Living a Lie
The Devil You Know
A Time for Us
Cradle of Thorns
Miss You Forever
Love Me or Leave Me
Tomorrow the World
The Gilded Cage
Somewhere, Someday
Rainbow Days
Looking Back
Let It Shine

The Woman Who Left
Jinnie

Bad Boy Jack
The Beachcomber
Lovers and Liars
Live the Dream
The Journey

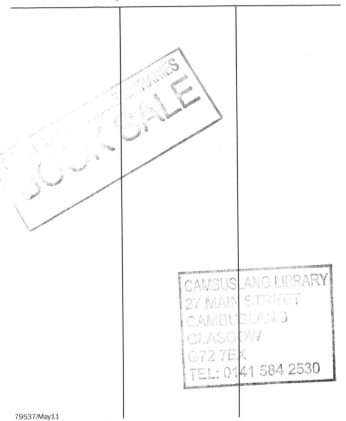

JOSEPHINE COX

~

Journey's End

HarperCollins*Publishers*

This novel is entirely a work of fiction.
The names, characters and incidents portrayed in it are
the work of the author's imagination. Any resemblance to
actual persons, living or dead, events or localities is
entirely coincidental.

HarperCollins*Publishers*
77–85 Fulham Palace Road,
Hammersmith, London W6 8JB

www.harpercollins.co.uk

Published by HarperCollins*Publishers* 2006
4

A catalogue record for this book
is available from the British Library

ISBN-13: 978 0 00 714617 8
ISBN-10: 0 00 714617 5

Typeset in New Baskerville by
Rowland Phototypesetting Ltd, Bury St Edmunds, Suffolk

Printed and bound in Great Britain by
Clays Ltd, St Ives plc

This book is for my Ken as always

Once in a while we are blessed with the friendship and love of someone who is uniquely special. When I was an infant and my mother gave birth to her fifth baby boy, I loved him from the moment I saw him; as we all did. She named him William, but he was always known to us as Billy.

Small and sturdy, with the funniest, most mischievous little smile, he was a rascal from the start. He grew up to be a fine man, with high principles and a fierce passion for family. He was at times infuriating, aggravating, bossy, but immensely lovable. He was our Billy, one of us and we all respected and loved him, without reservation.

A short time ago we celebrated his sixtieth birthday; it was a wonderful evening, with everyone there and our Billy in the midst of it all, laughing, teasing, innocently flirting, showing off his beloved grandchildren and happy to be with family and friends.

A short time later, he fell ill and, with very little warning, was all too quickly gone from us. With the memories of his birthday party still strong in our minds, we found ourselves mourning the loss of a much loved and very precious man.

God bless you, Billy boy, and keep you safe until we meet again. We'll talk about you and love you, and keep you proud in our hearts.

Most of all, we'll miss you desperately, our one and only Billy. There will never again be anyone like you.

CONTENTS

PART ONE

Late March, 1954

The Telling

Salford, Bedfordshire

CHAPTER ONE

S HE WOKE WITH a cry. It was the same dream as before – the same place, the same faces, the same jolt of terror; real in her dream, real in her life. Would it never leave her be?

The sweat dripping down her temples and her whole body trembling, she clambered out of bed and went to the window, where for a moment she stood, regaining her composure, collecting her senses.

Drawing back the curtains, she peered into the darkness, thick and impenetrable, like the deepest recesses of her mind. Dismissing the nightmare, she returned to the question that tormented her.

Should she tell? Would it destroy lives and minds? Would they hate her or, as she desperately hoped, would they thank her? But then, why would they thank her when the news she had to reveal was so unbearably cruel?

'Dear God, give me the courage to do what's right,' she prayed.

Maybe it would be better if the truth was never told. Yet that would be the coward's way out, and she might be many things, but Lucy Baker was no coward.

She glanced at the clock; it was five minutes past three – another day beginning. Taking her robe from the back of the chair, she slipped into it and sat on the edge of the bed, where she remained for a time. She sighed, a long, broken sigh. 'Oh, my dearest Barney, my joy, my life.' There was a murmuring of guilt, but never regret. 'I loved you then, and I love you still.'

Barney had been her only true love, and it was a love all-consuming, all-powerful. There was no way to describe how much she missed him. No words. Only memories.

The smile slipped away and in its place came a look of hatred.

While Barney had brought her joy, *Edward Trent had brought her tragedy.*

'Edward Trent . . . *monster*!' Her mouth curled with loathing, she spat out his name as though it was tainted with poison. His wickedness had caused such pain; she would carry the burden of it for the rest of her days.

Lucy was no stranger to nightmares. A thousand times, she had awoken terrified and sobbing, reliving the night when Edward Trent had kidnapped her little son Jamie, and caused him to drown.

In the sorrowful years that followed, Trent had haunted her every waking and sleeping hour. In the daytime she would be in the middle of a mundane task, like washing the dishes or drawing the curtains, and suddenly he was gnawing at her mind until she could hardly think straight. Then at night came the dreams which left her breathless and shaking. Eventually, over the past twenty and more years, she had grown used to them. Like the hatred, they had become part of her life.

In the dreams it was always the same: the darkness, the water, and the chase . . . that unforgettable chase, ending in such horror.

This time though, the dream had been different. There was no frantic chase, no rushing water as it tumbled downstream, tugging at her ankles and throwing her off-balance; there wasn't even the soul-wrenching sound of her child crying. This dream was like nothing she had ever experienced.

She had seen only his face, that swarthy, handsome face, his mouth frozen in an easy smile. Unlike before, he was not threatening her, nor was he reaching out. There was only the smile. And those mesmerising eyes, utterly chilling. And the silence – eerie, absolute.

'Take a hold of yourself, Lucy,' she said aloud. Grabbing the crumpled corner of the bedsheet, she wiped the sweat from her face. 'It was just a dream. *He* can't hurt you any more.' So many times she had tried to convince herself of that. Even so, the fear never went away.

It never would.

~

In the adjoining room, in that lazy space between sleeping and waking, Mary lay in her bed and listened. She heard her mother open the curtains, and she heard her muffled footsteps as they paced the floor. The young woman did not attempt to go in: she knew that Lucy would not want that. Instead, for the next hour, she lay waiting, the only sound the ticking of the clock.

This was not the first time she had heard her mother agitated, unable to sleep. The first time was many years ago, when she was just an infant. The sound of Lucy sobbing had disturbed her deeply. In her childish manner, Mary had gone to comfort her, but her mother sent her away. Since then, whenever she heard her mother weeping in the night, Mary would keep vigil, desperately hoping it would not be too long before her mother went back to sleep; as she always did.

Mary had known there was some secret torment in her

5

mother's past; some fearful thing that touched all of their lives in some way – herself, her mother, and Adam, that dear kind man who had always been there to protect them.

Only recently, Adam had taken it upon himself to tell the truth of what happened all those years ago. In the telling, he had betrayed Lucy's trust and broken his vow to his old friend Barney. At the time he believed it was for the best. Now, he was not so sure.

Mary was shaken to her roots by the story he told. Even now it was not ended. There were others who had to know: the ones who had gone away; the ones who had never known the truth of Barney Davidson's sacrifice.

In Mary's far-off memories, she recalled her father, Barney, who had died when she was a tiny girl. He had been a special kind of man, frail in body but powerful in spirit. She recalled how he would sit her on his knee and create magic through his vivid fairytales; he made her laugh with his comical mimicry, and sometimes when she woke crying, he would hold her up to the window and show her the stars and describe the beauty and wonder of the world they lived in. He told her she must never be afraid, because there would always be someone looking over her.

She loved him so much, and then he was gone, and their lives were never the same again.

When she was satisfied that her mother had gone back to sleep, Mary turned over and relaxed. Tomorrow, there would be no mention of this night. Mother and daughter would smile and chat, and talk of everything else, and it would be as though the nightmare had never happened. Because that was how Lucy wanted it.

CHAPTER TWO

BY HALF PAST eight, Lucy was out of her bed, washed and dressed and sprucing herself in the mirror. 'Not bad for an old 'un, if I say so myself!' Laying down the hairbrush, she ran her two hands through her short cap of greying hair, teased out a few stray curls and thought how, if it wasn't for the occasional lapse of memory and the age spots on the back of her hands, she could maybe pass for a young thing of fifty.

Sighing wistfully, she shook her head. 'Wish all you like, my girl,' she chided herself. 'It won't change the fact that you're past your prime, so stop fancying yourself in the mirror. Before you know it, the doctor will be here,' she frowned, 'not that you need him, because you don't – but it makes him feel wanted, so shift yourself, and be quick about it.'

She observed her image in the mirror. She did her best to keep what was left of her looks, but had not yet regained her strength since stumbling in the local churchyard a couple of years ago. The incident seemed to have sparked off a form of arthritis, but this was what you expected, wasn't it, at her age. You had to slow down, whether you wanted to, or not.

She gazed critically on herself; the skin was not as glowing as it used to be, and there appeared to be more of it which hung in little loose swathes round her neck, and there were lines round her eyes and mouth. But the small straight nose and heart-shaped face were still pretty, and the blue eyes as bright as ever. She had never been a beauty, that much was true, but she'd been better off than most women because, even though it was for a cruelly short time, she had had the love of a man like Barney Davidson.

Thoughts of her beloved overwhelmed her. She knew that Barney had never loved her as he had loved his wife, Vicky. In the end, Lucy may have filled his heart, but it was only ever Vicky who filled his soul.

Lifting the photograph from the dresser, she gazed down on herself and Barney, and the infant girl in his arms. It was a cherished picture, taken only a few months before Barney was lost to her, and even then, when the illness ravaged him, the goodness of the man, and his absolute joy of life shone out of his face – still a handsome face for all that.

Lucy choked back a sob. They had had so little time together, yet she thanked God for every second. They had shared everything – the anguish of seeing his wife and children leave him; the guilt and tears afterwards; the companionship between him and Lucy that grew into a kind of loving contentment, then the sheer joy and pride when Mary was born to them.

Through all the ups and downs of every passing day, they never forgot the others: Leonard Maitland, a man who had gone away knowing the truth, even though it meant he would never again have peace of mind, and Vicky and the children who had sailed with him, estranged from Barney and in total ignorance of the price he had paid for their new lives in America.

Lucy recalled the day when they left. 'There was no other way, Barney,' she murmured now. 'No other way . . .'

The loud spluttering of a car engine brought her hurrying to the window. 'Adam!' The brightness of a spring day was startling, and the skies above were blue and cloudless. For late March, it was unusually warm. 'Adam, what's going on?' she called down.

Covered in muck and oil, Adam was standing before the car in the drive of Knudsden House. He had the bonnet up and the starter-handle lodged into position.

'The damned thing's been playing up again,' he called back, 'and now it's completely given up the ghost. I've done what I can, but I reckon she'll need a new engine.' Diving his head under the bonnet again, he fiddled with a few nuts and bolts, before returning to swing the handle for the umpteenth time. There was a shuddering and a spluttering, and a shout of victory when he thought he'd done the trick, but then the engine fell silent again. 'It's no good.' Defeated, he gave a shake of the head. 'There's no spark at all now.'

Lucy shouted down: 'Leave it! Come inside . . . Come on.'

His heart warmed by the invitation, Adam waved up to her. 'I'll be there in a minute.'

Closing the window, Lucy smiled to herself. No spark, eh? She hoped the day never came when they said that about her! Life might be a bit more of a challenge these days and her health was not as robust as she would have liked, but by God, she wasn't done yet. Not by any means!

By the time Adam showed his face at the kitchen door, both Lucy and Mary were seated at the table, Lucy enjoying her eggs and bacon, and Mary toying with her scrambled eggs. 'Look at the state of you!' Pointing to Adam's mucky face and hands, Lucy asked him sternly: 'Have you had your breakfast?'

'Not yet, no.' Because the car had been playing up the previous day, he'd got out of his bed early this morning to work on the engine. 'There was no time for breakfast,' he explained. 'Two hours I messed about with that blessed machine this morning.' He groaned. 'I honestly thought I'd fixed it!'

Lucy felt as though she had known him forever. A loyal friend to them both, Adam Chives had been part of her life with Barney, and after Barney was gone, he had seen her through a bad time and remained ever close. Lucy had often wondered why he never married, until some time ago he confessed to her that she had always been the only woman he had ever truly loved.

Time and again Adam had asked her to be his wife and time and again she had gently refused. But knowing how persistent he was, Lucy was in no doubt that some time in the not too distant future, he was bound to try again.

Taking a gulp of her tea, Lucy discreetly regarded him. Homely, well-built, with thick greying hair and kind expressive eyes, Adam was an ordinary kind of man, but with an extraordinary sense of loyalty. When he made a friend it was a friend for life and when he fell in love, it was with heart and soul.

Over the years, Lucy had prayed that he might find a woman who would bring him the happiness he deserved; though in the beginning she had never believed it was herself he needed.

When some years ago, she expressed her hope that he might find a good woman to share his life, he told her he wanted no other wife but her. And that he would always be there for her as long as she needed him.

His confession had touched Lucy deeply.

'Right then, if you go and wash up,' she told him now, 'I'll see to your breakfast.'

'Thank you, Lucy, but no thanks!' Hungry though he was, he didn't want her fussing over him. 'I don't like to put you to any trouble, especially when you've got the doctor coming this morning.'

Brushing aside his protests, Lucy took another long gulp of her tea, before pushing back her chair and standing up. 'Breakfast will be ready when you are,' she assured him. 'And don't worry about the doctor. I can handle him.' She laughed. 'He seems a bit nervous of me. No sooner is he in the door than he's itching to get out again.'

'I'm not surprised. Poor devil!' Adam chuckled. 'I've seen how you boss him about.'

'Only when he tries to tell me what to do!' she retorted. 'I know I'm not as young and foolhardy as I once was; my bones ache like the devil and there are times when I want to run and can only shuffle. Some days it's like going through a fog . . . one minute it's clear as a bell and I can go forward, then the next I can't find an easy way and have to slow down.'

She smiled into his eyes. 'So you see, Adam, the bad times come and go, but I'm not bedridden yet, thank God. If I'm tired I rest, and if I feel all right I'll do whatever I please.' She gave a wry little smile. 'Either way, I expect I'll pop my clogs soon enough.'

Rolling his eyes to the ceiling, Adam gave a boot-deep sigh. 'You can't be serious for one minute, can you? Whatever will we do with you, eh?' He knew what *he'd* like to do. He'd like to sweep her into his arms and carry her off. But you didn't do that with Lucy. She was stubborn and a law unto herself. But that was the nature of her, and he would not have it any other way.

'And don't leave the sink with a rim of oil round it neither!' Lucy's voice sailed across the kitchen.

'Right, boss.' Bowing slightly, Adam gave a mock-servile tug of his forelock. 'I'll make sure I leave it ready for inspection.'

11

Having put the plug in the sink and taken the kettle from the hob, he began pouring the warm water into an enamel bowl. Looking over his shoulder with a cheeky wink, he made Lucy smile.

Through all this good-natured banter, Mary had remained silent, but now she told Adam, 'Best do as you're told. You know she'll examine your hands back and front before you're allowed to sit down – oh, and don't forget to wash behind your ears, or you'll be made to stand in the corner.'

Lucy wagged a finger. 'Behave yourself, young lady. I may be getting on a bit, and you a grown woman now, but I'm still capable of clipping your ear.'

Mary chuckled. 'I'm sure you are!'

At the sink, Adam took a moment to think. Getting on a bit? In his mind's eye he could see Lucy Baker, as she then was, as a young woman running barefoot across the fields, her long flowing locks lifted by the breeze, and on her face a smile bright and warm as a sunny morning. Sometimes, before the world was wide awake, when he was out walking across the headlands, he would see her by the river, seated on a fallen log with her feet dipped into the water. He had loved her then and knew how, for the remainder of his life, he would never love another woman. What he felt for Lucy was a love that would endure forever.

'Nay, you're far too full of yourself to ever get old,' he said cheekily.

'Well, thank you, Adam,' Lucy replied. 'I shall take that as a back-handed compliment, shall I – though I think you are seeing me through rose-coloured spectacles.' Something in his voice and the look in his eyes told Lucy that he might be ready to ask her again if she would marry him, and just for the briefest moment, her heart seemed to turn over.

'They say beautiful women never really know they're

beautiful,' he added softly. 'I reckon that's true where you're concerned.'

'Get away with you, you old flatterer!' Strangely embarrassed, she took a forkful of leftover egg and popped it into her mouth, and astonished Mary by blushing bright pink.

Graciously refusing Mary's offer to cook Adam's breakfast instead, Lucy threw two more rashers of bacon and some mushrooms into the pan. In no time at all, they were sizzling away.

A few moments later, having finished washing at the sink and making sure he'd wiped it round afterwards, Adam seated himself at the table, where his breakfast was put in front of him. 'Cor! Look at that – a real feast.' He hadn't realised how truly hungry he was until the aroma of hot food flooded his nostrils.

'Thank you, Lucy.' He turned to Mary with a wink. 'Your mother's not only beautiful, she's a good cook into the bargain.'

Lucy thought one fine compliment was enough in a day. 'Food is for eating,' she said, placing a platter of toast before him. 'So stop chatting and get it down you, before it goes cold.'

Smiling to herself at the way these two seemed to fit together like a hand in a glove, Mary was already getting out of her chair. 'I'll make some fresh tea.' She knew how much Adam loved her mother, and she also suspected that, although she didn't yet realise it, her mother had come to love him back.

Leaving them to talk, she took her time making the tea, while occasionally glancing at the two of them, now deep in conversation and looking for all the world like any other husband and wife; though they were neither of them ordinary. They were special, at least to her.

A short time later, having set them up with a fresh pot of tea, Mary excused herself. 'Ben will be here soon,' she explained. 'We're going into Shefford to look at a new tractor.'

'A new tractor, eh?' Lucy was delighted at how her daughter's friendship with Ben Morris, the owner of Far Crest Farm, had grown into a close and loving relationship. It had been her dearest wish for Mary to find a man who cared deeply for her, and she truly believed Ben to be that man.

'Talk of the devil, here he is now.' Adam looked out of the window and drew their attention to the dark-haired, good-looking man on his way up the drive; with his tall capable build and long, easy strides, he looked like a man who could handle whatever obstacles life put in his way.

A few years ago, emotionally and mentally drained by the break-up of his marriage, Ben had decided to uproot himself and build a whole new way of life. It was not an easy decision, but when he eventually moved to the area of South Bedfordshire, he kept in close touch with his only child, Abbie, who had a secretarial job in London and shared a flat there with friends.

On first arriving in Salford, Ben, a former architect knew next to nothing about farming. But thanks to his practical nature, and learning as he went, he now had a comfortable income and a way of life he couldn't have possibly ever imagined. And he had never been happier.

After the trauma and deceit that caused the end of his marriage to Pauline, he had not wanted another deep relationship. But then he met Lucy's daughter, Mary, and had soon come to realise that not all women were the same. Where his wife had been dominant and deceitful, Mary was kind and caring; though she did have a fiery side. Last summer while they were strolling across the fields, they saw a man kicking his dog, and before Ben could intervene, Mary had snatched the dog away and confronted the man with a passion.

This incident had only served to convince Ben that he was a fortunate man, because here was a woman he could trust and respect. And he had come to love her so much, it frightened him.

'BEN!' Knocking on the window, Adam hoped to catch his attention, but the younger man was already out of ear-shot. 'Don't you two go running off before I've had a chance to see him,' he said to Mary as she hurried from the room, 'I want to ask the lad if he'll have a look at the car. There's nothing I don't know about tractors, but I'm jiggered if I can fathom out what's wrong with this blessed car!'

He frowned. 'It starts then it dies away, coughing and spluttering. Ben knows his way round engines. With a bit of luck, he'll be able to make more sense out of that damned vehicle than I can.'

'Hey!' Lucy's voice followed them. 'That's quite enough of that cursing, if you don't mind.'

Half-turning, Adam gave another tug of his forelock. 'Sorry, boss,' he said nervously. 'I'll not do it again.'

Chuckling heartily, Lucy returned to her tea.

A few minutes later, when she started to clear away, a feeling of total exhaustion overwhelmed her. Sudden pains shot down the back of her neck, and her spine felt as though it was being squeezed. This had happened before; thankfully, the attack always passed, though lately the passing seemed to take longer.

Resting a moment to recover, she rolled up her sleeves and was soon up to the elbows in hot sudsy water. It was a hard thing to come to terms with, growing old, and she resented the years rolling away behind her. Life was too short, and love too fleeting.

She thought of Barney wistfully. She would never again hold his hand or experience that wonderful surge of joy as he slid his arm around her when she least expected it. Life could be so cruel. But she had Mary, and so she still had a part of Barney in her life.

Looking out of the window, she saw how content her daughter was. She saw Mary helping Ben off with his jacket, and she witnessed the way they briefly touched and held hands before he leaned into the car engine. They belonged together, Lucy had known that from the first minute she saw them together in St Andrew's churchyard all those months ago. That was why she had deliberately dropped her hand-bag there for Ben to find. When returning it to Lucy at her home, Knudsden House, he had met Mary again, and their romance had begun on that long, fateful night. And neither of them had ever suspected her part in it!

Ben reminded Lucy so much of Barney – oh, not in his physique, for Ben was taller and bigger-built than Barney and their colouring was different. But the essence of the man was the same; they each had a certain commanding presence. They smiled with their eyes and had that same kind of trustworthy, open nature.

Lucy's heart swelled with love as she gazed fondly on her daughter. Mary would never know how thankful she was that the girl had found someone she truly loved, and who loved her back in the same way.

She couldn't help but compare Mary and her sweetheart, to herself and Barney. She had loved her father in the same way the girl loved her Ben, deeply and without reservation.

She could see it all in her mind's eye – herself, Barney and Vicky, his true wife, soulmate, and the mother of his three other children. It was a devilish triangle, destined to torment them all, and Barney the unwilling centrepiece of a cruel game that no one could ever win.

She had often wondered what she could have done to save them all so much pain, and the answer was always the same: there was nothing. She could not have prevented what happened, at least not without hurting Barney, and she loved him so much she would gladly have died for him. God help her, she loved him still with every fibre of her being.

Her eyes swam with sadness as she followed Mary's every move. Oh, I don't fool myself, she thought, because even though for a glorious time we were together and you, my darling, were conceived out of love, your father was never really mine.

Barney *had* loved her, in his own way, but it was Vicky of whom he dreamed. Even after he had sent her away, she filled his heart and soul. Lucy had always understood: Barney and Vicky were made for each other, and Lucy could never take the other woman's place, nor would she want to. Vicky had been his first and only love . . . *just as you were mine*, she thought.

CHAPTER THREE

As LUCY CARRIED on rinsing the pots, dreaming quietly to herself, she heard Mary call out a greeting to someone. Lucy raised her gaze to see a familiar figure approaching up the path. 'Elsie!' Lucy was not expecting her so early.

Quickly now, she wiped her arms and rolled down her sleeves, and backing away from the sink, she sat at the table, for all the world as though she had been there all along.

As was her way, Elsie Langton burst in through the door like a wayward wind, her sharp eyes going straight to the sink, half-filled with sudsy water and the few plates resting on the wooden draining-board alongside.

'What's all this then?' she demanded, indignantly folding her arms. 'You've been washing up again, haven't yer? For heaven's sakes, can you never do as you're told and take it easy? What's more, I'd be obliged if you would stop doing my work. One fine day I'll come through that door and there you'll be, waiting with my pay packet and a "cheerio, how's yer father but I don't need yer any more". Then what will I do, eh? Tell me that if yer please!'

Lucy tutted impatiently. 'Don't talk so much nonsense, woman.' Clambering out of her chair, she confronted the little person with a sense of outrage. 'Anyway, who's in charge round here, you tell me that.'

19

As the bantering continued, Mary stood by the door, quietly amused. There was no harm in these fiery exchanges, she knew that. Her mother valued Elsie as part of the family. And as for the little woman herself, she was hardworking, funny and lovable, and totally devoted to Lucy; but when she had a bee in her bonnet she could be a real terrier.

'Out with it,' Elsie demanded grimly. 'What else have yer been up to? Sweeping the yard, taking down the curtains – what?'

With a measure of dignity, Lucy stood her ground. 'Just listen to yourself. You above all people should know I'm past doing those kind of things. Anyway, what if I *had* done everything you claim? It's my right. It's my house, isn't it?'

Exasperated, Elsie waggled her fat little head from side to side, which in turn wobbled the fat little shoulders. 'It's no use yer arguing with me,' she retorted. 'You had strict orders from the doctor . . . "gentle exercise and the occasional walk, as long as it's not too far", isn't that what the man said?'

Lucy glared at her. 'Good God, you make me sound like some poor old dog that needs to be put down!'

'Dearie, dearie me!' Elsie had a way of making you feel guilty even though you hadn't done anything wrong. 'If yer don't mind me saying, it's *you* that's talking nonsense now. My only concern is that you keep strong and healthy. I don't want to see you standing at the sink to wash the dishes, or turning the mattress, like you did the other day. And if I hadn't arrived in time when you were struggling to get the vacuum cleaner out of the cupboard under the stairs, like as not you'd have broke a limb. And only yesterday I caught you cleaning out the pantry. God give me strength, you're always meddling in places where you've no right to be. Cleaning, fetching and carrying is what *I'm* here for.'

When again she shook her head, her chubby little chops

shivered with irritation. 'It's why yer pay me, for goodness' sake!'

They both looked up as Mary stepped forward from the doorway. 'I'll make us a fresh pot of tea, shall I?' she suggested tactfully. 'That's if nobody has any objections?' Rona, Elsie's daughter, worked alongside Mary in her flower-shop in Leighton Buzzard, and the two young women were fast friends. She'd be sure to report the latest exchange to her!

Grateful for the intervention, Lucy gave a warm smile. 'Thank you, dear, that would be nice.'

But Elsie's feathers were still ruffled. 'I'll have two sugars in mine,' she snapped, 'and just a whisper of milk, if yer please. There's some Garibaldi biscuits in that tin. We're keeping the homemade ones for Doctor Nolan.' With that she took off her coat and hat and hung them up. 'Meanwhile, I'd best make a start on cleaning the winders . . . before somebody we all know takes a mind to do it herself!' With that she threw Lucy a withering glance and departed.

Lucy was left chuckling. 'Anybody would think I interfered with her daily routine.'

Mary turned with a wry little smile. 'You do.'

'Well, maybe I do, but I'm frightened that if I stop doing things, I might seize up altogether. Don't you know how hard it is for me to be still?'

'I think I know that more than anybody. Don't forget, I'm the one who has to live with you.'

'Do you think I should apologise to Elsie? She's such a treasure.'

'It wouldn't do any good if you did.'

'Why not?' Lucy had not expected an answer like that.

Coming to the table, Mary set the tray down. 'Because the pair of you will only be going at it hammer and tongs again tomorrow.'

Taken aback, Lucy stared up at Mary open-mouthed. 'Are we really that bad?'

'Worse!'

When the laughter carried outside to the men, they stopped work to look towards the kitchen. 'Something's tickled their funny-bones,' Ben remarked with a grin.

'Sounds like it,' Adam agreed; the merry laughter was infectious.

'That should do it.' Laying down the spanner, Ben asked Adam to start the car, and when it spluttered into life and seemed to run smoother than before, the older man gave a sigh of relief. 'Don't know how to thank you,' he said, and Ben told him he was only too pleased to have been able to help.

'I'd best get cleaned up, and take Mary to approve my new tractor.' Ben smiled at the prospect. 'After that, we've got the whole day to please ourselves what we do.'

Adam saw the gleam in Ben's eye and his heart warmed. 'You really love her, don't you?'

Ben's answer was instant and sincere. 'Like I've never loved anyone in my life,' he said. 'I can't recall what my life was like before she came along, and now I can't imagine a day without her.'

Suddenly, Mary was making her way towards them. Upstairs, hanging out of the window with her cloth, Elsie was shouting down to her, 'What were you two laughing about, eh?'

'It's Mum. You know what she's like.' Mary was still chuckling. 'She was saying how she'd best teach you your place, because you're getting too big for your boots.'

'Huh! It's the other way round, more like!'

When, a moment later, Elsie saw the doctor getting out of his car, she dropped her cloth into the bucket, ran to the landing and called down to Lucy, who quickly made her way upstairs, brushed her hair and sat nervously on the edge of the bed, waiting to greet him.

Though deep down she knew it was unfair, Lucy harboured a certain distrust of doctors. It had started when Barney fell ill and they could do nothing to help him. To Lucy's mind, doctors were all the same – authoritative and full of good advice, but as yet they had not managed to instil any degree of confidence in her. There was one exception and that was Dr Raymond Lucas, from her old home outside Liverpool. He had been a true and trusted friend, and even now Lucy valued his letters and friendship.

Interrupting her thoughts, the knock sounded on the door for the second time. 'Come in.' Like a rebellious child, Lucy remained seated.

The door inched open and a smiling face peeped in at her; with his cheeky grin and that ridiculous cap of thick brown hair, the doctor looked far younger than his early thirties. 'Am I all right to come in?' he asked gingerly. 'Or am I likely to get my head chopped off at dawn?' He knew Lucy well by now, and was aware that his visits were unpopular.

Lucy laughed and the atmosphere eased. 'I'm not that much of an ogre, am I?' she asked, shamefacedly.

'There are those who might argue the point.' Straightening his shoulders, he pushed open the door and sauntered in.

Lucy asked him pointedly, 'You're not about to put me through the grinder, are you?'

He took a deep breath. 'I'll do whatever's necessary to satisfy myself that you haven't been overdoing it.' He peeked at her with suspicion. 'And have you?'

'What?'

'Been overdoing it?'

'I don't think so.' Lucy hoped he would leave before

coming into contact with Elsie, who was certain to have her say on the matter.

'Mmm.' Slowly nodding his head, he made that peculiar sound that some doctors make when they're not quite sure what to say. 'Mmm . . . ah.'

'You don't believe me, do you?'

'I don't know what to think.' He ventured forward. 'And if I don't believe you, it's no one's fault but your own.'

'What do you mean by that?'

'I mean, I need you to be honest, but sometimes you tell me one thing and do another. How am I supposed to know if you're following my instructions when you won't tell me the truth?'

'Huh!' Lucy couldn't help but like him. 'So now I'm a liar, am I?'

Fearing he might have got on the wrong side of her, he suggested meekly, 'I'm sorry, Lucy, that is not what I meant at all. Perhaps we should forget the conversation so far and start again, what do you think?'

Lucy smiled her sweetest. 'I think that's an excellent idea.'

With a twinkle in his eye, he made the smallest bow and to Lucy's amusement, greeted her with a bright, 'Good morning, Mrs Davidson.'

'Good morning, Doctor Nolan.' Bright as a button, Lucy's quick smile betrayed her enjoyment. 'How very nice to see you,' she lied beautifully.

Placing the big black bag on the bedside table, Dr Nolan opened it and took out his stethoscope. 'And how are you today?'

'I'm fine, thank you, Doctor.' Unbuttoning the top of her blouse, Lucy prepared herself for the shock of the cold stethoscope against her skin.

'Have you anything to report?' he asked gently.

'No, nothing.' Sensing the game was over she replied in

serious tone, 'Everything is just the same as it was the last time you were here.' She was determined not to reveal how her arm still hurt like the devil after trying to shift that heavy cleaner out of the cupboard, for which Elsie had rightfully given her a scolding.

'So, no aches or pains then?' He proceeded to examine her, discreetly ignoring Lucy's visible shudder as the cold receptacle pressed against the flat of her chest.

Lucy shook her head. 'No more than usual,' she answered. 'There are times when my joints feel as though they've locked together, and other times when I feel I can carry the world.'

'No change there then?' he said, concentrating now on the job in hand of checking her blood pressure.

'Not really, no.' She laughed out loud. 'I was flattered this morning when Elsie accused me of being ambitious enough to take down curtains, and clean all the windows.' She rolled her eyes to the ceiling. 'Those days are long gone, more's the pity.'

Lucy remembered the time when she could throw a pitch-fork of hay on top of a wagon, or carry an injured lamb on her shoulders, but that was in another life. If she could bring it all back, she would. But it was gone, all but in her sorry heart.

A few moments later, after a thorough examination, the doctor put away his instruments and closed the bag. 'It seems you're no better and no worse, so you must be following my instructions after all.'

Lucy smiled triumphantly. 'Isn't that what I told you, Doctor?'

'So it is,' he replied. 'So it is – but you need to remember you're not the young woman you once were and your joints aren't quite so flexible. I'm not saying you can't do certain things – of course you can – but you must take care not to aggravate your condition. And that includes getting all hot and bothered about things.'

'I won't.'

'Good.' He wrote out a prescription. 'Your blood pressure is slightly up. Take one of these each morning, and an hour's rest in the afternoon. Right?'

'Whatever you say. You're the doctor.'

'I'll call again in a few days to check your blood pressure, just to be sure.'

Glad that the examination was over, Lucy relaxed. 'Are you ready for tea and biscuits?'

'Need you ask?' It had become a ritual; a bit of a banter, then the examination, before tea and biscuits. He had come to look forward to it. 'That's the main reason I come to visit,' the young man teased. He picked up his black bag. 'A few quiet moments in that delightful kitchen of yours sets me up for the day.'

Inching herself off the bed, Lucy slipped her shoes on. 'You haven't forgotten how I like mine, have you?'

He shook his head. 'Strong, with a little milk and two sugars.'

'That's it.' She waved him away with a gesture. 'Off you go then. You make your way down, and I'll follow on.'

By the time Lucy arrived in the kitchen, the doctor was pouring out two cups of tea and had got out a plate of Elsie's home-baked shortbread. 'I can't stay long,' he told Lucy. 'I must check on Maggie Craig; she's not too far away from giving birth.'

Lucy tut-tutted. 'That's her eighth in as many years. If you ask me, it's not Maggie as wants checking on, it's her old man. Quickest way to help Maggie and cut your work down into the bargain, is to chop it off for him. That'll give every-one a rest, won't it?'

The doctor laughed. 'It's a bit drastic, don't you think?'

Lucy shrugged. 'He's a selfish bugger, though. If it was *him* having the babies, he wouldn't be so quick to make them.'

She thought of her dead son, little Jamie, drowned these past twenty years or more, and her heart was sore. 'Mind you,' she went on in a softer voice, 'there is nothing more magical than holding a child in your arms.'

The doctor looked up to see the sadness in her eyes; he had seen it before and had been curious. Not for the first time, he sensed there was something in Lucy's past that she was unable to let go. He might have asked, but the young man's instinct told him Lucy would not thank him for it. So he waited until the sadness had passed, and she was smiling at him, as though everything was all right in her world.

'I expect you have a busy day ahead of you, Doctor?'

'I have, yes.' Finishing his tea, he munched the last of his biscuit, and when he thought Lucy wasn't looking, he tucked one into his jacket pocket. 'I really must get on now,' he excused himself. 'Remember what I said, won't you?'

Lucy nodded. 'I will, yes. Thank you, Doctor, and mind you don't crush that biscuit to crumbs in your pocket. Here.' Taking a napkin from the drawer she gave it to him with a knowing little smile. 'Best wrap it up in that, eh?'

Looking like a little boy caught with his hand in the sweetie jar, Dr Nolan did as he was told, and went sheepishly on his way.

~

Through the window Lucy watched him leave and when he was gone her gaze fell on Mary, who was walking with Ben towards the house.

'We're away now, Mother.' Mary arrived to kiss Lucy cheerio. 'Ben's just washing the oil from his hands, then we're off to organise the tractor.'

Lucy laughed. 'And what do you know about tractors?'

Mary made a face. 'Nothing,' she admitted. 'I know about cutting grass, about fertilising the soil, growing flowers and vegetables, plants from seed and collecting eggs from the chickens to sell at market, but that's as far as my knowledge stretches.' She gave her mother a curious glance. 'What are you smiling at?'

Lucy's memories had never jaded. She could remember Overhill Farm in the little Wirral village of Comberton by Weir as if it was yesterday, with Barney and his sons ploughing and seeding, and harvest-time, when the world was aglow with sunshine and the fields yielded their bounty. Somehow, without even knowing it, she had come to learn quite a bit about tractors and the way they worked. 'I was just thinking,' she said vaguely.

'From the look on your face, they must be pleasant thoughts.' Mary had often seen that look on her mother's face, a look of yesteryear, sometimes sad, sometimes warm with joy, and not once had she ever felt a part of it. 'What were you thinking about?'

'Oh, things that happened before you were born.'

'What things?'

Lucy was wary now. Even though Mary knew something about the secrets of the past, Lucy found it hard to discuss every little detail. 'I was just remembering how much I seem to have learned about tractors, that's all.'

Mary was intrigued. 'You loved helping Daddy on the farm, didn't you?' How she wished she had been a part of it all. But not the heartache, not that.

Lucy didn't get a chance to answer because now Ben was in the room, unrolling his sleeves and preparing to leave. 'If you're ready, we'd best be off now,' he told Mary, and to Lucy he suggested, 'Would you like to come with us?'

Lucy was tempted. 'That's very kind,' she said, 'but you

don't want me limping along, acting the wallflower. Besides, I've got things to do. You two get off and enjoy yourselves. You can tell me all about it when you get back.'

All too soon the two of them were climbing into Ben's car, laughing and talking, and Lucy was thrilled to see them so happy and content. 'See that, Barney?' she murmured aloud. 'That was you and me, in the short time we had together.'

Ravaged by emotions and memories she found difficult to cope with, Lucy went back to her room, slipped out of her shoes and lay down on the bed. Her gaze fixed on the ceiling, eyes closed, bittersweet tears trickled down her face. 'I want you back,' she whispered. 'Oh Barney, even now, after twenty years, I still miss you so much. I want you back – and I know it will never happen.'

For a time her heart was unbearably heavy. When she was quiet at last, she went to the bathroom and washed her face. Afterwards, feeling fresher and more able to face another day, she went downstairs, where Elsie was covering a large pie with pastry. 'Steak and kidney pie and mash for dinner tonight,' she advised Lucy. 'I'll cover it with greaseproof paper and set it on the shelf in the pantry. Oh, and there's apple crumble for afterwards. Won't take a second for Mary to heat up the spuds with a knob of butter, and to boil up some custard.'

Lucy was astonished. 'Good grief!' She stared at the pie and then at Elsie. 'You've got your skates on this morning, haven't you?' She glanced about the kitchen, which by now was spick and span. 'Are you in a hurry or what?'

For a minute it seemed as though Elsie had not heard Lucy's question, because she continued cutting the edge of the pastry to a pattern, then carried the pie to the pantry. Now she was at the sink, slapping her hands together to rid them of the flour before washing them under the tap.

Lucy spoke again. 'Elsie! Did you hear what I said?'

'I did, yes, and there's no need to shout.'

'Well then, have the manners to answer.'

The woman turned. 'All right – then yes, I am in a hurry.'

'Why?'

'Things to do.' Elsie never used many words when a few would do.

'What things?'

Elsie carried on wiping the table. After replacing the table-cloth she looked Lucy in the eye. 'Very well, if you must know, I'm taking Charlie to have his eyes tested.'

Lucy was open-mouthed. 'Can't he take himself?'

'No.'

'Why not? He's a grown man with a tongue in his head, isn't he?'

'That's the trouble.'

'What?'

'The tongue in his head. Gift o' the gab – that's his problem! If I'm not there to explain what's been going on, he'll convince the optician that he's fine. Then there'll be no spectacles and he'll carry on the same as before.'

'And what's wrong with that? Charlie is a fine blacksmith. Surely he doesn't need spectacles for shoeing horses?'

'Hmh! Shows how much *you* know.' Hands on hips, Elsie seemed ready for another fight. 'Last week, Ted Willis brought his old mare into the yard for re-shoeing and Charlie put the shoe on upside down; the poor animal went away limping worse than when Ted fetched her in. If Ted hadn't brought her back, she'd have gone lame for sure.'

Lucy thought the woman was being a bit harsh. 'Charlie doesn't often make a mistake like that. Does it really mean he wants marching off to the optician's?'

Elsie bristled. 'I think I'm the best judge of that, if yer please. And it weren't the only time he got it wrong neither.'

'Oh, you've always had a tendency to exaggerate,' Lucy scoffed.

Elsie was indignant. 'What about this then?' she demanded haughtily. 'A few days ago, Larry Barker brought his cart in for a new wheel to be put on, and when he came back to collect it, Charlie had only ruddy well changed the wrong wheel! Then the week afore *that*, I asked if he'd come into Bedford with me as I had a lot to carry home. We went round the shops and when we got back to the bus-stop there was a queue. When the bus arrived, blow me down if he didn't follow Maggie Craig on, grab her shopping-bags and sit himself beside her ... The silly article thought he were sitting next to *me*. I wouldn't mind if she hadn't got a back-side the size of the gasworks and a gob to match!'

At first, Lucy thought she ought not to laugh. Then she began to titter and suddenly the pair of them were laughing hysterically. 'Now you know why he needs the spectacles,' Elsie spluttered.

And Lucy had to agree.

'I've done all the chores for now,' Elsie said finally, wiping her eyes. 'See you same time tomorrow.'

As the little woman put on her coat, Lucy told her: 'Be gentle with him, won't you? I know what a bully you can be when the mood takes you.'

'Huh!' Elsie gave her a scornful glance. 'Look who's talking!' Off she went, shoulders high and head up, muttering to herself: 'Do this, do that ... never satisfied unless she's interfering! Besides, what does she know about my Charlie?'

'Have you two been arguing again?' Adam stuck his head round the back door.

Lucy swung round. 'That woman's getting more difficult by the day,' she said. 'Does as she likes and won't listen to a word anyone says.'

Adam smiled. 'Like someone else we know then, eh?'

Lucy laughed. 'You're right. I do have too much to say at times.' Whenever she was in Adam's company she felt content. 'Is the car all right?'

'Running like silk.'

'So, you'll be away on your errands now, will you?'

'That was the plan,' he answered quietly. 'Go into Bedford and collect the curtains you ordered, then visit the Post Office and the baker's on the way back. Then I've the rest of the day to put the new shelves up in the outhouse.'

'How long will you be?'

'I can't say for certain. Sometimes the road gets busy, sometimes it isn't.' Sensing her loneliness, he asked, 'D'you want to come with me?'

Lucy shook her head. 'No.'

Adam knew Lucy's every mood, and at this moment he knew he should not leave her alone with her memories. 'There's nothing so urgent that it can't wait till later,' he said softly. 'I'll keep you company for a while – if you want me to, that is?'

The tears still moist in her eyes, Lucy looked up. 'Thank you, Adam, I'd like that,' she whispered. No one alive knew her better than Adam, she thought fondly.

Relief flooded through him. When Lucy was sad, he was sad. And he was always content to be with her even if only as a friend; though one day, God willing, she might come to see him through more loving eyes.

He went over and settled himself in the chair opposite. 'What's wrong?' he asked. 'And don't say nothing, because I know you too well.'

'What makes you think something's wrong?'

He smiled knowingly. 'You're thinking of Barney, aren't you?' His voice was kind.

Lucy nodded.

'And you've been crying, haven't you?'

She nodded again.

'D'you want to talk about it?'

Drawing a deep sigh, Lucy confessed: 'I can't stop wondering about Barney's other family . . . Vicky and the children. Lately I can't seem to get them out of my mind, wondering where they are, and if they're safe.' She gave a nervous smile. 'I won't always be here, Adam. I'm getting old. How could I go to my Maker, with such a weight of secrets in my heart?'

Adam gave a slow, knowing nod. 'I understand how you feel, because I, too, often think about the others. To be honest, Lucy, I'm not sure if it would be kinder for them to know how it all came about. Or would the truth ruin what small contentment they might have found?'

Adam's concerns echoed in Lucy's mind. 'If they are to be told, it's me who should do the telling. And like I say, I'm getting on now, and time is rushing by. I must soon decide one way or the other.'

The very thought of not having her around filled him with dread. 'Don't talk as though you're old and decrepit because you're not,' he urged. 'God willing, you and I have many more years to enjoy, before our time comes.'

For a moment Lucy reflected on his words, and as always Adam had brought a kind of quietness to her heart. 'I hope so,' she murmured. 'But I can't shut out the past, and I can't see a way forward.'

Adam felt the same, but his first instinct had always been to protect Lucy. 'All I'm saying is, don't torment yourself. For all our sakes, try and let it rest. For now at least.'

Driven by doubts and guilt, Lucy reminded him, 'Some time ago, you insisted that Mary was entitled to know the truth, and you were right. So, don't you think *they* should know it, too? You say we risk ruining any contentment they may have found, but what if all these years they've never known peace of mind? What if the children have grown into adulthood, still carrying all the pain and anger that drove them away. And what of young Susie? Dear God, she loved her father with all of her young heart.'

Lucy recalled the powerful bond between Barney and his daughter. 'I can't get her out of my mind. I see the two of them sitting on the swing in the orchard, talking and laughing . . . happy and content in each other's company. She was so young, Adam. She knew only what she saw and heard, and that was a shocking thing. She never knew how Barney was suffering . . . how much he adored her. Susie was his darling little girl, and she went away hating him . . .'

Her voice breaking with emotion, Lucy bowed her head. For a moment neither she nor Adam spoke, but when he reached out to lay his hand over hers, she grasped it tight, drew it to her face and held it there for a moment.

To Lucy the moment was immensely comforting. Adam was right. He knew her as no one else could. He had travelled the years with her and Barney, and when Barney was gone, he was her beacon of light through days of darkness.

Though he could never be Barney, Adam was a very special man.

When the moment was gone, she released his hand and raised her eyes to his. 'I try, but I can't stop thinking about them – Susie, the two boys and Vicky, that lovely gentle woman who did all she could for me and Jamie – treated us like her own family. You know how devoted she and Barney were to each other, how they lived their whole life around each other. What happened to them, to the children, was so cruel, Adam . . . so terrible!'

So many sunsets had come and gone since those days over twenty years ago, she thought. In her mind she cast her memory back to the time when she could run like the wind and her life was filled with sunshine and the joy of youth. But there had been pain too; such pain she had thought never to recover from it. But somehow life goes on and takes you with it, whether you want it to or not.

Later, when everything else was lost, she and Barney had known their own joy together, and though it was for such a short time, Lucy had thanked the Good Lord many times over.

After Barney had died from the heart disease that had destroyed his last few years on this earth, her life seemed desolate. But then Barney had left her with a new life: Mary, their daughter, had been her salvation. Along with her dear friend, Adam, that patient, endearing man to whom she owed so much.

'Sometimes I think I'm the luckiest woman in the world.' Speaking her thoughts in a whisper, she hardly even noticed that Adam was beside her.

'Lucy?' Adam's quiet voice invaded her thoughts. 'What are you thinking?'

She looked up at him, her quiet eyes bathing his face. 'I was just thinking how Barney and I had so little time together. The days went all too swiftly, and even when we were making love and Mary was conceived, I always knew it was Vicky he needed, and not me.' Her smile was bittersweet. 'I didn't mind, not really. I would rather have had that small part of him, than live all of my life without him.'

Adam had never heard Lucy talk of her relationship with Barney in that particular, intimate way. He felt embarrassed and humbled, yet proud that she felt able to impart such a confidence to him.

Suddenly she had his face cradled in her hands, her warm blue eyes hinting a smile. 'I'm sorry.'

Relaxed in her gaze, he asked, 'Why should you be sorry?'

'I've been insensitive . . .' talking of private moments with Barney, when I know how you feel towards me.'

Adam did not want her to reproach herself, and so he led

her away from that place. 'Have you always known how much I love you?'

Lucy's smile was radiant. 'You were never very good at hiding it.'

'Did you think I was foolish?'

'Never! Besides, I always loved you back. But not in the way I loved Barney.'

Adam's face crumpled in a smile. 'It's an odd world,' he said. 'I love you; you loved Barney; and he loved Vicky. The eternal triangle.'

Letting go of him, Lucy sat back in her seat. 'We can't help the way we feel,' she answered.

With her touch still tingling on his skin, Adam waited a moment, before in a spurt of boldness he asked, 'Marry me?'

Momentarily taken aback, Lucy was about to answer, when he stopped her. 'You said just now you loved me, though I accept it could never be like it was with Barney. But I've never loved anyone else and never could. Think about it, Lucy. We're so good together. We can talk easily to each other . . .'

There was so much he wanted to say. 'We've known some wonderful times, Lucy,' he remarked thoughtfully. 'Some good, some bad. But we've lived through them together, always supporting each other. We make each other laugh, we're content and easy in each other's company. What more could we ask, at our time of life? And I'll always take care of you, Lucy. You know that.'

Lost for words, she took a moment to consider what he was saying. This was not the first time Adam had proposed, and she suspected it would not be the last. But this time there was a kind of desperation about his boldness, and it made her ashamed.

'Oh Lucy, I'm so sorry.' Wishing he had kept his silence,

Adam was concerned that he had turned her against him. 'Now I've spoiled everything, haven't I?'

Lucy put his fears to rest. 'No, you haven't, you darling man. We've always understood each other, and we've always been able to speak our minds. That will never change. You'll always be very special to me.'

'But you won't marry me?'

'I can't.'

'Never?'

Lucy had learned to count her life in minutes and weeks. 'Never is a long time.'

Sensing a kind of acceptance, Adam thought it wise to back away from the subject of marriage. 'I won't mention it again.'

Lucy chuckled. 'Yes, you will.'

'Do you want me to?'

Loth to mislead him, she made a suggestion. 'Why don't we just leave things as they are for now? When I have a change of mind, I'll be sure to tell you. Agreed?' She held out her hand for him to hold.

Adam was thrilled. Lucy had said, 'when I have a change of mind'.

That was his first real glimpse of hope. 'Agreed!' Reaching out, he took hold of her hand and kept it clasped in his for a moment longer than necessary, until Lucy gave him one of those reprimanding, twinkling looks that turned his toes up and set his old heart racing.

The conversation took another direction. 'Lucy . . .' He hesitated. 'Will you let me take you back?'

'*Back*?' She knew what he meant, but could not bring herself to acknowledge it. 'What do you mean?'

'Back there . . . to Jamie.' Before she could protest, he went on, 'For your own peace of mind, you must go back. Do you think I don't know how it haunts you? Sometimes, when your mind wanders, I know you're thinking of him, reliving that night, remembering every little detail. I feel your pain, Lucy. You need to be there. It isn't enough that you've arranged to have his grave looked after, and no, Bridget did not tell me about that. She didn't have to.'

Lucy felt the weight of his every word. 'Are you judging me?' she whispered.

Adam shook his head. 'I would never judge you, you know that,' he assured her. 'We all need to deal with things in different ways. I knew you could never come away and not have someone look after Jamie's resting-place. Bridget was the obvious choice; she's loyal and honest, and she thinks of you as family.'

Lucy gave a wistful smile. 'She's always been there for me, and now she's there for little Jamie. I owe her so much.'

'I know that. And it's a good arrangement, but it isn't the same, is it? Forgive me, Lucy, but anyone can pay weekly visits and place the flowers there, and I know Bridget is a long and loyal friend, but she is not his mother. *You* are.'

Pausing a moment, he then went on in softer tone, 'I know how, deep down, you long to go back. Let me take you, Lucy. Please! Let me do that much for you at least?'

'I can't!'

'Why not?'

For a long moment Lucy lapsed into silence, her mind alive with the past, then in a fearful voice she asked, 'What do you think happened to Edward Trent?'

Adam snorted with disgust. 'We can only hope and pray he's already got his comeuppance. A man like that must incur enemies and loathing wherever he goes.'

'Why do you think they never caught him after . . . after he . . .' Her voice broke.

'Because like all rats he knows all the dark places where he can scurry away and hide.'

'Do you think he's still alive?'

Adam shook his head. 'Who knows? If there's any justice, he'll be rotting in the fires of Hell where he belongs!'

When now, Lucy turned away, her face cold and set with loathing, he asked tenderly, 'Let me take you back, my darling. It might help to lay the ghosts.'

But Lucy would not be persuaded. 'I don't want to talk about it any more,' she replied quietly.

Realising that Lucy had put up the barriers and he had no chance of getting close, Adam departed, leaving her to ponder on what he'd said.

~

Strolling to the dresser, Lucy held Barney's photograph and for a time she looked at his familiar face, the strong set of his jaw, the light in those wonderful eyes, and the boyish, mischievous smile that played about his mouth. A sigh rippled through her body. So much to think about. So much guilt. And what about Vicky and the others? Should she write to them, or should she leave well alone?

The thought of revealing Barney's long-held secret was almost unbearable. Lucy asked him: 'How can I tell her how you put yourself through Hell, so she and your children could have peace of mind and security?'

She lingered a moment longer, tracing the profile of his face with the tip of her finger, and turning the whole idea over in her mind. 'If the truth *must* be told, I pray they will find the strength to deal with it,' she whispered.

As she walked away, Lucy turned back to the photo one last time. She thought of those on the other side of the Atlantic, and at last she knew what must be done. 'I know I will have to tell them, Barney,' she said out loud, 'and I know it will come as a terrible shock. If I had it in my power,

I would make it less painful for them.' Her heart sank. 'But it's not.'

Squaring her shoulders, she searched inside herself for an answer, but there was none. 'They would need to find the strength to live with it.' The smallest hint of bitterness shaped her words. *'Just as we did, all those long years ago.'*

~

Outside, Elsie was chatting with the coalman, conveniently forgetting she was in a rush and making him chuckle as always. 'I saw you in front as you came down the lane,' she told him. 'I might have begged a lift only you were too far away.'

A bumbling, homely sort with a wonky shoulder got from years of carrying heavy bags, the coalman joked, 'So you don't mind your arse being covered in coaldust then?'

'Not really, no,' Elsie replied. 'I might tell yer, I've had worse than that in my time. But I've never had a ride in a coalcart.'

'An' would you enjoy two grown men fighting over yer?'

'Hmh? That'll be the day.'

'What would your Charlie say, if I let you sit on my cart?'

Elsie laughed. 'I've no idea, but I'm willing if you are.'

'I'd watch what you say if I were you.' The coalman gave a naughty wink. 'There's many a man might take advantage of a remark like that.'

'You behave yerself, Bert Peters!' Elsie chided. 'I'm too old in the tooth to be flirting with the likes of you – and besides, if I were to pounce on you now, you'd run a mile. Don't deny it!'

Bert roared with laughter. 'Aye, an' if you *were* to pounce on me now, I'd more likely collapse. I've carried that many bags o' coal today, me legs 'ave gone.'

Back in Knudsden House, Lucy heard their shrieks of

laughter echo across the valley, and couldn't help but smile. The world might be crumbling round your ears, she thought, but somehow, life went on.

Her thoughts returned to what Adam had said earlier, and her mind was made up.

Suddenly she knew what she must do. She looked up to the heavens, a deep yearning for peace flooding her heart. 'I will go back and face the demons,' she declared. 'Maybe then, I can find some kind of peace.'

It would not be easy, she knew that. It had been a lifetime since she had travelled that particular road. When she left that familiar and much-loved place, she left behind a wealth of laughter, sun-filled days and happiness. The pain she took with her, for it had never gone away.

Her train of thought turned to the monster who had snuffed out her baby's life.

'Edward Trent, may you rot in Hell for what you did! You murdered your own son!'

She had no idea where he was. After the tragedy he had fled into the darkness of the night, and was never heard of again.

Many times over the years, Lucy had prayed that, somehow, he had been made to pay for the evil thing he did.

In the beginning, the hatred had eaten into her very soul, but now as the years caught up with her, after World War Two had changed everybody's lives forever, she had learned not to let it rule her life. By contrast, with the passing of time, memories of Barney and the personal sacrifice he had made grew ever stronger; as did the need to put things right before it was too late.

She thought of how it had been, and her heart was sore. 'I'm going back, Barney,' she murmured. 'Then I'm going to tell it all, to try and bring a measure of peace to Vicky, and the children.'

First, though, there was someone she needed to see.

CHAPTER FOUR

T HE GOVERNOR WAS busy poring over official documents
when the knock came on the door. 'Yes, who is it?'

The prison officer told him, 'I've got Carter with me
now, sir.'

At once the Governor's face betrayed his repugnance.
'Right! Let's have him.'

Momentarily disappearing, the prison officer threw open
the door and thrusting Edward Carter inside, positioned
him before the desk. 'All right, Carter! Stand up straight!'
he growled. Digging him in the back with the flat of his
hand, he pushed the prisoner forward.

For a seemingly long time, the Governor remained in
his seat, his head bent and his long bony finger flicking
over the pages of his document. He neither spoke nor
looked up.

When, beginning to tire, the prisoner lolled to one side,
his hands sliding deep into his pockets, he was caught up
short by another dig in the back, this time rougher and
more meaningful.

Without raising his head, the Governor peered over his
rimless spectacles. 'Remember where you are, Carter. Hands
out of your pockets . . . NOW!' he ordered.

Wary of this new Governor, who had already proved

himself to be a harsh disciplinarian, the man quickly did as he was told. After all, he had secrets to hide. Moreover, he had almost served his time and did not want to jeopardise his date of release.

Intending to unnerve the prisoner, the Governor continued to stare at him, his observant gaze taking in every detail of the man: the strong, stocky build, the inherent arrogance, the thick shock of greying hair and the deeply-etched lines on the once-young and handsome face.

Here was a puzzle, he thought. Carter was a devious cunning sort, capable of anything, a man seemingly without a background; though if it was ever uncovered, it would probably betray him as an evil and merciless creature.

While the Governor studied the prisoner, the prisoner did the same in return. He observed the lank dark hair and the small beady eyes behind the spectacles; the long sinuous fingers now drumming on the desktop, racking his nerves and sending a ripple of murderous intent through his every sense. There were many men inside this prison he would like to strangle, but the greatest pleasure would come from feeling his hands round the Governor's slender white throat.

His train of thought was abruptly broken as the Governor smiled directly into his face. 'You'd like to kill me, wouldn't you, Carter?' he asked tantalisingly. 'You'd love to get your two big hands round my throat and squeeze the life out of me. I'm right, aren't I? You hate me so much you can taste it.'

Gulping so hard his Adam's apple bobbed up and down, the prisoner lowered his gaze, his thoughts going wild. Jesus! How did he know that? He must be a bloody mind-reader . . . but he was right. The prospect of choking him until he stopped breathing filled him with excitement.

The scraping of a chair told him the Governor was standing up. He could feel the coldness of his gaze as it fell on him. 'Look at me, Carter.' The sound of air being drawn through his nose was oddly loud in that warm, uncomfortable room. 'LOOK AT ME, I SAY!'

Carter looked up. 'Sir!'

The Governor came close, so close his smoke-stained breath fanned the prisoner's face. 'You broke both his legs, Carter.' The voice was almost tender. 'You went into the showers and broke both his legs. Why would you do a thing like that?'

The big man looked up. 'I didn't do it. I never touched him.'

'Liar!'

'No, sir. I'm no liar.'

'So you say.' The Governor put his hands behind his back and strolled about for a while, eventually coming up behind the prisoner. 'If *you* didn't do it, who did?'

'Don't know, sir. It pays to keep yourself to yourself in this place. All I know is, it weren't me.'

'You were seen.'

'No, sir. It weren't nothing to do with me.'

'There was a witness, Carter! You were seen . . . slithering into the space beside him. One minute he was washing, and the next he was writhing on the floor and you were gone.'

'No, sir!' As he glanced up, rage fired his eyes. If ever he found out who had grassed on him, he'd slit their throat without a second thought. 'Who was it, sir? Who lied about it being me?'

Silence fell, and in that moment the air was charged with a sense of danger. Eventually the Governor spoke, his voice so soft it was barely audible. 'Did I tell you to look up?'

The prisoner dropped his gaze. 'No, sir.'

'Did I give you permission to speak . . . to ask *me* questions?'

'No, sir.'

'Mmm.' The smaller man remained still for a moment, then he strolled round the room, and after a time he returned to stand before the prisoner. 'You were *seen*!'

Cursing himself for almost losing control, the prisoner gave no reply.

'You had an argument with him earlier. Later, you saw your opportunity, and you viciously broke both his legs.'

Slowly shaking his head, the prisoner remained silent.

'They say you threw him to the ground and stamped on his legs, so hard that they cracked under the weight. Did you do that, Carter? Did you?'

Sweating profusely, the prisoner looked up and in hesitant voice denied it yet again. 'No, sir. I swear it.'

'I see.' Anger and disappointment coloured the man's voice. 'This is not the first time you've been brought before me, Carter,' he snapped. 'Time and again you've caused trouble amongst the prisoners. You're a nasty, evil sort who belongs more in a cage than a prison.'

He took a step away, as though he suddenly could not bear to be near such low-life. 'I know you did this, Carter, I'd gamble my life on it. But you're such a devious devil, I can't prove it. Y'see, they're all too cowardly to come forward, but you already knew that, didn't you?'

He leaned forward, his face almost touching that of the prisoner. 'You may be off the hook on this one, but there will come a time when I get you bang to rights. So watch out, Carter, because from now on, you won't be able to scratch your backside without me knowing.'

Turning to the officer, he ordered briskly, 'All privileges stopped for the foreseeable future. Now get him out of my sight!'

With that the prisoner was dismissed, and when he was gone, the Governor sat at his desk, muttering under his breath, 'Nasty piece of work! No background, no past. It's as though he was never born.'

Taking off his glasses, he placed them on the desk and with both hands he wiped the sweat from his face. 'I wish I knew what made the bastard tick. If I knew that, I'd be able to finish him once and for all.'

Replacing his spectacles, he resumed his paperwork. But the leering face as it went out of the door burned in his mind, until a few minutes later, he had to stop work, go to the cabinet and taking out a bottle, pour himself a much-needed drink. There were times when he wondered if he really needed this job after all.

~

That evening, when the lights were out and only the narrow-est shaft of silver moonlight filtered through the window-bars, Edward Trent – for Carter was only an assumed name – lay in his bunk, his eyes closed and his mind full of thoughts about the woman he could not get out of his mind, and the child called Jamie, his one and only son, who was lying in a cold churchyard because of him.

'I don't suppose you've got a ciggie hid away somewhere, 'ave ye?' The voice with the Scots accent belonged to the man in the lower bunk; young and bold, he feared no one, except maybe the man above him, who was renowned for his quick temper and cruel punishment of anyone who set against him.

The answer was instant and sharp. 'If I had, what makes you think I'd give it to you?'

'Well, for one thing, I thought you might appreciate the way I kept my mouth shut when questioned by the Governor this morning.'

'You had a choice. I didn't ask you to keep quiet about that weasel in the shower.'

There was a low peal of laughter. 'What d'you take me for? What would have happened if I'd told them how I saw you go in, I heard him squeal, and then I heard the crunch of his bones? I also saw you come out and slink away. I knew what you'd done, all right. I could have shopped you if I'd wanted.'

'Why don't you then?' Hanging his upper end over the bedrail, Trent hissed at the young man, 'Go on! Call for the screw and tell him what you know, you Scottish nonce.'

'Oh yeah? And have both my legs broken tomorrow? No thanks. I'll settle for a ciggie.'

There was a pause while Trent stared down on the bold young man. Then he swung away, delved into the curve of the wall and a moment later threw down a hand-rolled cigarette. 'Two draws and no more,' he warned. 'If they get a whiff of smoke they'll be in here to search the place from top to bottom.' He gave a devious grin. 'It wouldn't do for them buggers to poke about where they're not wanted.'

The young man sat up. 'I need a light.'

Another moment and the match was thrown into his lap. 'Two draws and no more,' he was reminded.

Having struck the match on his shoe, the young man lit the cigarette. He took a deep, satisfying draw. Then: 'D'you mind if I ask you something?'

'I don't know till you ask me.'

'Have you ever killed anybody?' Taking a long smooth drag of the cigarette, the young fella looked up, startled when he was suddenly grasped round the neck and hoisted into the air. 'Woah, woah! I didnae mean nuthin'.'

He was hoisted almost to the top bunk, shaken hard, then dropped to the ground where he lay for a moment, choking on the smoke he already had in his throat. 'You're a damned lunatic!' he gasped. 'Isn't a man allowed to ask a question without the wind being knocked out of him?'

Above him the big man leered over the edge of his bunk. 'Twice,' he said softly. 'I killed twice; one was a thieving bastard who thought he could get one over on me . . .'

'Hmh!' Clambering up, the young man brushed the dust from his prison nightwear. 'He won't be thieving from you again then, will he, eh?'

'Too right he won't.' Lying back in his bunk, the big man was in a confiding mood, especially as he knew his cellmate was not the gabbing kind. 'I've got this temper, y'see? When folks rile me up the wrong way, I lash out. I can't help it.'

'Is that right?' No sooner had the young man taken another deep drag of the cigarette, than it was torn from his mouth. 'Jesus! You've ripped the skin offa my lips!'

'I said two draws. It's mine now.'

'Who was the other one?'

'What other one?'

'You said you'd killed twice.'

The answer was slow in coming. 'A child ... I killed a child, but it was an accident.' Suddenly he was back there, the dark rage alive in him as it was then. 'The bastards should never have chased me! If they'd stayed back like I asked, it never would have happened. I knew she wouldn't come with me, so I took the kid, but she ran after me ... the other man was coming upriver and I felt trapped. I didn't mean for it to happen. It was as much their fault as mine. *They should never have come after me!*' The last words were a howl.

'Whose kid was it?' The young man knew his cellmate was a bad lot, but a child! That was a terrible bad thing.

'It was mine.'

'Christ Almighty! You killed your own child?'

He might have said more but when two iron-like fists tightened round his head, he thought he too was about to die. 'All right! All right! It was an accident – I understand. Let go, you crazy bugger, let go of me!' In the second before the other man let go, the young Scotsman was sure his head would burst.

Trent went on, his voice thick with emotion: 'His mammy was the best woman I ever had. I didn't realise how much I loved her until I'd let her go, then she went off with some other man, and I couldn't get her back. She turned me away, told me she wanted nothing to do with me ever again.' Anger quivered in his voice. 'Have you any idea how that makes a man feel?'

For a time he was silent, reliving that night. 'I was crazy . . . out of my head. I grabbed the boy and carried him off, hoping she'd change her mind and come with me, but instead she went wild! She came after me and I panicked. She tried to snatch the boy and somehow it all went wrong. It was the river, y'see? The river took him away. It was Lucy's fault. If she'd agreed to make her life with me, it never would have happened.' His voice broke. 'I don't suppose Lucy will ever forgive me.'

'What happened to her?'

'I don't know. I ran as far away as I could . . . went back to sea for many a long year. When war broke out I was over in Canada – went to work in a logging camp for the duration. Didn't see why I should get a bullet in the arse from Hitler while I could avoid it.'

The other prisoner, who had been too young to fight, didn't think much of this attitude, having lost an elder brother and an uncle, both soldiers, in the war. However, he wisely kept silent, although something of his feelings came over when he asked: 'So, they didn't put you away then?'

'No.'

'And you got away with it?'

'Yes.'

'And the other one?'

'What other one?'

'The one that stole from you.'

'I was clever. After I'd killed him, I put him where he'd never be found. He was a nobody, a thief and vagabond; it was easy enough to take on his name. I made sure I stayed away long enough to build up my new identity.' Arrogant as ever he went on, 'Twenty year and more, I managed to stay out o' the limelight, then one night on shore leave in Liverpool I got drunk and picked a fight which ended up nasty, and got me sent down.'

'Is Edward Carter your real name?'

A moment, then: 'More questions, eh, Scotty?' Trent grew cautious. 'Sounds to me like I've said more than enough.'

'You're a lucky man. By rights you should have been hung from the neck for what you did.'

With amazing agility that belied his age, the big man swung himself down from the bunk, caught the young fella by the shirt-collar and yanked him to his feet. 'You should be honoured,' Trent growled. 'You're the only person I've ever confided in. Maybe it was a bad idea. Maybe you know too much for your own good.'

Tightening his grip, he drew the younger man closer still. 'Have I made a big mistake? For all I know, you might be the sort who would like to make a few bob out of what I've told you. Are you? Are you the gabby sort?'

Eyes wide with fear, the young man assured him, 'You know I'd never do a thing like that. I'd have to be some kind of a fool! I value my legs too much. I wouldn't want to be left crippled or worse, just 'cause I don't know how to keep my mouth shut.'

The big man hissed, 'What do you know about me?'

'Not a thing! Not a single thing!'

'Very wise.' Flinging him aside, Trent hoisted himself back on his bunk. A moment later the cigarette end was thrown down to the other prisoner. 'I often wonder about her.'

'Who?' Thankful to still have the use of his legs and

another couple of draws into the bargain, the young man was still shaking.

'Lucy Baker. She was the most exciting woman you could ever meet. She wasn't what you might call a beauty – not dazzling or glamorous or anything like that.'

'If she wasnae glamorous or beautiful, what attracted you to her?'

'Lucy was different somehow, hard to forget. She was childlike – pure and innocent, but mischievous, too. She was more alive than any other woman I've ever met. Her smile was more radiant than a summer's day, and when she laughed it turned your heart over. She was small and homely, with eyes that sang. They kinda latched onto you and wouldn't let go.'

'What happened to her?'

'I don't know.' He dreamed of her. 'She's older now, like me. I often wonder if she still has that magical quality, or whether she's all shrivelled and ugly. I've taken good care of myself over the years, but I can't tell what she looks like. I've still got this image in my mind . . . might be a shame to spoil it with the real thing.' He gave a wry little laugh. 'I daresay I'd be shocked if I were to see her now.'

'Have you ever been back . . . to that place?'

'No. I want to, though. I've always wanted to, only I might stir it all up. There was a bloke, Barney Davidson his name was. Likely as not if he saw me, he'd come after me. From what I recall, he wasn't a big man, but he had this bull-like strength about him. There's bound to be trouble. I don't know if I should risk being carted off and strung up for what happened that night.'

'So, you won't ever go back there then?'

The big man gave a gruff laugh. 'I've been thinking about it a lot lately. I just might decide to go there and find out if she's still around. First though, I have to keep my nose clean and get out of here.' He hung over the end of the bunk. 'But don't think I won't seek you out, if ever you open your mouth about what you heard here tonight.'

The young man handed back the tab end of the cigarette. 'I might be bold and reckless at times – it's what got me here in the first place. But I'm not wrong in the head. Your secret's safe with me, so you needn't worry.'

His cellmate gave a soft, sinister laugh. 'I don't intend to,' he replied confidently. 'I'd rather let *you* do the worrying.'

Long into the early hours, the young man lay awake to consider his companion's veiled warning. There was no doubt in his mind; if he ever talked of what was discussed this night, he would be made to pay a terrible price.

All the same he was intrigued by what he'd heard of the child and the woman; and how, even now after all this time, the big man was still besotted with her. This Lucy: she sounded like the woman every man needed in his life – not glamorous enough to attract other men, but with a special inner beauty that shone out.

What was she doing now? What did she look like? Was she shrivelled and ugly as Carter feared, or was she still the same magical person she had always been? Most of all, what were her feelings towards him? After all, indirectly or not, he had murdered her child.

One thing was certain. It was only the fear of capture for what he had done that had kept Carter away all this time.

Glancing up to make sure his cellmate was asleep, the Scotsman mulled over the story he'd been told. He muttered softly as though talking to Lucy direct, 'Seems to me, the madman still has a craving for you.'

Closing his eyes, he made the sign of the cross on himself. 'God help you, lady. I've got a feeling you're not rid of him yet!'

CHAPTER FIVE

'**D**O YOU WANT to help?' Emerging from the barn at Far Crest Farm, Ben made his way over to Mary, who was leaning on the fence. 'Look what I've found.' Holding out a pair of wellies he told her, 'They're a bit big, but I'm sure you'll manage.'

With his brown cords tucked into his own wellingtons and wearing a woolly polo-neck jumper under his knee-length coat, she thought he looked every inch the farmer. 'What? You want *me* to help round up the sheep?' she said nervously. 'I wouldn't have a clue how to start.'

He smiled patiently. 'And you never will if you don't let me show you how.' With the confidence of a man who was content with his lot, he came up beside her and slid an arm round her waist. In each other's company they were quiet and easy, lingering a moment to enjoy the feast of Nature spread out before them.

'This is the time of day I love the most.' Ben never failed to be amazed at how quickly he had forgotten the city life. His work and his heart were now firmly rooted here in Salford. 'There are three times in the day when I feel closer to the land,' he confided now. 'First thing in the morning when the world still sleeps and the dew is on the grass; the end of the day when the sun is going down and the sky is shot with colour; and now when it's turning midday, with the morning slipping into afternoon.'

Reaching across, he kissed Mary softly on the face. 'Before I met you, I was a lonely man,' he murmured in her ear. 'I watched the days change and pass, and with the ending of each one, I felt even lonelier. Because there was so much beauty around me, I learned to live with my loneliness and enjoy what I have here. But now I have you to share it all with, and I've never been happier, or more content.'

Taking her by the shoulders, he gently turned her round to face him. For a long moment he looked on her face, on those deep, lavender-blue eyes and the shock of thick fair hair that framed her pretty features. 'I love you,' he whispered. 'Now that I've got you, I never want to be without you.'

'If I have my way,' Mary teased him, 'I promise you will never be.' Her thoughts turned to her parents, Barney and Lucy. 'Sometimes though, I can't help but feel frightened,' she added.

Ben held her close. 'Frightened of what?'

'Of the way we are, you and me.'

'Why should you be frightened?'

'Because of my parents. They loved each other too, yet after a pitifully short time they were parted.' After years of waiting for the right man, Ben had brought her alive, and at the same time made her more afraid than she had ever been. 'I couldn't bear it if I lost you, Ben.'

Ben held her close. He understood her fears, for didn't he feel the very same? 'When you love someone,' the feel of her silky hair against his face was wonderful, 'you have to take each day as it comes and live it to the full. The truth is, you have two choices, my darling: on the one side, you have to accept that there can never be a happy ending for one or the other of you . . . unless somehow you were to leave this earth at one and the same time.'

Mary had not thought of it that way, but now she realised how starkly true that was. 'You said there were two choices?'

He nodded. 'On the other hand, you can choose never to commit yourself to anyone. But if you do that, you will never know what it's like to love someone the way your mother loved Barney, or the way we love each other.' He slowly shook his head. 'I wouldn't want to miss out on what we have now.'

Mary had no doubts either. 'I'd rather suffer pain and loneliness for part of my life, than never know what it was like to love you,' she told him.

Holding her at arm's length he was astonished to see the tears bright in her eyes. With the tip of his finger, he wiped them away. 'You and I have been very lucky because some-how, we found each other. So, for the moment let's just be grateful and, as I said, take each day as it comes.'

Having returned from his wanderings, Ben's faithful old Labrador Chuck ran to meet them, excitedly yapping. 'I think he's trying to tell us something,' Mary laughed.

Ben leaned down to pacify the animal. 'All right, all right! Calm yourself down.' Looking up to Mary he asked, 'So, are you willing to give it a go? Do you want to help with the sheep?'

Never having done it before, Mary took a moment to answer, but when she did, it was with enthusiasm. 'Very well. I'll give it a go.'

'I knew it!' Ben exclaimed. 'We'll make a farmer of you yet.'

~

As it turned out, Mary had never enjoyed herself so much. The dog was a master at rounding up the sheep. 'Gently now, boy!' Ben kept him under control so as not to send the

57

sheep into a run, which could damage the pregnant ewes.

In no time at all, the flock were teased into the pen, ready for Ben and Mary to weed out the more heavily pregnant sheep and release the others.

With great care and tenderness, though never losing authority, Ben examined each and every one. The heavily-pregnant ewes were given over to Mary, who then led them into the smaller adjoining pen which ran behind the field-gate, while one by one the others were returned to graze the main field.

When the flock had been sorted, Ben and Mary took a breather. 'I'm proud of you,' Ben told Mary. 'You're a born farmer's wife.'

The twelve pregnant ewes were next ushered into the smaller paddock nearer to the homestead, where Ben could keep an eye on them. 'I think we've earned a break,' he yawned.

Mary agreed and the two of them made their way to the cottage, where they kicked off their boots, hung up their coats and washed the smell of sheep and muck off their hands.

Inside the cosy parlour, Ben soon had a cheery fire going, while in the kitchen Mary made the tea. She loved this pretty little place; with its low-beamed ceilings and big open stone fireplace, it was like a cottage you might find on a picture-postcard.

When the fire was roaring up the chimney and each of them had a warming drink, Ben sat in the armchair, while Mary curled up at his feet, her face aglow from the fire's heat, and a contented smile on her face.

When she lapsed into a long silence, Ben leaned over her shoulder. 'What's wrong, sweetheart?'

Mary shook her head. 'Nothing.'

But Ben knew different. 'Hey! This is me you're talking

to. Something's playing on your mind. If you're worried, I'd like to know.'

Reaching up, she took hold of his hand. 'I'm sorry, Ben.' She didn't want to spoil the moment, but she really did need to talk. 'It's something you said . . . about my parents. It's been a year since we were told, and I still can't take it all in – Barney sending his family away like that, making them hate him while all the time he was so ill, and in desperate need of them. And Mother, loving him like she did, when all the time he loved someone else.'

'That must have been so hard for her,' Ben remarked thoughtfully. 'To work all the day long with someone you love, and to know that he only has eyes for his wife . . . although that's exactly how it should be in a happy marriage.'

Mary had been thinking along the same lines. 'It must have been Hell for her. And yet she stayed, content enough just to be near him.'

'She and Barney were together in the end though,' Ben reminded her. 'And I for one am grateful for that, because if they hadn't, then you would never have been born, and I would never have known you.'

'What will she do, Ben? Will she ever bring herself to tell Barney's other family what happened? Or will she leave them to live out their lives, in ignorance?'

Trusting him implicitly, she opened her heart. 'I need to know where they are. I need to meet them and talk with them, about my father, and the way it was. I want them to know what he did for them . . . that he never stopped loving them, and that he sent them away because he didn't want them to lose the opportunity of a new life in Boston by finding out that he was terminally ill.'

Since Adam had confided the truth, Mary had thought about little else. 'Do you understand what I'm saying, Ben?

Do you think it's wrong for me to meet my other family . . . Thomas and Ronnie, and Susie? As for little Jamie, he was just a baby of two when he drowned, and Mum won't talk about him. I have to know my roots, where I came from. I want to go back there, to Liverpool where it all happened!'

Her voice broke. 'Oh Ben! If only I could remember clearly. Why won't she take me there? Is she trying to protect me? Is she afraid I'll be hurt by it all? But I'm hurting now, can't she see that? Why doesn't she understand that I desperately need to see where it all unfolded, if only to gain some peace of mind? I only know half the story and she won't talk to me about it. I need to stand in the fields where they worked; I have to walk by the river where they fought to save little Jamie. I have to see where he lies and make my own peace with him.'

Taking her in his arms, Ben quietened her. 'I know it's hard, but it's hard for your mother too. She lived through it, and now she's having to live with the consequences of it all. Give her time. It will take a lot of strength for her to face it all again, but your mother is a strong, determined woman. She *will* go back. She *will* show you where it all happened, I know she will. Be patient, my darling. She needs to be sure; when the time comes for her to face all those demons, she's bound to want you there beside her. Because you're hers and Barney's child, and because going back will be one of the hardest things she's ever had to do.'

The two of them talked a while longer, until his embrace tightened and the kisses grew more urgent, and soon, right there on the rug, they made love for the very first time. It was a joyful, fulfilling experience, a bonding of heart and body, when the love between them was forged even stronger.

Afterwards, with passion melted and bodies exhausted, they lay in the warm glow of the fire, thinking and dreaming of their future together. They didn't speak for a long time, because their hearts and minds were in harmony. There was no need for words.

After a time, while Mary was dressing, Ben ventured outside. A moment later, he was calling her. 'MARY! Quickly – come and see!'

Not knowing what to expect, she ran out to find him beckoning to her, his face alight with excitement.

'Look!' He pointed to one of the ewes. Head down, almost on her knees, and with the whole of her weight pressed against the fence, she was in labour, and seemingly oblivious to their presence.

The next few minutes were magical. Inch by inch, the newborn appeared. Bathed in fluid, the lamb wormed its way out until, with the slightest plop, it slid to the ground. For what seemed an age, the mother did not move. Instead she stood, head hanging, resting. Then suddenly she turned to her offspring and began licking away the slimy, covering membrane.

Moments later, the lamb stood up, its legs unsteady and its head seeming far too large for its tiny body. It gave itself a shake, fell over and struggled up again, and in an incredibly short time, it was searching out its mammy's teat.

Mary was thrilled. 'It's beautiful.'

'Have you never seen a lamb born before?' Ben had seen it many times now, and each time was just as wonderful as the last.

'I've never seen one actually being born,' Mary admitted. 'I've walked the fields at different times and I've seen the newborns playing and skipping, but I've never actually seen a ewe giving birth.'

'Have you ever touched a newborn lamb?'

'Never.'

'Would you like to?'

She was surprised. 'Won't the mother be hostile?'

Ben shook his head. 'No.'

'Then yes, I'd like that.'

They waited a while, until mother and newborn had bonded and the young one had its fill of milk. Then, with great care and talking to the mother as he went, Ben led Mary across the paddock.

He did not take the newborn straight away. Instead he gestured for Mary to be still; he murmured to the sheep that he was just as proud of her baby as she was, and that he meant no harm except to show her off and then return her. But the mother displayed little interest in them, and when he reached down to lift the newborn into his arms, she merely stood and watched, almost as though she knew he meant no harm.

At first, the little one struggled, but Ben secured the squirming bundle and holding it towards Mary, told her to smell its coat.

Nervously, Mary leaned towards the tiny creature and sniffed at its coat. 'It smells warm, and tangy . . . like fresh-made marmalade,' she laughed. 'Can I touch her?'

When he nodded, she reached out and stroked her fingers over its fleece; the sensation was like nothing she had ever experienced. Beneath her touch, the tight curls of fleece felt hard and wiry. She was amazed. 'I thought it would be *soft* to the touch,' she said in wonderment.

Before returning the lamb to its mother, Ben dipped a finger in the fluid which had cradled the newborn and was now lying in little pockets in the grass. He then wiped it over the back of the lamb and returned it to its anxious mother, who ran her tongue over its back before leading it away, contented.

Mary was curious. 'Why did you do that?'

Ben explained, 'Sometimes, a ewe will reject a lamb if she's not sure it's hers. We've both handled the lamb and we've left our smell on it. By wiping the fluid on its back, I made sure she could smell and recognise her newborn, so there would be no doubt in her mind.'

This had been a day that Mary would always remember. She had made love with her husband-to-be and witnessed the miracle of birth, almost as a sign of the babies that she might have, one day in the future. But for now, she was anxious to get home and talk with her mother. For the moment, there were other important issues that needed to be resolved.

~

Lucy saw them arrive. 'They're back now,' she told Adam, who had been polishing the car and was now enjoying the sandwich Lucy had brought him.

'Good!' Finishing his sandwich, he excused himself. 'I'll away and get out of these overalls.'

'Don't be long, will you?' Strange how with every passing day, Lucy needed him to be more a part of everything she did.

Adam was thrilled but doubtful. 'Are you sure you want me to stay?'

'Yes, Adam, I'm sure.' Lucy had no doubts. 'You've always been a part of all this.'

'Right then. I'll go and get washed up. Give me ten minutes or so. Oh, and thanks for the sandwich.' He handed her the plate. 'It was tasty as always, though a bit more pickle would not have come amiss.' With that he gave a mischievous wink and hurried away.

Lucy went outside and waited for her daughter and Ben to climb out of his car. 'You've had a delivery this morning,' she told her daughter. 'It's near the greenhouse.'

Mary, who was looking more beautiful than her mother

had ever seen her, had completely forgotten. 'What sort of a delivery?'

'A load of rotting manure,' Lucy groaned. 'Adam helped to fork it off the cart, and by God does it stink! I can even smell it from the kitchen.'

'You won't grumble when I've dug it into the ground to produce fat cabbages and juicy carrots,' Mary grinned. 'Anyway, we had another sort of delivery today, didn't we, Ben?'

Ben was absent-mindedly running the flat of his hand along the side of Lucy's car. 'Adam keeps this car beautiful,' he said. 'It's a credit to him.'

'Ben!' Mary gave him a nudge. 'I was just saying, we had another kind of delivery today, didn't we?'

'We certainly did . . . the first of the spring lambs decided to make an appearance,' he announced proudly. 'And we saw the whole thing, from birth to suckling.'

Mary eagerly imparted the bones of her little adventure. 'I stroked its coat. I always thought it would be soft and downy,' she told her mother excitedly, 'but it was harsh to the touch, and tight as a coiled spring.'

'I could have told you that,' Lucy teased. 'Your daddy once had a whole flock of sheep. Spring was always the best time, when the lambs were born and I could sit on the tree-stump by the edge of the woods and watch them frisking and leaping about.'

Before her memories could overwhelm her again, she announced briskly, 'Come inside. I have something to tell you.'

By the time they strolled to the kitchen door, Adam was already there, washed and changed and looking apprehensive. 'Hello, you two!' he greeted them. Stepping aside, he waited for the family to pass before following them across the hallway and into the drawing room.

When they were all seated – Ben and Mary on the sofa together, Adam in the leather armchair and Lucy in the matching chair beside him, she told them all, 'For a long time now, I've been toying with the idea of going back North.' As she went on, the nervousness disappeared and a calm strength emerged. 'It won't be an easy thing for me to do. There will be other people living in Barney's old house now, and strangers farming the land.'

She grew wistful, eyes downcast. 'The memories will still be there though, in the fields and the cottage. Memories that will never leave me . . . such joy and regret, and oh, the laughter we all shared.' Such laughter, such joy, friendship and the yearning for a man she believed could never be hers.

Swallowing hard, she looked up to see her daughter silently coaxing her to go on. Bracing herself, she cleared her throat and in a firm voice told them, 'A visit is long overdue, and now with time seeming to pass ever more quickly, I won't leave it any longer. I have a very old friend in Doctor Lucas, as I'm sure you're all aware of by now. He knows me well,' glancing at Adam, she instinctively reached out and took hold of his hand, 'almost as well as my good friend, Adam.'

Turning a deep shade of pink, Adam smiled. 'Doctor Lucas is a fine man,' he remarked. 'It will be good to see him again, I'm sure.'

Mary had a question for Lucy. 'Have you told him you're coming?'

'Not yet, no.'

'When do you intend going?'

Lucy shook her head. 'I'm not sure. I've only just made the decision. In a couple of weeks' time, maybe? I'll write to Doctor Lucas. There are any number of good hotels in the area.'

Mary had another question. 'Mother?'

'Yes, dear?'

'Can we come with you – me and Ben?'

Lucy quickly reassured her. 'I wouldn't dream of going back without you,' she said. 'When we left there, you were too young to remember what it was like . . .'

Nostalgia flooded her senses. 'I need to show you the fields where your daddy and the family worked alongside each other, and the cottage where we lived. I can't wait to see Bridget, either. From her letters, she's still full of life, with the dancing and the singing and the shameless flirting. She's married four men and dumped them all one after the other, and doesn't seem to have changed one bit. But oh, how wonderful it will be to see her again. I bet she's grown old disgracefully, and made a fortune out of everything she's ever touched.'

Ben was intrigued. 'Have you never met up in all this time?'

Lucy shook her head. 'Bridget's been too busy making her fortune, and until now, I've never really mustered enough courage to go back.' She laughed heartily. 'I wouldn't mind betting she looks exactly the same, and as far as I can tell, she's still up to her old tricks, wheeling and dealing, and playing havoc with the men.'

Caught up in Lucy's enthusiasm, Mary ran to sit on the arm of her mother's chair. 'Oh Mum, I'm longing to meet her! And I want to see it all – the fields and the cottage, and the river . . .'

She paused when Lucy looked at her through agonised eyes, almost as though her mother knew what was in her mind at that moment. 'Will you take me to see where he is, Mother?' Sliding a hand into Lucy's, Mary gently persisted, 'Will you take me to the churchyard where little Jamie lies?'

In her mind Lucy saw it all – that night, and the horror

– and thrusting it to the back of her mind, she avoided the question. 'So there you are, my dear,' she said brightly, and turning to Ben, she asked, 'You will come with us, won't you, Ben?'

Just as she had hoped, Ben did not hesitate. 'I'd like that. Thank you, Lucy.'

Lucy clapped her hands. 'Good! That's wonderful. I'm sure Adam will organise it all.' She winked at him. 'Of course, it would be nice to have a date for the wedding too, so we can start planning for that as well. Ben's daughter Abbie will make a beautiful bridesmaid, don't you think, Adam?'

Mary flung her two arms round her mother's neck. 'You're a conniving old biddy,' she chided, 'but I wouldn't swap you for the world.'

Lucy would not be deterred. 'Well, Ben? Is there soon to be a wedding or not?'

Delighting in Lucy's character, Ben promised, 'I think you should get your hat and outfit ready. I wouldn't be at all surprised if it didn't happen before too long, isn't that right, Mary?'

Mimicking her mother, the girl was a little coy. 'We'll have to wait and see, won't we?' With that, she took her leave. 'Who wants a cup of tea?'

For now, the discussion was over, but there was much to look forward to.

And much to fear.

CHAPTER SIX

Bridget had taken flowers to the churchyard every Saturday, and this Saturday was no different.

Twenty years ago, she had made a promise to a friend, and though she had been many things in her life, some of which she was not proud of, it was not in her nature to break a promise.

Stooping to lay down the posy of white and yellow narcissi, she dug into her pocket and took out a white envelope. Then she held it up, almost as though she thought little Jamie could see it. 'I had a letter from yer mammy this morning,' she murmured in her soft Irish lilt. 'At long last, she's coming to see us. What d'you think o' that, eh? Ah, sure, it won't be easy for yer mammy . . . what with a family in the cottage an' the river only a spit away, as if nothing bad ever happened there. But we all know different, don't we, eh?'

Drawing a deep breath through her nostrils, she blew it out in a great sigh. 'Ah, but she's a brave woman, yer mammy. After you were took, she went away with dear Barney. She made a new life and though we've written time and again, we've not clapped eyes on each other these many years.'

When a dewdrop appeared on the end of her nose she

cuffed it away. 'There's a chill wind brewing,' she said. 'I'd best be going, or my knee will seize up again.' She chuckled. 'I'm not so young as I was, more's the pity, but I can't let the years get the better of me, 'cause once I do that, I'm finished.' She squared her shoulders. 'Inside, I'm still the young woman who fought and clawed her way to the top.'

After rearranging the posy in a nicer position, she clambered to her feet, groaning as she straightened up. 'The old bones are beginning to complain, but the mind's as quick as it ever was.' Bridget was thankful for the good health she enjoyed. It meant she could keep to her schedule and stay one step ahead of advancing years.

She rubbed her sore knees and for a moment was quiet in contemplation. 'In some ways it might be better if yer mammy never came back, poor wee thing,' she said, 'but then I wouldn't see her, would I? An' she wouldn't see *you*, an' that would be a terrible shame, especially when it's taken her so long to make this particular journey.'

The man's kindly voice startled her. 'You know what they say about people who talk to themselves?'

Swinging round, she almost fell over. 'Jaysus! I almost had a heart attack. What d'you want to creep up on me like that for?'

The man apologised. 'I wasn't creeping up on you,' he said. 'It's just that I've seen you so often down here, I thought I might come up and say hello.'

Slim and tidy, with a pleasant bearded face, something about him jogged Bridget's memory. 'Have I seen ye somewhere before?' she asked. 'You look familiar.'

He laughed at that. 'Isn't that what the men are supposed to say when they see a woman who takes their fancy?'

Bridget could see the funny side. 'Ah well now, it's not that I'm after taking your fancy,' she joked in return. 'I really do believe I've seen ye somewheres before.'

Offering the hand of friendship, he introduced himself. 'The name's Oliver Rogers.'

Bridget shook his hand. 'An' how d'you do then, Oliver Rogers.' Suddenly she was blushing to the roots of her hair. 'Ah, now I know where I've seen ye. That's it! You used to visit my old place . . . Gawd Almighty! Sure, that's more years ago than I care to remember.'

He laughed. 'You're right. It must be at least twenty-four years since I climbed the steps to spend an hour or so with one of your girls.'

Bridget nodded. 'If I remember aright, you always asked for Judy.'

'That's right, I did.' He seemed embarrassed. 'But only because she was the nearest to you I could get . . . same red hair and that wonderful bubbly nature. It was always you I wanted, Bridget. You were the loveliest of them all, but you were always just out of reach.'

Like a young schoolgirl on her first date, Bridget protested, 'Away with you! Why would you want me, when you could have the pick of my girls?'

He gazed at her for a moment, before answering softly, 'We can't help who we fall in love with, can we?'

For the first time in her life, Bridget was lost for words. When she did speak, her voice was alive with anger. 'Soft talk, is it? I expect you've found out that I've made it good and you want a slice of it. Well, aren't you the cunning blighter, eh? In love with me, you say? Hmh! I know what you're after, so I do.' She wagged a finger at him. 'I'm far too canny to fall for all that nonsense, so ye'd best be on yer way, before ye see a side to me you wouldn't like! Go on, be off with you! I've no wish to renew our acquaintance. What's more, I can't be wasting the day talking to the likes o' you. I'm a busy woman, so I am.'

With that she turned on her heel and went smartly down

the path, muttering to herself and cursing. 'Bloody maniac! Coming up behind me like that. Does he think I were born yesterday? Sure, I've worked hard to get where I am today. I started with nothing and fought my way up. Now I've got a good life and a healthy bank-balance, I'm not about to share it with some crafty, grasping old bugger!'

She stole a glance behind. Looking very sorry for himself, the man was standing right where she left him. 'Be Jaysus! I've a good mind to go back and smack him one, so I have.' She clenched her fist and thrust it into her pocket. 'Just let him try it again, that's all.'

'Bridget!' His voice followed her. 'I didn't mean to offend you. Come back . . . let's talk.'

'Sod off!'

'Please, Bridget! I'm sorry if I spoke out of turn.'

'Ye heathen! You'd best be gone, or ye *will* be sorry!'

'Don't go . . . BRIDGET!'

Ignoring his plea, Bridget climbed into her beloved Hillman Minx. Losing no time in case he might follow her, she shut the door and turned on the engine.

'Bloody cheek!' Stamping her foot on the clutch, she slammed the car into gear. Lurching forward, it jerked into a spasm and for a moment she almost lost control. 'Come on, come on!' She kicked on the accelerator and it took off at a crazy pace, throwing her back in the seat.

Oliver Rogers was right behind. When the car shot forward, with the wheels skidding and squealing, the hail of dust and muck thrown up from the hoggin-path covered him in a thick cloud. 'You're still a damned lunatic!' he yelled. But Bridget was already out of earshot.

He brushed himself down. 'That's my girl,' he chuckled. 'You might think I'm after your money, but nothing could be further from the truth.'

Walking the few steps to the large, sleek Humber, he

climbed in and watched as Bridget's car skidded and danced all the way down the road. 'You're a bit older, with a few more wrinkles and greying hair,' he nodded approvingly, 'but you're still the same lively little devil you always were.'

Slipping into gear he manoeuvred the vehicle onto the road. 'You're a right handful,' he laughed. 'That's what I like most about you. And that's why I mean to have you before we're both too old to enjoy what's left.'

~

Driving like one demented through the streets of Liverpool, Bridget had pedestrians leaping out of the way. 'Don't you swear at me!' she had snapped at an angry young couple who had the misfortune to step out in front of her, and now she didn't see the old dear who ran back to the pavement in fear for her life. 'Sorry, love, but ye should have the good sense to look where you're going!' Bridget tutted as the old woman waved her stick at her. 'Hmh! From the way she scooted up onto the pavement, she doesn't need that stick at all.'

As she slowed down a little, Bridget grinned to herself. 'I wouldn't mind betting she only carries it about to whack folks on the head,' she said aloud, and was still laughing as she pulled up outside an imposing office. Situated on a wide quiet street just a brisk walk from the city centre, it boasted her name above the entrance:

The Bridget Business Agency

Climbing out of her car, Bridget stood for a moment as she always did, filled with pride and a sense of accomplishment to see what she had achieved.

The Bridget Business Agency. Even now, after so many years, she could hardly believe that this imposing building was really hers, paid for lock, stock and barrel. 'You've done well, Bridget my girl,' she told herself. It was a far cry from that little house in Viaduct Street, with its poky rooms and second-hand furniture.

At one time, these offices had been two shops; one a man's tailor's and the other an ironmonger's; the upper floors provided spacious living accommodation.

Having outgrown her previous offices, and wanting to stay fairly central, Bridget bought the two shops and gutted them. She redesigned the building and filled it with the most expensive furniture, creating the air of discretion and professionalism that her clients preferred.

She had eight attractive young women working for her, and nowadays, the business was of a more respectable and lucrative nature. Most of the work was done over the telephone and through appointments, with the majority of clients being genuine businessmen needing escorts; though of course there was always the occasional gentleman who wanted a little more than that. After thoroughly vetting them, Bridget did occasionally turn a blind eye.

But that was the exception rather than the rule for she had built up an admirable reputation in Liverpool and protected her standing like a tiger protecting her cubs.

Making her way upstairs, Bridget burst into reception in her usual robust manner. 'Top o' the morning, Amy, me darling.' She strode across the room. 'You're looking pretty, I must say. Off out, are you?'

Middle-aged and still single, Amy had taken the place of Tillie Salter as Bridget's right-hand helper. With her baby-face and sad eyes that made a body want to hug her, she never over-dressed or went out of her way to show herself off; in fact, quite the contrary.

At home, she would wear anything and everything as long

as it felt comfortable. But while at work she was always smart and trim, with her hair tied back and her white shirt stiff and starched. But not this Saturday morning, for she had her hair washed and loose, and curled up at the ends, and she wore a soft blue blouse with a little daisy brooch on the lapel.

'Will ye look at you!' Bridget loved to tease her. 'Don't deny it – you've got a date, so ye have.'

'No, I haven't!'

'Why else would ye be done up all pretty, with yer eyes shining and a smile on yer little face?'

Amy blushed to the roots of her hair. 'You're imagining things, like you always do. I'm not going on a date.'

'Hey now!' Bridget wagged a finger. 'You might be in charge when I'm not here, but I'm the boss and I'm allowed to think and say what I like. So don't you forget it, young madam!'

In charge of the offices, Amy had been with her for a good while now. She was an excellent organiser and had a flair for figures – which had never been Bridget's strong point.

Amy explained, 'I thought I might go to the pictures this afternoon, that's all. It's a Norman Wisdom film.'

Bridget glanced at the clock. 'In that case, you'd best make tracks or you'll miss the matinée,' she told her. 'I should never have asked you to come in on a Saturday. It was unfair of me, so it was.'

'Don't worry about it,' Amy assured her. 'I didn't know myself about the film until I got out of bed this morning. When the postman told me that he was going to see it, I just thought it would make a nice treat for me too.'

Bridget chuckled. 'So, it was the postman put the sparkle in yer eye, was it?'

'No, it was not.'

'Ah, don't gimme that now. I've seen your postie and he's a fine body of a man, so he is.' She made a smiley face. 'It's him that's taking you to the pictures, is it?'

Pretending to tidy some papers, Amy looked away. 'He's not taking me,' she protested, 'though it's likely we could bump into each other . . .'

When Bridget opened her mouth to speak, Amy cautioned her, 'Don't leap to conclusions, because there's nothing going on, and that's an end to it.'

'Sure, I wasn't about to say anything at all.'

'Yes, you were. I saw it in your face.'

'Well, all right, yes, I was about to speak. But it was nothing to do with the postman.' She couldn't resist another little jibe. 'If you fancy a torrid affair on the quiet with him, who am I to judge?'

Ignoring her teasing, Amy asked, 'So, what were you about to tell me just now?'

Feigning indignation, Bridget pouted, 'Ah, sure, I've changed me mind. I'm not telling you now.'

Amy laughed. 'You're itching to tell me. So, come on. What is it?' Leaning over the desk, she folded her arms. 'I'm not doing any more work until you tell me.'

'So! Refusing to work now, is it?' Bridget was enjoying the little exchange. 'I hope ye realise, I could sack you for that.'

'But you won't.'

Bridget's smile grew wider. 'I got a letter this morning.'

'Oh? An old boyfriend, was it?' Amy knew how to turn tables.

'No, 'twas not!' Waving the letter under Amy's nose, she said, 'You'll never guess who it's from.'

'Aw, Bridget, stop teasing.' With sleight of hand, Amy tried to get at the letter, but Bridget was too quick for her.

'Don't be impatient.' She could be a real torment.

Amy tried another tack. 'Well, I'd best be going now. I've updated the appointment book. There's just a bit of filing to be done, but that can wait until Monday.' She began to turn away.

Horrified, Bridget grabbed hold of her arm. 'Aw, go on then,' she said, and thrust the letter at her. 'Open it, why don't ye?'

A moment later, Amy was clapping her hands and shrieking, 'Oh my God, it's Lucy! She's coming to see us!' Running round the desk she caught hold of Bridget and wouldn't let go. Then she was crying and laughing all at the same time. Tears of joy ran unheeded down her face.

'Behave yourself,' Bridget chided. 'Sure, I know you're thrilled and so am I, but will ye stop the damned bawling . . . oh, now will ye look at that! You're plastering snot all over the sleeve of me coat!'

Amy wiped her eyes with the back of her hand. 'I'm sorry,' she whimpered, 'but I can't believe it. All this time, Lucy kept her distance, not wanting to see us and not wanting to come back, and now she'll soon be here, and I can't believe it. Oh Bridget!'

'Hey!' Taking her by the shoulders, Bridget warned, 'Don't start bawling again, or I'll have you locked away somewheres, then you won't see her at all, will ye?'

Amy laughed at that. 'Oh, but isn't it wonderful?'

The other woman agreed. 'It is, yes – though I'm not sure why the sudden change of mind after all this time.'

Amy's eyes widened. 'You're right. She hasn't said why she's coming to see us. Oh no. You don't think she's poorly, do you – really poorly, I mean? Oh Bridget, I couldn't stand it if she was coming back to tell us that.'

Although the very same thought had initially occurred to Bridget, she immediately put Amy's mind at rest. 'Oh for heaven's sakes, will ye stop yer blathering! Think about it. If

Lucy was that ill, she wouldn't be travelling all this way to see us, would she, eh? Instead, I'm sure we'd be asked to go to *her*.'

Amy gave a sigh of relief. 'You're right. Oh, and it will be lovely to see her, won't it?'

Bridget smiled, that deep-down smile that spoke more than words. 'Yes. Now get off, or you'll miss the start of the picture, so ye will.'

While Amy went to fetch her coat, Bridget threw herself into the high-backed leather chair.

'I'm away now,' Amy said, then had a sudden thought. 'Lucy won't arrive today, will she?'

'O' course not. I only got the letter this morning. You read it yourself. She'll write again with a date to expect her. So, get off now, or you'll miss the postman.' She winked knowingly. 'And ye wouldn't want that now, would ye?'

'Bridget! You shouldn't be saying things like that. It could cause all manner of trouble if that kind of silly gossip got out.'

Bridget tutted. 'Oh. Married, is he?'

'No, he's not married, and as far as I know, he's not planning to, though from the sound of it you'd have us both marching down the aisle whether we want to or not.'

Bridget gave a naughty wink. 'Whatever gives you that idea?'

Amy shook her head in frustration. 'I'll see you later.' That said, she hurried out of the room.

'Wait on!' Behind her, Bridget gave a loud groan. 'Oh Amy, you little darlin', I don't want you to miss the Pathé News, but you couldn't fetch me a bowl of hot water, could ye? All that walking. Jaysus! Me feet are like two roasted chickens.'

Amy looked at her watch and gave a shrug. 'I don't suppose it will matter if I miss the first ten minutes.'

78

She returned to make Bridget more comfortable, though on delivering the bowl of hot water she gave her a lecture. 'You're too hard on yourself,' she chided. 'You do too much, always on the run, and frightening the life out of anybody who gets in the way of you and that mad machine. You need to remember, you're not getting any younger.'

Bridget was indignant. 'I didn't build this business by sitting on my backside,' she retorted. 'And because there's more competition ready to muscle in on me, I need to work at staying on top. I haven't got time to grow old, thank you very much, and I don't need reminding how I'm not getting any younger.'

Dipping her bare feet into the bowl, she gave a long, delicious sigh. 'As for my mad machine, that car is a godsend to me. It saves my legs and gives me the freedom I need.'

Leaning over, Amy gave her a peck on the cheek. 'I'm sorry,' she told her. 'I worry about you, that's all.' If she lost Bridget it would be like losing her best friend, and entire family.

'Well, there's no need.' Bridget dismissed this with a wave of her hand. 'Now, be off with ye.'

As she went, Amy remarked once more on Lucy's imminent visit. 'I can't wait to see her,' she said. 'I wonder if she's changed?'

'Well, o' course she's changed!' Bridget scoffed. 'We all have. We're older and slower, with wrinkles and greying hair.'

Amy laughed at that. 'Not *you*!' she called out as she went through the office. 'You have your hair dyed and slap enough make-up on to frighten the devil. And you're still as mad as a hatter.'

With that she closed the door and went on her way, leaving Bridget wondering about Lucy, and remembering how it was, before she went away. 'Aw, Lucy my old friend, you had it hard, so ye did. What with losing the bairn and then Barney, and ye never even told us about him until a year later. But I think I understand why you needed to shut us out.' She lounged deeper into the chair. 'You thought to save us any distress, and like a wounded animal, you needed a place to hide.'

She closed her eyes and gave up a heartfelt prayer. 'God willing, you maybe found a measure of peace, in your far-off hideaway.'

CHAPTER SEVEN

NORMALLY, ON A Sunday, Bridget would not see hide nor hair of Amy, and if by chance she did pop round to see her boss, it was never before midday. 'I like my extra hour or two in bed of a Sunday,' Amy would declare. And if truth be told, Bridget also enjoyed her bit of a lie-in.

But not today, because on this warm, bright Sunday in April, Lucy was coming to see them. 'What time do you think she'll arrive?' Amy was like a cat on hot bricks.

'Sit down and stop wearing out my floor, if ye please, and turn that blessed wireless off. I'm in no mood to listen to the Goons!' Bridget groaned. 'Like I've told ye for the umpteenth time, Lucy has a long way to travel. Who knows how long it might take. She'll be here when she arrives – no sooner, no later.'

In fact it was a quarter to four when Adam drove through the main streets of Liverpool; on this Sunday as on every other, the heart of the city was quiet, with only the odd window-shopper strolling about.

'All this time and nothing seems to have changed,' he remarked.

Adam had hardly got a word out of Lucy all the way up from Bedfordshire, and now as he tried hard to draw her into a conversation, he could only imagine the emotions raging through her. His own heart, too, was churning at seeing his familiar old hometown.

Loth to betray her feelings, Lucy was deeply moved at seeing all the familiar haunts. Greedy to keep and hold it forever, she took in everything; the church on the corner, the avenue of shops, the street-lamps, and even the kerbs and pavements worn down over the years by the feet of many, including Barney's and her own.

'You're wrong, Adam,' she answered quietly. 'It *has* changed. There was a time when I thought Liverpool would always belong to me. When I last walked down these streets, they were comforting and friendly, because Barney was still alive. If I was out shopping, he was always at the back of my mind, and I knew that when I got home he would be there, waiting for me – that warm, wonderful man.'

Yes, Liverpool was still here, she thought, and yes, it *looked* the same – the proud old buildings, the old cobbler's on the corner, and the tearooms where she and Vicky often took a rest from the shopping.

Even the pub where she had seen Barney and the street-woman on that dreadful day – that was still there. Everything looked the same, but it didn't feel the same, because now they were all gone – her darling boy Jamie, Barney, Vicky and the others.

It was gone four by the time they booked into the hotel. 'Do you want to rest before we do anything else?' Adam was concerned for her. 'We could give it an hour or so, before we go to Bridget's. I could order tea and sandwiches, and you could have half an hour or so in your room resting.'

'Are you tired, Adam?'

'Not really, no. We had an hour's stop. That was enough to refresh me.'

'Good!' Lucy was adamant. 'There'll be time enough for us to rest later. I really do need to see Bridget, and Amy, and . . .' She paused. 'Leave the porter to take up our bags, Adam. I'd like to go to Bridget's straight away.'

The porter was instructed and they climbed back into the car. 'Do you know where you're going?' Lucy asked. 'If I remember rightly, Duke Street is situated in the posh area along by the marketplace then second right, turning past the cinema.'

Adam laughed. 'Unless they've moved the streets, I know every twist and turn,' he assured her. 'We'll be there in a few minutes.'

Adam was as good as his word. In no time at all, they were turning into Duke Street; tree-lined and flanked with expensive houses. 'I'd forgotten how posh this area was,' he said.

As he drove slowly by, Adam carefully read the names and numbers of each house. Every one was different – some with high gates, others with no gates at all, but each one oozing money and affluence. 'Bridget wasn't exaggerating when she wrote and told you she was comfortably off,' he said.

Lucy smiled at his remark. 'I always knew Bridget would move up in the world,' she said proudly. 'This is all a far cry from the old place.'

∼

Having been back and forth to the window this past hour and more, Bridget saw the car draw up and Adam get out of the driver's seat. At first she didn't recognise him, but then as he opened the rear door for Lucy, he looked towards the house and Bridget was sure. 'It's them!' Raising her voice she called Amy, who had been keeping vigil at the window but had now gone to sit by the fireside. 'AMY! It's them!'

Excited, Bridget hurried to the front door and flung it open, and there after all these years was her dear friend Lucy, still strong, still defiant against all odds. Even though she leaned on her walking-stick, there was a grim determination in her step as she began her way up the path.

Her hair that once hung thick and loose over her shoulders, was now gathered into a clip, and she appeared slimmer, her shoulders upright and straight. Over the years, Lucy had carried a great burden on those slim shoulders, but she had borne her troubles well, and never once had she leaned on others who would have helped if only she had asked.

Now, as she paused in her steps to look up, her eyes were warm and clear, shining with goodness.

'Hello, my darling Bridget.' The voice was Lucy's. The woman was the girl again, and the girl was the same, with this precious moment frozen in time. They were young again, and the years were as nothing.

Bridget had vowed not to cry or be emotional, but as she ran to meet her old friend, the tears flowed, and when she called Lucy's name her voice broke and faltered. 'Oh, Lucy . . .' Unable to speak any more, she snatched Lucy to her, and they held each other in a close embrace; it was the most magical moment. One brief moment, born out of tragedy and joy, and a friendship which from a distance had spanned a lifetime.

Adam stood by, a lump in his throat and his heart soaring. These two should never have been parted, he thought, but Lucy had done what she felt she must do, and now thank God, she was back.

With her arm secure round Lucy, Bridget opened her embrace to include him. 'Oh Adam, you don't know how wonderful it is to see you both.'

He went to them and they stood a moment, holding each

other as though they would never let go, and the pain in Lucy's heart was eased. This is right, she thought. This is how it should be.

When Amy came running down the steps, Lucy took her into her arms. 'Amy!' She kissed her face and smiled. 'You look taller, and smarter.' Amy had made a special effort to look good for Lucy. She had on a pretty cream-coloured jacket and brown skirt, her hair was especially bobbed and she had on a touch of lipstick.

'You look every inch the businesswoman.' Lucy had been told how Amy ran Bridget's business almost single-handed. 'But to me, you'll always be shy little Amy.'

Amy laughed. 'Not so shy now,' she said. 'And not so little, either. I've put on a few pounds since you last saw me.'

'Come inside.' Bridget led them onwards, Amy and Adam talking softly behind, with herself and Lucy in front. 'We're like two old soldiers,' Bridget joked tearfully. 'Back from the wars, licking our wounds and ready for the next battle.'

Lucy smiled at that. All my battles are done, she mused. But then she thought of Edward Trent, and her heart fell.

Inside the house, while Amy went to the kitchen, Bridget took Adam and Lucy on a tour; first stop was her large office overlooking the garden. 'This is the room where I enjoy a drop o' the good stuff, put me feet up and think o' the old days,' she confided. 'Back there I had a humble little place with a backyard and men who visited discreetly for pleasure, and now I have a house with beautiful gardens and a posh office, and I'm still in the same business of providing lovely girls for lonely men, only this time it's more business than pleasure.' She shrugged philosophically then confided, 'And would you believe, I'm making ten times the money.'

'I can see that.' Lucy was taken from room to room, in and out of five large bedrooms, all furnished in the latest style; two enormous bathrooms shaped in marble and glass, and then down the wide staircase into a drawing room with French doors leading out to a magnificent garden.

'You have a beautiful house, Bridget.' Lucy fell thankfully into the wide armchair; Adam sat close and when Amy brought in the tray of sandwiches and tea, the four of them reminisced about the past. 'Will you ever come back here to live?' Amy asked hopefully, and Lucy told her she would not; that though she had fond memories, the bad ones were still too real.

'Besides,' she said, 'I'm too old in the tooth to be moving house and starting over.'

Adam told them he felt the same. 'Liverpool will always be where my roots are,' he confessed, 'but my home is in the south . . .' no one missed the adoring glance he shot in Lucy's direction, '. . . with Lucy and her daughter.'

'And how is your daughter, Mary?' Bridget enquired of Lucy. 'Sure, I thought you were bringing her with you, and this young man of hers – Ben, isn't it?'

'They'll be along shortly,' Lucy promised. 'Mary called on us this morning before we set off and said how Ben's sheep had all started lambing. The pair of them were up all night, and the lambs were still coming when we left.'

'And do they know where to find us?'

Adam intervened. 'I copied out the directions you sent to Lucy,' he said. 'I'm sure they'll find you, no trouble.'

'Good!' Like Amy, Bridget was longing to see Lucy's daughter. 'Oh, I can't wait to meet her,' she told Lucy. 'When you took her from here, she was just a tiddler, so she was.'

There was something else Bridget wanted to know, but she wasn't quite sure how to broach it.

Anticipating the question, Lucy enlightened her. 'We didn't go to the churchyard,' she said quietly. 'If that's what you're wondering?'

Bridget nodded. 'You read my mind, pet. I was just after asking if you might have called there first.'

When emotion threatened to creep up on her, Lucy merely shook her head. The memories were vivid as always: after little Jamie's second birthday party on that joyous November night, Trent had appeared at her cottage, wanting her back, beseeching her to leave Liverpool with him. Then, when he realised that her love had turned to hate, he had snatched her child and disappeared into the night.

Mortally afraid for little Jamie, Lucy had pursued him, but he was like a madman fleeing through the pitch-dark fields. Stumbling and calling, she had gone after him, but he was always a distance away. And then he was crossing the river, carrying the child over the slippery boulders that straddled the water above the weir, now in full flood. Screaming hysterically, Lucy had followed him. And it was while grappling with him that Edward Trent began to lose his footing in the raging torrent.

It all happened so quickly. She pleaded with him to give her the child, but he was so crazed and evil there was no reasoning with him. Then Barney came out of the darkness and shouted for her to go back, to leave it to him, but instead, fearful for little Jamie, she followed her instincts and reached out for her baby. Then suddenly it all went wrong. In one frantic, desperate moment, she and Trent lost their footing, and their son was gone. And as the water carried him away, she prayed, like she had never prayed in her life before or since.

Caring nothing for his own life, Barney had gone after the child but it was all too late, and since that terrible moment when he had carried Jamie's lifeless body to her, she had blamed herself. If only she had listened to Barney when he told her to get back. If only she had not pursued Edward Trent, he might have returned her child safely. If only he had not made for the river . . . if only. *If only*. Dear God, would the heartache never end? And now here she was, where it all happened, and for her own peace of mind, she must visit little Jamie's last resting-place.

The prospect was unbearable to Lucy, and yet she desperately needed to stand where he lay, to speak with him and in her heart and mind to hold his hand and reassure him that she had not forgotten, that she still loved and remembered him and would do so until the day she followed.

So often she had mentally prepared herself for this day, when she would be with him, yet each time she had resisted. Because she knew how hard it would be, how devastated she would feel. But it was ever in her mind and heart. These past twenty years and more she had thought of little else.

'So, will ye go?' Soft and encouraging, Bridget's voice entered her consciousness.

Lucy nodded. 'You know I will.' Of that there was no question.

'Not today though, eh, Lucy?' Adam could see how tired she was. He above all others knew what an emotionally draining experience it would be when Lucy finally returned to her baby's resting-place. 'I think we should go back to the hotel and take it easy for the rest of the evening.'

As always, his only thought was for Lucy. 'I'll take you to the churchyard first thing in the morning, when you've had a good night's sleep. What do you say, Lucy? It's been a long journey. You need to take it easy now.'

Lucy took a while to answer. To the others, she appeared calm and controlled, while inside, her heart and mind were in turmoil. How could she go there? How could she not? Yet she must. She must! Oh, but where in the name of God would she find the strength?

Suddenly her heart was open and her mind at peace.

From Barney, she realised; that's where she would find the strength.

'You're right, Adam.' She smiled on him and his heart warmed. 'It might be best to leave it until morning.'

Bridget had a suggestion. 'I wouldn't mind betting ye haven't had a good meal all day, am I right?'

Up to now, Lucy had not felt hungry, but suddenly she was famished. 'Why don't we all have dinner at the hotel?' she suggested, perking up.

'Well, I never!' Bridget cried excitedly. 'You took the very words out of my mouth. It'll be my treat, so it will, and no arguments.'

Neither Adam nor Amy needed much persuasion and so it was arranged. 'You take yerselves off, and me and Amy will be there soonever we've painted our faces and put on our glad rags.'

At seven-thirty they gathered in the hotel bar. Having rested awhile, Lucy was now bathed and changed. She had on a black straight-skirted dress with blue collar and cuffs, and her hair was swept back into a loop and fastened with a daisy-chain pin. 'You look lovely!' Even if she was dressed in sacks, Adam would still think the same. In his eyes, Lucy was everything perfect.

All the same, Lucy was flattered. 'You don't look so bad yourself.' In his dark suit and pale green shirt, he made a handsome figure.

Amy and Bridget arrived on time; Amy looking young and fresh in a brown two-piece, Bridget painted to the eyeballs with dark rouge, crimson lipstick, and the smartest bright green two-piece. 'Don't tell me,' she laughed. 'I look like a leprechaun.' She cast a scathing glance at Amy. 'Sure, haven't I already been told that?' Doing a twirl she fished for compliments, and got them a-plenty.

Spending a few minutes in the bar for a pre-meal drink,

they were delighted when Mary and Ben came through the door. 'What a lovely surprise! You're just in time for dinner.' Lucy gave them each a hug before proudly presenting them to Amy and Bridget.

'Gawd love us!' Bridget wrapped herself round Mary and squeezed her so hard, Lucy warned her she'd have her eyeballs out. 'Look at her . . . she's all grown up, so she is!' There was no stopping Bridget once she started. 'Oh, and isn't she like her daddy! Oh Lucy, I can't believe it.'

Becoming emotional, she was almost in tears, until Lucy told her firmly, 'Behave yourself, and let the young 'uns get ready for dinner.'

An hour later, they all went through to the dining room.

The evening was perfect, the food was done to a treat, and the conversation at different times both sparkling and nostalgic; with Bridget unable to take her eyes off Mary, and Mary content to see her mother's eyes shining with pleasure at being with her old friends.

Later, when they had a few minutes alone, she mentioned to Ben that tomorrow would be a difficult day for Lucy. 'God only knows how she'll cope when she goes to the churchyard and sees little Jamie's grave. It's bound to bring it all back with a vengeance.'

Ben had few doubts. 'Your mother will cope like she always does,' he assured her. 'She's the strongest, most determined woman I've ever met.' Looking down at Lucy's daughter, he observed the fine straight features and honest clear eyes, and his voice softened. 'And you, my lovely, are a chip off the old block!'

~

The next day started badly for Lucy. She had not slept well. She saw the dawn light the skies and she heard the first birdsong, and for a time, she sat gazing out the window, her mind shot with all manner of mayhem.

This morning she would see the little cottage given to her by Leonard Maitland, her employer up at The Manse in the village of Comberton by Weir. This was the cottage where she and Barney had lived for a while before moving down to Salford, the cottage where Mary had been conceived, in love, in anguish. The same cottage where she had spent several idyllic months with her young son, enjoying the countryside and the company of their friends, the Davidsons. The cottage where she had shed so many tears, mourning the loss of his bright presence. Bittersweet memories that would never leave her.

Oh, why ever had she come here to this place which she had deliberately shut out of her life for so long? How would she cope? How could she force herself to go through with it all? Had she made a terrible mistake?

All the yearning in the world could never bring back what she craved; her firstborn son, her youth, Barney's love – albeit a love that could never be as powerful and absorbing as hers was for him. It was all gone now. Time had rolled it away, out of sight but not out of mind. And some day, time would roll her away too, and Adam, and everything else she cherished.

It was a sobering thought, which made her even more appreciative and protective of the family she still had – Mary and Adam, and now Ben – and she still had her friends – friends she did not deserve, for hadn't she deliberately distanced herself from them all this time?

After washing and dressing, and feeling more settled in her mind, Lucy went downstairs, where Adam was already waiting. 'Sleep well, did you?' His wide smile was all-enveloping.

'Not too badly,' she lied. 'What I need more than anything right now, is a refreshing cup of tea and a plate of scrambled eggs on toast. That should set me up for the day.'

'Then you shall have it.' Holding out his arm he escorted her to the dining room, where they were led to a small round table by the window.

In no time at all, Lucy had her eggs and a handsome pot of tea, with the daintiest cup and saucer, and a jug of milk filled right to the top. 'Just what the doctor ordered,' she said, and Adam agreed, while eagerly tucking into a full and generous breakfast.

'Talking about doctors,' he remarked, 'when do you intend seeing old Doctor Lucas?'

Lucy had been thinking about that. 'Later,' she said. 'First of all, I'd like to show Mary the cottage where she was born, and the fields where her daddy and the rest of us broke our backs to bring in the harvest, but oh, Adam, they were such wonderful times, weren't they?'

'They certainly were.' His eyes dimmed with emotion. The memories were powerful, painful in their beauty. Reaching out, he laid his hand over hers. 'Wonderful times, yes,' he agreed. 'Sadly, long gone.'

He smiled encouragingly. 'But we're still here, you and me, and Mary, and soon, God willing, once she and Ben are wed, you might be a grandmother, and how would you like that, eh?'

Lucy smiled wistfully. 'Grandma Lucy. Who would ever have thought it, eh? That young wild creature running bare-foot across the fields . . . a grandmother.'

Just then Mary and Ben showed at the door. Catching Mary's attention, Lucy gave a wave and the two of them came across.

'I slept like a log,' Mary said. 'I think the long drive must have tired me.'

Ben told her jokingly how he was the one who should be tired, because he had done all the driving.

The waiter came across and they ordered bacon and eggs for Ben, and toast for Mary.

Through breakfast they discussed plans for the day, and while Adam explained how Lucy wanted to take them to see the cottage and the fields, Lucy's courage began to falter; until Adam sensed her dilemma and winked at her in his usual cheeky manner.

The intimate gesture seemed to harden Lucy's determination. 'We'll go out to the cottage,' she declared. 'Then we'll visit the churchyard, and after that it's on to see Doctor Lucas.'

Lucy and Adam finished their breakfast and left Ben and Mary to finish theirs. 'We'll see you in the foyer in half an hour,' Lucy said. With that she took her leave, and Adam went with her up the staircase. When they reached Lucy's room, he excused himself. 'I'll see you downstairs in half an hour then.'

With that he hurried away, thinking how he would have preferred to be going into the room with her. But maybe that was for another day, when he had persuaded her into being his wife.

Some short time later, the four of them climbed into Ben's car; they drove away from the city of Liverpool and on, towards the outskirts and the open fields of Comberton. Lucy was apprehensive, but knew that she must not shirk from doing what she came here to do. Just once, that was all, and afterwards she would never visit the old places again.

Sitting in the back of the car with Adam beside her and her daughter and Ben in front, she felt strangely isolated, and so incredibly lonely, it was almost unbearable. Then Adam reached out and, tucking her hand into his, he shifted closer to her. His nearness, the touch of his hand and the way he looked at her, as if to say, 'You're not alone, we're all here with you,' gave Lucy a warm feeling.

In all her life, she had learned never to lean on anyone.

But now here she was, leaning on this dear man. And somehow it felt so natural.

Following Lucy and Adam's directions, Ben headed the car away from the main road. As they trailed the curve of the lanes, she was taken back to those far-off days when she worked in those same fields with Barney and his family.

'In here, Ben.' Excitement trembled her voice. 'Pull in here.' On the way over, Lucy had known every twist and turn, and now as they neared the cottage, her heart lurched as she recognised the meandering avenue of oak trees, and the orchard where little Jamie had so often played.

When the car was stationary, she climbed out; for a moment she stood by the gate, her hungry gaze taking it all in. Instinctively now, she went through the gate and following the very same path she had so often followed before, she climbed to the peak of the hill, her every step a trial.

Behind her, Mary prepared to get out of the car. 'Not yet.' Adam felt for Lucy and he knew she would need to be alone. 'Let's give your mother a few minutes, eh?'

Mary nodded, and so they stayed. They watched the small figure climbing and saw how her steps occasionally faltered.

At the top of the rise, Lucy stood tall and proud, her face turned towards the cottage and her gaze marking the spot for all time.

In her mind's eye she saw herself outside the cottage, laughing and playing with Jamie, swinging on the branch of the tree, and gathering fruit from the orchard. She saw Barney and Vicky, sitting on the swing-seat that Barney had created out of old rope and fallen trees, and then there was the party; the barn was still there, its roof sagging and the door hanging lopsided on its hinges. She could even hear the music and the dancing.

It was all there, caught in time forever. And she was content to have been a part of it all.

'It's still here, Barney,' she whispered. 'This wonderful place, that gave us all such happy times.' Rolling down her face and wetting her lips, the tears burned her skin. 'I came back, Barney,' she murmured. 'I came back.' Suddenly she was sobbing, unable to speak for the emotion raking her soul. With her hands over her face, she took the moment to feel his presence and when she looked up again, she was calmer. 'I came back to see if it all really happened,' she whispered, 'but I can never come back again, Barney. It's too much . . . too painful. I'll take it with me, but I know now, it's time to say goodbye.'

She gave a small, choking sob. 'I'll always love you, Barney, you know that, don't you?'

After a restful interlude, she looked up to find the others beside her. 'It's beautiful here.' Sliding her hand into Lucy's Mary admitted, 'The descriptions you gave were so lovely, I thought you might have exaggerated. But you didn't, because it's everything you said.' In her distant memory she felt a part of it, too, yet not in any detail. It was more a deep-down feeling of belonging.

And so they stayed awhile. Drenching her mind with images she had never forgotten, Lucy told them stories of how it was. Adam also had a few comical tales to tell.

'I remember when me and Barney were painting the out-side walls of the big barn. We ended up with more paint on us than on the walls . . . and another time he hosed out the pig-pen and didn't see me in the corner. Talk about a drowned rat!' Everyone roared, and then he added, 'It's a wonder I didn't go down with pneumonia!'

So many memories, alive as though they had happened only yesterday. 'Another time, he nearly killed me when he felled a big old tree that was rotting from the roots up. If Vicky hadn't called out, I'd have been flattened like a pan-cake on the ground.'

They talked and smiled and laughed out loud, and Lucy felt the anguish draining away. People often said that anticipating an event could sometimes be worse than the doing, and so far it seemed they were right, she thought. Instead of pain, the visit had brought a measure of joy.

After a while they walked on down to the river.

On the night they lost little Jamie, the river had been a raging torrent, but now it was unusually quiet, with the shimmering waters gently rolling over the boulders before leaping and dancing on their way down to the valley below.

In her mind, Lucy relived that awful night for the ten-thousandth time, right up to the sight of Barney walking towards her through the water, the tiny lifeless body in his arms and his desolate face preparing her for the worst. Dear God Almighty, how had she lived with it since? How could she go on living with it?

'Come away, my dear.' Lucy was startled by the touch of Adam's fingers as they closed gently round her arm. 'You've lingered enough,' he told her. 'Please, Lucy . . . come away now.'

Turning away from the waters, Lucy assured him she was fine, though at that moment, she wished she could be anywhere but here, in this particular place. It was not over yet, she thought. The next stage of her journey would be the worst.

~

The flowers that Bridget had taken to Jamie on Saturday morning were still fresh and colourful. Even from a distance, the yellow and white spring blooms brightened the little boy's grave.

As she walked through the churchyard, Lucy kept a steely determination not to break down.

In truth, it was Mary who broke down.

Having learned only a year or so ago about her baby brother, she was very emotional. 'You did wrong,' she said, rounding on Lucy, her voice shaking. 'You should have told me long ago. I had a right to know,' she sobbed. Though this trip had been an ordeal for her mother, it had proven difficult for her, too.

Before she could run away, Lucy took hold of her. 'I'm sorry, sweetheart,' she whispered. 'You're right, I should have told you about him – our little Jamie. But it was so hard. I couldn't bring myself to speak of it. I thought if I shut it all out it wouldn't hurt, but it did, and now *you're* hurting, and I won't forgive myself for that.'

For what seemed an age, Lucy held her daughter, as the scent of narcissi rose in the air and surrounded them like a prayer. She let her cry and cried with her, and afterwards, Ben came and took Mary away, while Lucy stayed with Jamie for a while longer. 'I'll always love you,' she murmured. 'As long as I live, I will never forget you. I had to come back, to see you one last time.' Wiping away a solitary tear, she then stroked her fingers tenderly over the name on the granite stone. 'My darling little boy, thank you for the joy you brought me.'

After a while she walked away; leaving the car and the others far behind she went to the edge of the churchyard, where she leaned on the fence and let her mind wander over the fields, as though drawing every memory to her, so that when she left this place it would come with her.

She didn't hear his footsteps as he came to stand beside her, nor at first did she realise he was there, until he spoke softly. 'I can't help you, Lucy, my darling. I want to help you . . . but I don't know how.'

His words touched her deeply. Turning to him, she smiled with all her heart. 'You *have* helped me, Adam,' she said. 'All these years you've been there for me.'

He was leaning on the fence, with his hands clasped before him, when suddenly she reached out and slid her hand into his. 'You're a remarkable man, Adam; kind and caring, always backing me up, always there for me.' She paused, searching for the right words, wanting to convey her feelings. 'The truth is, you mean far more to me than you could ever know.'

When it seemed he might speak, she put her finger over his lips. 'No, Adam, I need to tell you how I feel.' She took a deep breath. 'Coming here, seeing everything again, things I tried so hard to shut out for so long, has made me realise what a fortunate woman I've been, and still am. There have been two men in my life – Barney and you. Both good, unselfish men.'

After faltering a moment, she regained her composure. 'You know I could never love you in the same way I loved Barney, but lately I've come to realise just how much I do love you.' Her eyes told him all he needed to hear. 'Dear Adam, I couldn't bear it if I lost you.'

'You'll never lose me,' he promised. 'Because wherever you are, that's where I'll be.' He saw the tears shining in her eyes and he felt the honesty of her words, and he was the happiest man on God's earth. He ached for her to be his wife; he needed to know that she loved him that much. But his instincts told him that this was not the time nor the place. And so he kept his silence, slid a protective arm round her shoulders, and together they made their way back to the car.

Mary and Ben saw them coming. 'Look at the pair of them, like two sweethearts,' Ben remarked. 'Who knows? We might be having a double wedding, eh?'

Calmer now, Mary was thrilled to see how easy they were, talking and smiling and so comfortable in each other's company. 'Coming here must have made them realise how quickly time flies away and that we must take whatever chances life brings us. Those two were always meant for each other. At one time when I was small, I even thought Adam was my father. He was always around, always looking out for us.'

She paused. 'But there was always Barney. Mother made sure I knew my father, she spoke of him all the time, until I could see him clearly in my mind's eye; I felt as though I knew him as well as she did. There was never any other man for her. But Adam is special. He knew Barney like a brother. Then afterwards, when Mother was left alone, Adam was there; he has grown old with her, and with every year his love for her has become stronger. I know, because I saw it, every day of my life.'

Ben was intrigued. 'And now they're together here, putting the past to rest.'

Their story was amazing, he thought. And now, he too was a part of it, and proud to be so.

CHAPTER EIGHT

T HAT EVENING THEY paid a visit to Dr Raymond Lucas, their former local doctor of twenty years ago. He knew all of them – Barney and his family, Lucy and Adam. The old man was delighted to see them. 'Still the same pretty girl that went away,' he said, kissing Lucy on the cheek.

She laughed. 'You old flatterer, you. That girl is long gone. What you see before you is a woman past her prime, carrying a stick and aching from top to toe. I feel as if I've climbed mountains today,' she groaned. 'Oh, but it's so good to see you.' She thought he had not aged too well. His skin was creased and leathery, his hair almost all gone, and his shoulders had sagged, but his smile and friendly manner were the same.

'You already know Adam Chives?' She brought him forward. 'My dearest friend and confidant.'

The elderly physician shook hands with Adam. 'It's been a long time,' he said. 'I'm glad you brought her to see me . . . thank you.'

Adam chuckled. 'It's more a case of Lucy bringing *me*,' he declared. 'What Lucy wants, Lucy gets. But I'm so glad we're here. To my mind, this visit is long overdue.'

Drawing Mary forward, Lucy was proud to tell him, 'This is Mary . . . mine and Barney's daughter.'

The old man was visibly taken aback. 'Good heavens above! She has a definite look of him.' He held out his hand in friendship. 'You were a beautiful child and you've grown into a lovely woman. Your father would have been proud of you.'

Mary thanked him and linking her arm with Ben's she explained, 'This is Ben, my fiancé. We plan to wed very soon.'

'Then we must celebrate!' Tugging on the bell-rope by the fireplace, Dr Lucas summoned the housekeeper. 'Lizzie, are you able to squeeze another four in for dinner?'

Lizzie did not hesitate. 'Of course,' she replied indignantly. 'Don't I always make extra, and isn't there always enough of this or that in the pantry to conjure up a fine meal?' Large-boned and formidable, she gave the appearance of being an ogre, when in fact they discovered afterwards that she was a real gem, and that the doctor valued her above all else.

Lucy was horrified at the doctor's suggestion. 'We can't put you both to all that trouble, and besides, we're not dressed for a social occasion.'

Dr Lucas would hear none of it. 'You look all right to me,' he protested. 'You're here now and we've so much to talk about. There's a great deal I want to ask, and besides, I need to make the acquaintance of your daughter and her good fellow.'

And so it was settled.

Brushing aside Lucy and Mary's offer of help, Lizzie advised them firmly, 'I was a master cook in my time. Worked in a top hotel, I did! At times we were lucky if we got half an hour's notice to prepare food for upwards of sixty guests; hard work, but good training. Ever since then, I've always been prepared, never caught offguard, and if the spare food isn't eaten, it'll always warm up and do for another day.'

That understood, she marched out and set about preparing the meal.

'I've never dared to argue with her,' the doctor confided jokingly. 'And I don't mind telling you, she frightens the life out of me at times. But she's worth her weight in gold. A real treasure, she is.'

After making sure they were settled and comfortable in the drawing room, he poured them each a drink; a gin and tonic for Lucy, a glass of sherry for Mary, and a measure of whisky each for Ben and Adam.

'That'll warm the cockles of your hearts,' he remarked jovially.

For the next half hour they discussed anything and everything from the old days, content just to reminisce. At first the talk was light-hearted and there was much laughter. But then the talk grew serious, and the doctor recalled how, 'I was devastated when it was discovered that Barney was so ill. Of course, I couldn't tell anyone. Barney made me promise not to, but even so, I have an oath to my profession, so of course I couldn't tell . . . not even when I saw him falling apart.'

He sighed from his boots. 'What happened to Barney was tragic,' he muttered. 'In all my years as a doctor, I have never seen a man so hellbent on hiding his condition from his family; especially when he desperately needed them, more than at any other time in his entire life.'

He glanced at Lucy, who had been intently listening to him. 'I found his actions so hard to comprehend. I could understand why he was reluctant to tell them how ill he was until the last possible moment, but to make them hate him! To deliberately make them believe he was a drunk and a womaniser; to alienate himself from the family he doted on, so they would embark on a new life without him. Dear God! I can only imagine what that must have done to a man like

Barney . . . so in love with his wife, and doting on his children the way he did. Anyone could see how Barney's family were his entire world.'

He glanced at Mary. 'Your father was a remarkable man.'

'I'm beginning to realise that more and more.' Mary answered him softly, her thoughts taking her back to the daddy she remembered, the kindly man who would sit her on his knee and enthral her with magical tales.

An anger took hold of her. 'He needed them so much! Why didn't he tell them how ill he was? He should have told them. HE SHOULD HAVE TOLD THEM!'

'No, Mary.' Lucy calmed her. 'You're so wrong, my darling.' Lucy herself had often wondered why Barney did not put himself first, especially when he was so desperately ill. Deep down though, she knew he had done the right thing – for his family if not for himself. 'If he had told them how ill he was, they would have stayed. They would have seen him suffer the way I saw him suffer, day and night, hurting, fading away until he was like a helpless baby.'

She paused and swallowed, then went on in hushed tones: 'After they were gone, he was so lonely. He would have given anything for it not to have happened. He desperately needed Vicky and the children to be with him to the end, to support and help him, and lift his spirits when he was down.'

'Then why didn't he tell them?'

'Because he was a bigger man than that. He sent them away, out of love. He knew he was not able to go with them; that the opportunity had been cruelly snatched from him. But, by turning them against him, he gave them all their once-in-a-lifetime opportunity, a chance to go to America and build the kind of life they would never be able to find here.'

Adam intervened. 'I can't begin to imagine how he must have suffered, to see his beloved family sail away without him. Barney Davidson loved his family like no other man I know. Yet he made them believe that he didn't care for them any more – that he despised them. He wanted them to believe that he was rotten to the core, a drunkard who preferred the company of street-women to his own darling wife.'

He took another swig of his whisky. 'God only knows where a man could find the strength to do a thing like that.'

The talk now focused on Barney's family, with the doctor asking, 'His daughter Susie will be what . . .' He did a mental calculation, '. . . thirty-five, six?'

'Older, I think,' Lucy answered. 'Ronnie would be about thirty-nine, and Thomas, a couple of years older.' She shook her head in disbelief. 'It seems incredible. In my mind's eye I still see them as young people. I often wonder, if I saw them in the street, would I even recognise them?'

She thought of Barney's wife, that lovely, vivacious creature he adored, and her heart was sore. 'As for Vicky, she was a few years older than me.' Adding up the years, she was shocked. 'Good Lord! She must be well into her sixties by now.'

'Do you think they've made good, the way Barney hoped they would?' That was Mary's question.

Lucy pondered for a moment. 'Yes,' she answered. 'No doubt Susie will have gone on to be a designer of sorts. Thomas was always the shrewd businessman – there was a lot of Barney in Thomas. As for Ronnie, well, I wouldn't like to say. He was headstrong and never seemed to have a particular direction in his life, and after what happened with Barney and everything, I don't know. There was a lot of bitterness in the end. Who can tell how they all survived the trauma of what happened?'

Mary acknowledged her mother's words with a thoughtful

nod of the head. 'You're right,' she murmured. 'It doesn't bear thinking about.'

The old doctor remembered each family member with affection, but as he recalled, Barney's wife was an exceptionally delightful creature. 'Vicky has managed to survive intact, I believe. Marriage to Leonard Maitland has given her security and companionship.'

Lucy said stoutly, 'Yes, Vicky would have kept them all together. She was strong in nature, and very protective of them all. On that last day when she came to see Barney, it was to plead with him. Even after all he had done, she was ready to forgive him. But he played his part well. He sent her away, and that must have broken her heart; it certainly broke his. But, yes! I think somehow or another, Vicky would have kept them all going despite their problem.'

'You did know that Leonard Maitland was in love with Vicky?' the doctor said.

Lucy smiled. 'I think most people knew that – even Barney. He would tease Vicky about it. But it made no difference to either of them, because they had eyes only for each other.'

She imparted a secret she had kept for too long. 'One day, soon after Mary was born, Barney and I were sitting outside on the swing, when he spoke of Leonard. He told me how he had always known Leonard was a good man, that he had confided in Leonard and made him swear never to tell anyone the truth. He also said that he had asked Leonard to take care of Vicky, and marry her when he was dead, because he knew how much in love with her he was.'

Adam nodded. 'Knowing that Leonard had promised to take care of Vicky would have given Barney some peace of mind.'

During the course of the conversation, they touched on

most things. There was talk of Lucy writing to Vicky, and she said it was something she had to do, and very soon.

'One thing at a time though,' she said. 'Coming here has taken up all my energy. But I have it in mind to contact Vicky.' She looked at the old doctor. 'I haven't been able to write before, because I had no way of knowing where they were. But I have a sneaking feeling that you have their address. Am I right, Doctor Lucas?'

A shy little smile crept over his features. 'You've caught me out,' he admitted. 'I do have the address of Leonard's office in Boston. On the day he sailed for America, he said if there was anything that Barney needed, I was to let him know straightaway.'

He gave a long, drawn-out sigh. 'Of course, I never asked him for anything. Firstly because Barney would not have wanted me to, and secondly, because there was absolutely nothing that Leonard could have done for him. When all was said and done, I thought it best to cut away from them, for the family's sake, and because Barney had gone to such horrendous lengths to make sure they would not come back.'

'Would you mind giving me the address?'

'Not at all. I know exactly where I have it.' He struggled out of his chair and picked up his stick. 'In fact, I may as well find it now, and then we can simply enjoy our evening together.'

As he went from the room, Mary crossed to the window and peered out. 'Such an interesting garden,' she observed. 'I do love the conservatory.' Stroking her chin with the tips of her fingers, she mused aloud, 'I wonder if there might be space for us to have one built at home?'

When she beckoned for the others to come and see, Lucy and Ben made their way over to join her. Adam, however, had other ideas. Leaving the room, he stood a while in the hallway, listening intently. When he heard the doctor muttering and moaning, he followed the sound down the passage towards the old man's study, and tapped on the open door. 'Do you think we could have a word?' he asked as the doctor swung round to face him.

'But of course. Come in!'

Adam thought he had never seen such a chaotic room.

The study was piled high with boxes of old files and documents; boxes on the desks, boxes against the wall, and more boxes on top of the filing cabinet. 'I'm always meaning to set about tidying this place up,' the old man explained, 'but somehow, I never seem to get round to it. Lizzie kindly offered to sort it all out, but I can't let her loose on this little lot. The poor darling would not know what goes where, or how to decipher half of it. Besides, most of these are patients' private records. They need to be carefully gone through and meticulously filed, and that's my job.'

He carried on muttering as he threw boxes out of the way. Then: 'There it is!' Digging into one of the half-open desk-drawers, he waved a piece of paper in the air. 'I knew it wouldn't be far away.'

'I just need a minute of your time, if that's all right?' Adam thought that Raymond Lucas was more like an absent-minded professor than a doctor.

'Sorry!' He sat on the edge of the desk. 'You have my full attention now, so please fire away. What's on your mind?'

'May I close the door?'

Dr Lucas frowned. 'If you must, yes . . . close it.'

Adam quietly did so. 'It's just that I wouldn't want Lucy to overhear this.'

'Well, go on then, man! What is it?'

'It's just that, well, as you have the contact address for Leonard, I wondered if you might also have information regarding another ghost from the past.' He lowered his voice. 'Edward Trent . . . the man who caused little Jamie's drowning. Lucy still has nightmares about that. She doesn't know whether he's alive or dead, or even if he might turn up at any minute. So, if it turned out that somebody had finished him off, it would give us all some peace of mind.'

The old man understood immediately. 'That was a terrible thing and no mistake,' he said sombrely.

'So, have you any idea what happened to him?'

'No,' the doctor apologised. 'None whatsoever. It's a mystery to me why they never caught him, but then we knew him to be a cunning fox. Either he had an argument with some other lowlife and was left for dead in some dark, God-forsaken place, or he managed to get far enough away to escape the law.'

'So, God forbid, he could still be on the loose somewhere?' Adam was bitterly disappointed, because even though many years had passed, Edward Trent still cast a dark shadow over their lives.

Though Adam would never mention it to Lucy, not a day went by when he didn't fear for her safety. 'When Lucy rejected him that night, he seemed to lose his sanity. I would feel much safer if I knew where he was today. Somehow, I don't believe he's a man who would easily forget being rejected by a woman.' A thought occurred to him. 'I hope you never give out Lucy's address?'

The older man was wounded. 'Good God, man, what do you take me for? Haven't I kept her address safe these many years?'

Adam apologised. 'I'm sorry. It's just that I do worry about her. There's always the chance that he might come back and look for her.'

'I doubt that. He may be dangerous, but he's not mad. Even if he is still alive, why would he take a chance like that now?'

All the same, he understood Adam's concern. 'Let's hope we'll never see hide nor hair of him again, and Lucy can learn to forget.'

But Adam was unconvinced. 'She will *never* forget,' he murmured. 'And neither will I.'

CHAPTER NINE

L UCY HAD RETURNED home to Salford with the intention of writing to Vicky at the earliest opportunity.

Unsure of how to start, she took a moment to reflect.

Looking out across the garden of Knudsden House, her mind was alive with memories of her incredibly eventful life. Where had they gone, all those years? How did they fly away, without her even noticing?

Tears of regret burned her eyes. Fate was so cruel. She brought you joy, filled your heart with love and hope, then just when you were beginning to feel safe and content, you turned around and it had all been taken away from you.

Releasing a great sigh that seemed to move her very soul, she stood before the desk in the sitting room, her gaze falling to the blank page awaiting her, her voice whisper-soft as she spoke her thoughts aloud. 'Oh Vicky, I'm so sorry!'

Slowly shaking her head, she let her gaze momentarily drift to Barney's photograph. For a long, agonising moment she soaked the contours of his familiar features into her senses, the bright eyes, the winning smile, the wonderful energy in his face. Such a man, she thought. Such a joy.

She returned to his smile, though whilst his was sunny, her smile was sad. 'You should never have left me,' she chided. 'Oh, dear God, Barney! Look how long I waited to be with you . . . then suddenly one day when I wasn't looking, you were gone.'

When emotion threatened to overwhelm her, she sat herself down at the desk, and picked up her fountain pen.

Three times she started the letter, and three times she tore it up and threw the remnants in the waste-paper bin.

Leaning back in the chair she closed her eyes, let her mind reshape her thoughts and started again.

My dearest Vicky,

I know this letter and its contents will come as a shock to you, and for that I deeply apologise. But there is something you should know.

All those years ago, you left for America, wrongly believing that Barney had forsaken you. He made you think he did not love you or his children, that he wanted rid of you all. You must have been heartbroken. I can't even begin to imagine how desperately hard it was for you.

Sadly, Barney had a reason for wanting to make you believe he had turned bad. I knew the truth and I wanted to tell you, but I could not, until now . . .

Throwing down her pen, she snatched up this page, too, and tore it into the tiniest fragments. 'It's not right!' She was angry, with Vicky for not being here where she could explain face to face, with Barney for having created such a dilemma, and with herself for not being strong enough to do what she knew in her deepest heart must be done.

'Why can't I say the right things?' she asked herself. 'Why can't I say them in a way that won't cause her any more heartache?'

She gave a wry little laugh. Look at her – trying to protect Vicky, when what she really wanted to say was that, whatever

Barney had done or said, Vicky should have trusted and loved him enough to know that when everything bad was happening, she should have questioned it more. As his wife, Vicky should have known that being cruel or spiteful was *not* in Barney's nature.

Pushing the chair back, Lucy began to pace the room, her own heart beating fast in agitation. Vicky should never have left him! Never have doubted him! When he needed her, she should have been there for him. Instead, his wife had left him alone . . . deserted him and sailed to the other side of the world, just when he needed her the most.

After a time, anger and confusion subsided. She regained her composure and returned to sit at the desk, where she laid out a clean sheet of paper and began to write. 'It has to be done,' she murmured as she formulated her thoughts. 'Painful or not, Barney's family must be made aware of the truth.'

As she wrote, the years rolled away and memories sharpened into focus: of Barney, Vicky, their three lovely children and the times they all enjoyed together.

Though determined not to avoid what she now considered to be her duty, Lucy was later to recall writing that letter as one of the most painful episodes in her life.

~

The room was small. Smelling of new polish and aging leather, it had magnificent panelled walls and narrow high windows, and behind the long table, the four men talked amongst themselves in whispers.

Eventually one by one they straightened their shoulders and all raised their heads to look at Edward Trent; though of course he was known to them as Edward Carter.

'Pay attention, Carter,' the Governor snapped. 'We have

looked at the facts and examined your record here. Unfortunately, it seems you have excelled yourself in making trouble and undermining the discipline of this establishment.'

Grim-faced and unforgiving, the man who spoke recognised that he had a personal dislike of this particular prisoner; though it would jeopardise his own position if he was not seen to be impartial. 'In our view, and it is unanimous, your record is such that you should consider yourself fortunate not to have your sentence lengthened. You're a threat to every prisoner here; whenever there have been stabbings or punishment attacks, your name comes up time and again.'

His expression hardened. 'We know you're behind it, Carter, but you have such cunning that so far you've managed to escape blame.'

He finished with a dire warning. 'You're being watched, man. It's only a matter of time before you're caught red-handed.'

His stiff gaze rested on the prisoner a moment longer, before stamping the document with a flourish. 'Appeal denied!'

Instructing the officer to take him away, he was deeply shaken when at the door, the prisoner turned to stare at him, and in those brooding eyes, he saw a glimmer of pure evil.

With the prisoner gone and the room plunged into silence, he turned to the men around him. 'There goes a bad lot!'

'He deserves to be locked up for good,' said one. 'Two men scarred for life; another terrorised out of his mind, and another in hospital for three months. And we all know who's responsible.'

'Yes, but he's so devious,' said another. 'The other prisoners are in such fear, we've never been able to prove anything against him.'

The Governor had to agree with his colleagues. 'We all know he's the culprit, and so far we've managed to keep him detained. But I'm very much afraid there will come a time when we can't keep him under lock and key.' Anger coloured his voice. 'Unless he happens to slip up, or some brave man steps forward to point the finger.'

There was a lull in the conversation, during which every man there felt helpless.

When after a few moments someone spoke out, it was with deadly earnestness. 'So, what you're saying is, we may have to let him go, the next time he's brought before us?'

A quieter voice intervened. 'Even if he gets out, he'll be back soon enough. A man like that . . . it's only a matter of time before he kills.'

PART TWO

~

October, 1954

Barney's Family

Boston, Massachusetts

CHAPTER TEN

LATE AUTUMN IN Boston was a time when the magnificent colours of the trees, which had created magic to the eye only a few weeks before, were already drifting away as their leaves fell, heralding the onset of winter. But in spite of all that, it was Mrs Vicky Maitland's favourite season.

'I always enjoy our evening walks alongside the water,' Vicky tucked her arm through her husband, Leonard's, 'but autumn is best. The trees may be shedding their leaves, but the beauty never fades.' She playfully kicked the leaves along under her feet. 'It's just different,' she mused. 'A quieter, deeper kind of beauty.'

Leonard smiled down on her. 'You see beauty in everything,' he said lovingly. 'But yes, I know what you mean – and you're right, as always.'

They strolled on for a time, eventually sitting down to rest where the overhanging branches of a giant tree dipped into the water.

For what seemed an age, not a word passed between them. Over the years they had grown so close, they almost knew what the other was thinking. And just now, in that moment, Vicky was thinking of another stretch of water, the Atlantic Ocean, and a journey that she would never forget. It seemed a lifetime ago when she and her children boarded the liner

119

that would carry them away from their homeland forever.

She thought of Barney, and the way their marriage had ended. What he did had broken her heart. It had almost ruined one of their sons, made the other forever bitter, and taken away their daughter Susie's childhood. Each and every one of them had changed because of what Barney had done, and for that, Vicky could never forgive him.

In the beginning, there was deep shock, and a yearning to punish him for splitting the family asunder. But though she might blame him for the pain he had caused, Vicky could never stop loving him. Barney was her first and last real love. Nothing could ever change that.

Eventually, she forgave him for what he had done to her. But she could never forgive him for what he had done to the children – Susie in particular. She had been made to grow up before her time.

'A penny for them?' Leonard's voice cut across her thoughts.

'Oh Leonard, I'm sorry,' Vicky apologised. 'I was just thinking.'

'You were miles away.' Sliding an arm round her shoulders, he drew her to him. 'You were thinking of Barney again – I can always tell. But it's all right, my dear. I understand, I really do.'

Vicky felt ashamed. 'You're such a good man,' she muttered. 'I don't deserve you.'

'No, you don't,' he agreed, 'because you deserve the best – and in your eyes that will always be Barney Davidson. I don't pretend to match up to him, because I never will, nor would I want to. Yes, I know he caused you all such pain. But it's never the *bad* things we remember about the person we love. It's always the good times – the laughter and the joy.'

Pausing to gather his thoughts, he watched the rowboat go past. He saw some children running along the riverbank trying to keep up, and it made him smile. 'We do the best we can,' he said. 'We strive and struggle, yet sometimes it's not enough. We must never forget, Barney was very special. A strong, determined man, he was totally devoted to you and the children. You can't dismiss a man like that – and no one would expect you to, least of all me.'

In the deepest recesses of his mind, he recalled the night he had found Barney huddled by the tree trunk, desperately ill and almost out of his mind. That night, he had made a sacred promise to Barney, and for Vicky's sake he had kept that promise; though with every passing year, the burden of guilt weighed heavier.

Deeply moved by his quiet words, Vicky reached up to kiss him softly on the mouth. 'You know me so well,' she chided. 'I can never keep a secret from you.'

She needed to tell him something now – something she had never said before. 'What you say is true, Leonard – I do still love Barney, and I will love him to the day I die. But I love you, too. I love being your wife, and I love the way you took me and the children under your wing. You're kind and thoughtful, and I'm so glad you were there for us.' She moved closer to him. 'Have I been a good wife to you, Leonard?'

He squeezed her tenderly. 'You know you have.'

'I always knew you had a fancy for me,' she chuckled. 'Barney was the first to notice it, and he would tease me mercilessly. It's strange how things worked out,' she mused. 'Do you think some things are meant to be?'

'In what way, exactly?'

'You and me . . . do you think there really is something called Fate, which channels our lives into a particular direction?'

In answer, he took her by the elbows and stood her up. 'I'm certain there is,' he replied. 'I think it was Fate that made me get rid of that monstrous fiancée of mine; it was Fate that made me fall in love with you, and it was Fate that brought us here to this land of America, where I won your heart . . . not your soul because that belongs to Barney. But we're here together, safe and secure. And yes, I do believe we have Fate to thank for that.'

Vicky nodded. 'Or some almighty hand that guides us to our destiny.'

They resumed their stroll in silence.

After a time it was Vicky who spoke. 'Leonard?'

'Yes, my darling?'

'Will Ronnie ever come home to us?'

Leonard nodded his head. 'I hope so. He's already made a start by coming to work on the estate.'

'I really thought he would go to gaol after that last court hearing. Drunk in the road . . . cursing and fighting with the officers when they tried to arrest him. In some ways, you would think he was seventeen, not a man of nearly forty. Oh Leonard, I wish now that we had let him fight in the war, even though it would have broken my heart to see him go. It might have got rid of some of his demons.' Her heart turned over at the thought of it all. 'He carries such anger inside.'

'I know. But he does seem to be coping with life better these days. Perhaps he's turned the corner at long last.'

In his heart, Leonard held out small hope. Ronnie had always clung to his father; all his young life he had modelled himself on Barney, and after they were made to leave him behind, Ronnie never really got over it.

~

'To hell with it!' Sliding out from underneath the tractor, Ronnie threw the wrench across the ground. 'The damned thing was rotten right through. It's snapped in half now and I can't shift it no way!'

Having stood patiently by while Ronnie tried to replace the bolt in the floor of the tractor, Thomas picked up the wrench. 'Don't get all worked up,' he told him sternly. 'You're always in too much of a hurry, that's your trouble.'

'Huh! Well, that's rich, I must say. I've been working at it for half an hour.'

Getting down to his knees, Thomas peered beneath the tractor. 'Ten minutes, not half an hour,' he reminded his brother. 'You've been at it for *ten* minutes, and in that time you've managed to cause chaos. You caught the fuel pipe and almost ripped it off in a panic, and now you've chopped the bolt off so there isn't enough left to grip hold of.' He gave a weary grin. 'Do me a favour, will you?' he asked light-heartedly.

Ronnie groaned. 'Now what?'

'While I'm under here, I want you to stay right where you are. Don't do anything! Don't try to help, and don't move, not even an inch. Do you think you could manage that?'

Ronnie had to smile. 'I reckon so,' he answered sheep-ishly. 'I'm sorry, Tom . . . bad night, worse morning. One o' them days, eh?'

Thomas crawled under the tractor. 'I know what you mean,' he remarked cynically. 'Since first light this morning you've been a right pain, moaning and groaning, dropping this and throwing that. To tell you the truth, I'd rather you stayed away when you're in one of those moods.'

'All right, all right! There's no need to keep on, dammit!' Kicking the tractor with the flat of his foot, Ronnie cursed under his breath when his foot began to throb. 'It's just that, well, these days, I've got things on my mind. I can't seem to concentrate.' A wry smile lifted the corners of his mouth. 'Everything I touch seems to go wrong.'

Thomas smiled up at him. 'You're a walking disaster,' he agreed. 'Now just remember to stay right where you are – at least until I get out from under here. That's all I'm asking.'

Ronnie nodded. 'Sure.'

'Oh, and by the way, what happened to that good-looking woman I saw you with at the park . . . Norma, wasn't it?'

Ronnie tutted. 'Nancy! Her name was *Nancy*.'

'OK, so what happened to Nancy?'

'It wasn't working out.'

Thomas slid out from under the tractor. 'What you mean is, she got fed up with your fiery moods and quick temper, and she dumped you. Am I right – *is* that what happened?'

'Something like that, yes.' Ronnie shrugged his shoulders. 'She went off with some wagon-driver. It doesn't bother me, though. She wasn't so perfect either, when it came right down to it. Truth is, I think I'm well out of that one.'

Tapping him on the shoulder with the wrench, Thomas warned his younger brother, 'One of these days you'll find somebody you really love. You'll drive her away with that raging temper of yours and live to regret it.'

'So what?' Ronnie gave the tractor another vicious kick. 'It wouldn't be the first thing I've lived to regret!' With a parting shot he strode off. 'Tell Mom I'm staying in town tonight.'

'Why don't you stay home, just this once?' Thomas asked angrily. 'You know that's what she wants.'

'Oh yeah?' Ronnie turned on him. 'Well, we don't always get what we want out of life, do we, eh? I wanted her to stay and work it out with Dad, but she refused. When we got here, I wanted her to go back and try again, but oh no! And when it was too late and we heard that Dad had died, it didn't take her long to marry Leonard, did it? All women are bitches, in my opinion.'

'It wasn't like that, and you know it!'

Grabbing him by the shirt-collar, Thomas reminded him, 'Leonard has been good to us. If it hadn't been for him, God only knows where we might have ended up. As for Mom, she was devastated when Dad did what he did . . . parading himself through the centre of Liverpool with tarts and drunks. And don't forget how he turned on her when she tried to reason with him! I'll never know why he changed like he did. But he did, and it hurt. It hurt us, and it hurt her more. Don't tell me she didn't try to rebuild the family, because she tried time and again, belittling herself for our sakes, but Dad was so far gone he didn't want to know! As for her marrying Leonard, what would you have her do, eh? Spend the rest of her life being lonely, brooding over what happened?'

He gave Ronnie a shake. 'Did you really want her to go back and beg Dad to change his mind? Did you want her to suffer another round of shame and rejection? Is that what you wanted? Is it?'

There were tears in both men's eyes.

Thomas, too, had been affected by leaving his father in Liverpool, but through it all he saw himself as the man of the family. With Susie and his mother in pieces and Ronnie getting involved with all manner of bad things, it was up to him to reassure the others, when all the time he was feeling heartbroken and bitter. He loved his father. But seeing him turn into a stranger had been devastating. To his dying day he would never understand why it happened the way it did. But it did, and they had to live with it – Ronnie included!

Suddenly, the younger man was crying, loud bitter sobs that shook Thomas to his roots. 'I didn't mean to blame her,' he wept. 'I know it wasn't her fault.'

Wrapping an arm round him, Thomas held him in a brotherly hug. 'Just remember, she did what she could,' he said quietly. 'She secured us a future, and I for one am glad she has somebody else to look out for her. Leonard is a good man, you know that.'

Ronnie didn't look up. Instead, he nodded his head. Then he turned and walked away.

Thomas watched him go. He saw the hunched shoulders and the dogged steps, and it tore him apart. 'Ronnie, come back . . . RONNIE!' Instead, Ronnie broke into a run. He ran down the dip and on towards the lane, where he jumped the five-bar gate, and was quickly gone.

Behind him, Thomas leaned against the barn door, his sorry gaze following Ronnie as he disappeared out of sight.

He was torn two ways. He knew how hard his younger brother had tried to stay out of trouble, and for a time he had managed it. He stayed home and worked the land with Thomas. He slotted back into the family fold and was even forging a friendship with Leonard. But like always, this period of peace was short-lived. Somehow he always drifted back to the bad ways, hanging out with ruffians on the wrong side of town, getting drunk in bars and causing mayhem wherever he went.

Seeing his brother so damaged, was deeply troubling to Thomas. There seemed no peace for him, no salvation. Inevitably his thoughts returned to the day they sailed out of Liverpool, when he had seen young Ronnie hiding behind a column on deck, looking back, tears in his eyes as he searched for the figure of his father; there was no sign of Barney, only the Mersey docks, getting smaller and smaller, until they disappeared altogether.

Time and again over the years he had tried to reach out to Ronnie, but when he was in one of his black moods, there was no reasoning with him.

The boy had gone, the man had emerged, but the heart was still raw with loss. And because Barney was not here to ease his pain, he blamed everyone else – his brother, his mother, and most of all, Leonard.

Susie was the only one he would talk to, because she knew how he felt. She, too, had gone through all the emotions, the bitterness and hatred, the longing and regrets. But over the years she had poured all her energy into work, and somehow had managed to come to terms with the upheaval that had turned all their lives upside down.

On seeing his mother return with Leonard, Thomas quickly went into the barn and resumed work on the tractor.

When he heard a noise at the barn door, he looked up to see his mother standing there. 'Is everything all right?' she asked worriedly. 'Was that Ronnie I saw running across the fields?'

Thomas told her that Ronnie had been helping him service the machines. 'He had to go,' he explained. 'Things to do, or so he said.'

Vicky came closer. 'Don't fob me off, young fella,' she said. 'Ronnie was running like the devil was on his heels. Something's wrong, I know it.' She saw the pain in her elder son's eyes and her heart sank. 'What's wrong this time? Where was he headed? Please, lad, tell me the truth.'

Thomas straightened his shoulders. 'He's gone,' he said simply.

'Gone where?'

'God knows.'

'Why did he go? WHY?'

'Who can tell?' Anger and frustration rippled through him. 'One minute he was working under the tractor, then we were talking and now he's gone, like you say . . . running as though the devil was on his heels.'

Vicky didn't need to ask but she did anyway. 'What exactly were you talking about?'

'Nothing in particular,' he said cautiously. 'This and that.'

'It was Barney, wasn't it?' Where Ronnie was concerned, her instincts were always right. 'You were talking about your father, and he got himself all aerated?'

Thomas was stuck for an answer. So many times he'd been caught in the middle, not wanting to hurt Ronnie, not wanting to hurt his mother. 'All right, yes, we were talking about Dad, or at least Ronnie was,' he said finally.

She nodded an acknowledgement. 'And he was blaming everyone. You, for not persuading me to go back and try to reunite the family, and Leonard for marrying me?'

'Look, Mom, Ronnie's got it all wrong. He took it bad when the family broke up.'

Vicky put up her hand to stop him. 'We *all* took it bad!' she reminded him. 'You, Susie, and me. We've *all* had to deal with it. Did you tell him that it was twenty years ago, and that he must learn to come to terms with it? Otherwise it will ruin him, and if it ruins him, it will ruin us too.' A thought crossed her mind. 'What else did he say?'

Thomas knew his mother would not let it go until she had the whole story. 'He said you should never have married Leonard,' he muttered, hating to say the words.

'I see.' She bowed her head. 'He still dislikes him, doesn't he?'

'No, I don't think he dislikes him. It's just that he sees him as having taken Dad's place.'

Vicky's quiet voice reflected her thoughts. 'He doesn't know how wrong he is. No one could ever take the place of Barney.'

His sorry eyes belied the bright smile on her face. 'Ronnie will be back,' she assured him. 'He needs us, just like we need him, so let's not worry too much, eh?'

As she walked away, the tears burned brightly in her sad eyes. In the curve of the lane she paused to look up at the skies; just then the clouds shifted and from somewhere deep in the Heavens, the sky was lit with a warm glow. 'Help him, Barney,' she pleaded. 'He's so bitter and unhappy, and he won't let any of us near. He's your son, my darling, and he's in turmoil. Help him, please.'

After a while she blinked back the tears and walked on.

She knew how Ronnie felt and she could not blame him. There were times when she, too, felt the pain and loneliness of not having Barney in their lives. Yes, she had made a new life with Leonard, and yes, she had her family around her. But every day, every minute something was missing. That something was Barney.

In the beginning she had often been tempted to go back, to make contact with him and talk it through, until she reminded herself that it was Barney himself who had made the choice; it was Barney who had broken all their hearts and sent them away; and it was Barney who had cruelly rejected her, time and again. For whatever reason, their happy life together had been poisoned for all time.

That was when the pain turned to anger, and she hardened herself to move on, away from the past and into the future.

For all their sakes, it had seemed the only way.

CHAPTER ELEVEN

SUNDAY-EVENING DINNER with the family had become a regular event. This Sunday was no different, except by the time Vicky had set the table ready for serving, Ronnie had still not shown up. 'He's deliberately staying away again, isn't he?' She was at her wits' end. 'He can't even bring himself to sit at the table once a week with his own family!'

Leonard had seen it all before and try as he might, he could not get through to Ronnie. 'I'm sorry, sweetheart, but you know what he's like. He'll either turn up or he won't. Either way there is little we can do. We can't frog-march him here.'

Vicky still blamed herself. 'If only he would talk to you, it might help.'

'No, it wouldn't.' Leonard shook his head. 'I've tried to be a father figure, but he's not having it. I can't force myself on him, sweetheart. It's got to come from him.'

Leonard had kept his promise to Barney. In all this time he had not once betrayed that amazing man. It frightened him that if they ever discovered he had known the truth all along, none of them would forgive him, least of all Vicky. So he remained silent; though there was not a minute in the day when he didn't feel the weight of that fateful promise he made to Barney.

There was an element of guilt, too. Through no fault of his own, Barney had lost everything – the family he cherished and his own precious life – while he, Leonard, had gained everything – a new life here in America on his grandfather Farley Kemp's huge farm, now restored to its former productivity and wealth, and most of all, he had Vicky.

He observed her now, her slim figure, the pretty hair that was once rich and golden with youth, now plaited back, the telling streaks of grey betraying her age. The handsome features were still strong, and just as he had done since the first moment he saw her, he loved her with every fibre of his being.

'With luck he'll turn up, there's still time.' Vicky set her younger son's place along with the others. 'I'd best get back to the kitchen, or the meat will be like charcoal.' Vicky had not changed from the woman she had been; always happiest when caring for the family.

'I don't know why you won't have a cook to do all that for you.' Leonard had tried in vain to persuade Vicky to have more help in the house. 'It's a big place for one woman to run by herself.'

'I don't run it by myself,' Vicky reminded him. 'I have Beth.'

'Yes, but she only comes in twice a week to do the bedrooms. You take care of the rest – polishing and cleaning, cooking and gardening. There's no end to it!'

'I'm a born housekeeper,' Vicky told him with a smile. 'Now, will you please stop nagging, and put the glasses out. The family will be here soon.' She glanced out the window. 'Ronnie too, I hope.'

It was eight-thirty when the family started arriving.

Thomas was the first, along with his wife. Tall and willowy, with bobbed black hair and dark eyes, Sheila was a stunning beauty, even at the age of forty. Married these sixteen years, she and Thomas lived close by, in a fine house they had designed themselves.

Unbeknownst to Thomas, who adored the ground she walked on, Sheila had indulged in several affairs, all of them brief and sordid. When the novelty wore off and the fun was over, she would pay off her sexual partners with a wad of money to keep their silence.

'Vicky, how are you?' Kissing her mother-in-law on the cheek, Sheila made a show of affection. 'You're looking wonderful as always.' She observed Vicky's long red dress and that ever-slim figure, and though Vicky was far older than her, with her best years behind her, she could not suppress a vicious surge of envy.

'Thank you, Sheila, I do the best with what I've got.' Vicky was always pleasant and friendly, but she had no illusions where her daughter-in-law was concerned. She had long entertained suspicions about the woman's fidelity, but that's all they were . . . suspicions. She so much wanted to believe that Thomas and his wife were truly happy together. Certainly Thomas was, and for that she must be grateful.

It had been a bitter disappointment that there were no grandchildren on the scene. It was probably too late for Thomas and Sheila, but there was still Ronnie; and though Susie was edging past the child-bearing years, there was time enough for her to become a mother. Having devoted all her time and effort to her business, Susie had yet to find the man she loved, but God willing, he was out there somewhere.

Like a caged cat looking for an escape route, Sheila glanced about the room, her eyes alighting on Leonard. 'Oh, there you are, Lenny,' she gushed. 'And how are you?'

Leonard got out of his chair to kiss her fleetingly on the cheek. 'I'm fine, thank you, Sheila.'

She traversed her gaze around the room. 'No Ronnie then?'

'Not yet, no.' Vicky showed no concern. 'But I'm sure he'll be here any minute.'

'Really?' Sheila's sly grin made Vicky clench her fists. 'You know very well he won't turn up,' she gloated. 'He never does.'

Thomas stepped in. 'Sheila! That's a hurtful thing to say.'

'Maybe, but it's true. He doesn't give a damn about anybody but himself, least of all his family.'

'Enough said!' Stepping forward, Vicky thrust a tea-towel into her hands. 'The roast potatoes need taking out of the oven. Would you mind, please?'

The two women stood eyeball to eyeball, the older one smiling calmly and the younger one silently seething, but she knew better than to show her resentment. 'Of course I don't mind,' she replied with a shrug. 'But I'm surprised you're so behind with the cooking, Vicky, honey. Normally you have the food all ready for serving.'

Turning on her heels she went away grumbling. 'I guess it don't matter that I've just painted my nails, and if the grease spills down my new expensive jacket, who is there to care?'

Vicky knew her daughter-in-law was goading her, but she did not retaliate. She had more important things on her mind than exchanging verbal blows with the spiteful Sheila. What she really wanted was for Ronnie to show his face. But she was not fooling herself. Sheila was right; he probably would not turn up, more's the pity.

~

A striking figure in a blue pencil skirt with matching bolero and cream-coloured blouse, Susie climbed the three flights of stairs to her brother's apartment in the heart of Boston.

As she climbed, she kept a wary eye about her. This was not the best of neighbourhoods.

Yet again the elevator was out of order, and on the stairs that wound up the outside of the building, a lone visitor was a prime target for the hopeless bums who frequented this area.

'Ronnie Davidson, you're a hopeless bugger!' she muttered as she traipsed upwards. 'Hiding in your room skulking – I'm fed up with it! You live in a slum, you think the world's against you, and you abandon your family at the drop of a hat. I won't have it, d'you hear? You're still my brother and God help me, I care about you . . . we all do.'

Tripping over an empty box flung across her path, she kicked it aside. 'You can moan and grumble all you like, but I don't intend to let you waste your life like this!'

Holding onto the handrail she followed the row of doors; damaged doors with broken windows, doors without any windows at all; doors that were kicked in and hanging on their hinges – and when she reached the door that had the name RONNIE painted on it in big, clumsy letters, she stopped, took a deep breath and knocked. 'Ronnie! It's me, Susie. Open up.'

After a few more determined knocks and a series of loud shouts through the letter-box, the door slowly inched open, to reveal Ronnie's unshaven face. 'I thought I told you never to come here,' he said in a surly voice. 'It's not safe for a woman on her own.'

Susie pushed past him into the sitting room. 'You know what they say: if the mountain won't come to Mohammed and all that?'

He glared at her. 'What d'you want, sis?'

'What do you *think* I want?'

'I won't know if you don't tell me.' Scratching his head, he sauntered across the room. 'Banging on the door, yelling through the letter-box like a crazy woman!'

Ignoring his rantings, Susie instructed him to get dressed.
'I am dressed!'

Shaking her head, she regarded his appearance: the shirt-tail hanging out, the crumpled trousers and the hair standing on end. 'I'm not taking you out to the spread looking like that,' she said. 'You've got ten minutes,' she warned. 'I want you washed and dressed and fit to sit at the table with ordinary human beings.'

'I'm not going to Mom's house.'

'You are!'

'No, I'm not. And there's nothing you can say that will make me change my mind.'

'All right then.' Hands on hips she gave it her best shot. 'What if I was to say that if you don't come with me now, I will never visit you again? I'll forget I ever had a brother called Ronnie, and when you need me – which you frequently do – I'll refuse to see you. I'll cut you out of my life and leave you to sulk and hide and feel sorry for yourself, and when they drag your worthless body out of here, with your clothes stuck to your back, your teeth all rotten and your hair all gone, I'll look the other way and make out I don't even know you. Now then, what d'you say to that?'

Ronnie burst out laughing. 'You're a lunatic!' But he loved her. When he didn't want his mother to know how deep he had sunk, and Thomas was driven to distraction, it was always Susie he turned to, always Susie who would sit for hours and listen to his sorry tale, and never judge or condemn. She simply came to his rescue, without question or reprimand. But not today. Today it seemed he had overstepped the mark with her.

Susie cocked a thumb towards the bathroom. 'I assume you have soap and water?'

'Somewhere, I suppose.'

'Then go wash!'

Ronnie was still laughing at her previous remark. 'I think I'd better,' he said. 'I don't want to end up being dragged out of here with my clothes glued to my back ... no teeth, no hair ... whatever would the neighbours say?' Then: 'You'd make a good horror-writer, sis. I have to say, you certainly paint a gruesome picture.'

Still chuckling, he made his way to the bathroom, where he ran the tap and stripped off, with the intention of making himself respectable.

While he was splashing and scrubbing, Susie's voice sailed in from the other room. 'This place is a disgrace! The holes in the carpet, if you can call it that, are filled with cigarette butts, the springs in the sofa are poking through, and the curtains are hanging by a thread.' There was a pause while she ran the tip of her finger along the window-sill. 'Dust an inch thick everywhere. Dirty socks in the corner. The place stinks to high heaven. How in God's name can you live in a dump like this?'

While she went about the room tidying everything away, Ronnie mimicked her in the bedroom, where he was sorting a decent pair of trousers from the pile on the bed. 'The place stinks ... dirty socks, raggedy curtains, holes in the carpet.' He chuckled, 'I should think myself lucky to have a carpet – not everybody round here has that luxury.'

A moment later he burst out of the bedroom. 'Right then, kiddo, do I look human enough?' He made a handsome figure; tall and slim, with his thick mop of fair hair brushed back from his face, which was now shining clean and free of whiskers.

Susie approved of the new Ronnie. 'Where did you get the trousers from?'

'I've had them for ages, why?'

'They're too big.' Susie observed how the belt was too long to fit the buckle-prong into the holes, so it was wrapped round and round, with the tail end tucked into the pocket of his trousers.

'I've lost weight.' Thrusting his hands into the pockets, Ronnie looked set for a confrontation. 'So now you're about to have a go at me for that, are you? No doubt you'd rather have me fat and flabby with drooping jowls and a huge belly hanging over my belt.'

'Oh, don't be silly!'

'You're right, I am silly. Silly to think that somewhere in that hard heart of yours, you might find a snippet of praise for the effort I've made.'

'Is that the only belt you've got?'

' 'Fraid so.'

With time marching on, Susie was considering how she could rectify the situation. 'Have you by any chance got a pair of scissors?'

'Nope.'

'A sharp knife then?'

'Nope.'

'What do you use to cut your cheese?'

'I don't. I just take a bite whenever I feel the urge.'

'That's disgusting!'

'No, it's not.' He cocked his head. 'You should try it,' he advised. 'It tastes better when you tear off a chunk with your teeth.'

While he ranted on, teasing and taunting, Susie dug into her handbag. 'Got it!' Brandishing a pair of nail scissors, she advanced on him with a determined gleam in her eye.

'Hey!' Backing off, Ronnie demanded to know what she was about.

'Stand still, and stop your moaning!' Grabbing hold of him, she whipped the belt from his trousers and while he struggled to hold them up, she gouged a couple more holes in the belt. 'Here, try it now.'

He slid the belt round his waist and was delighted to find that it fitted snugly with the new holes. 'You're not just a pretty face, are you, sis?'

Snipping off the tag end of the belt, she stepped back to view her handiwork. 'There – that looks better.' Grabbing his jacket from the chair she threw it to him. 'We'd best get going, or we'll miss dinner altogether.'

He frowned. 'Do I have to come?'

Her answer was to drag him out of the door. 'If anybody needs a good meal inside him, it's you. So come on, move yourself, and when you get there don't sulk in a corner, and don't refuse the drink Leonard is bound to offer you.'

As they went down the fire-escape to the sidewalk she was still giving out her orders. '. . . And don't drink too much, or you'll only end up saying the wrong thing.'

'Gee, Suze, I never knew you were such a nag!'

'Get in the car.' In minutes she had him inside with the door shut, and after scrambling into the driver's seat she went off down the road at such a speed he hung on to his seat for dear life. 'Slow down, you're driving like a damned lunatic!'

'Rubbish! I'm only doing fifty miles an hour.'

'That's what I mean. I'm too young to die.'

The banter continued all the way out of town and on towards the big farmstead.

'If you get us there in one piece I'll eat my hat!' Ronnie promised.

'For God's sake, shut up and relax. I know what I'm doing.'

By the time they arrived, Vicky was about to serve the first course. Placing the tureen of soup on the table, she ran out to meet them. 'You decided to come after all. Oh Ronnie, I'm so pleased.'

'Your bullying daughter dragged me here,' he moaned.

'She also made me wash and shave, she cut off a chunk of my belt, and nearly killed us both on the way here.'

'Take no notice of him, Mom.' Kissing Vicky on the cheek, Susie explained, 'It wasn't my driving that made him a shivering wreck. He was already like that when I found him.'

Leonard was delighted to see Ronnie. 'Your mother was worried about you,' he said.

Ronnie never had much to say to Leonard, and tonight was no exception. Without replying, he addressed Vicky. 'There's no need for you to worry. I'm quite capable of taking care of myself.'

'I only wish that were true!' Vicky knew her children like she knew herself, and she never cared much for the way Ronnie deliberately excluded Leonard from any conversation. 'But I'm glad you're here, all the same. We all are, aren't we, Leonard?'

His stepfather smiled at Ronnie, a smile that said, 'Even if you don't accept me, I'll still be here whenever you need me.'

'I think Ronnie already knows,' he replied. 'I'm always glad to see him.'

Vicky gave Susie a grateful glance, discreetly thanking her for bringing Ronnie home, even if it was only for a short time. He was the stray sheep that had not yet found its way back to the fold.

'Right,' she announced, 'dinner's ready. There's pea and ham soup to start, thick and rich, the way you all like it.' It had been one of Barney's favourites.

~

The evening went just as Vicky had planned, with everyone together, all eager to catch up with the latest news and gossip. 'Now that we've managed to secure Baron's Farm, that will bring our holding up to close on a thousand acres of prime productive land.'

Leonard had been after the 200-acre farm for some long time, and now that he had secured it into the family holding, he was desperate to persuade Ronnie to come back and work with them. It was what he wanted and, more importantly, it would make Vicky a contented woman.

Vicky picked up immediately on his piece of news. Addressing Ronnie, she told him, 'Leonard has it in mind to renovate the old farmhouse. It's yours, if you want it.' Under the table she kept her fingers crossed, hoping he might leap at the chance. 'You know the place,' she reminded him. 'It's in a lovely spot, and you can be as isolated as you want. Please, Ronnie, we all want you to come home. Say you'll take it.'

All eyes were on Ronnie as he seemed to be considering the proposition. When at length he gave his answer, it was not the one Vicky wanted to hear, yet it was the one they all expected. 'Not yet, Mother.' He gave a determined shake of the head. 'I'm not ready. It's not that I don't want to, you know that.'

'So, what is it then?' Thomas was quick to lose his temper where Ronnie was concerned. 'You don't seem to know how lucky you are. Leonard is offering you a tidy house, and a chance to come back where you belong. At least give it a try. If it doesn't work out, then you've got choices.'

But Ronnie could not be persuaded. 'Like I said, I'm not ready. It's a wonderful offer and I appreciate the thought, but I can't be shackled. I need the freedom to work when I can and wander when the mood takes me.' He looked at his stepfather. 'Sorry, Leonard. Like I say, it's not that I don't appreciate the offer.'

While Susie had kept her silence, Sheila was bolder. 'You must be mad!' This was the first *she'd* heard of Baron's Farm being sold to Leonard. 'If it's not wanted, we'll take it, won't we, darling?' Snuggling up to Thomas she made cow eyes. 'We could really do something with that old place, and like Lenny says, it's in a lovely spot.'

Like everyone else, Thomas ignored her comment. He, more than most, knew how Sheila was never satisfied with what she had. To her, the grass was always greener on the other side.

'The house was not offered to us,' he said coolly, 'and even if it was, we don't need two houses. End of discussion.'

'The farmhouse is yours, whenever you're ready,' Leonard assured Ronnie. 'You're an important part of the family business, and we all want you with us, like I say . . . whenever you're ready. At the moment, the house is being totally renovated. The builders reckon it should be finished in about six months' time. Take it or leave it, but it's yours. The deeds will be in your name, and the keys put aside for when you decide to come and collect them. There's no pressure. It's entirely up to you.'

Ronnie thanked him sincerely, and now that the discussion was over and the mood had lightened, Susie had a thing or two to say. 'I wouldn't give him a choice,' she teased. 'I'd lock him up in the house until he came to his senses. Anywhere is better than that hellhole he lives in.'

Grinning, Ronnie shrugged his shoulders. 'It's *my* hellhole,' he objected. 'It's where I want to be . . . for now.'

Vicky had listened to all of this, and her heart ached for Barney's youngest son. Like the rest of them he was still hurting, but instead of getting on with life, he had immersed himself so deeply in the past, he just couldn't let go. All she could do was wait and pray, and hope that sometime soon, Ronnie would find peace in his heart and the need for his family about him. More than that, she could not do.

She now turned her attention to her daughter. 'And what's happening in the world of hats?'

Susie swallowed a forkful of potato. 'Well, I too have bought property – I acquired the old butcher's shop, and I'm already having plans drawn up to change it into a fashionable milliner's. It's in a good area, on a corner position, with two panoramic windows and huge floorspace. It's got great potential.'

'Well done, sis!' Thomas exclaimed. 'I'm proud of you.'

Everyone raised their glass in celebration, even Sheila, though her comment was a touch sarcastic. 'What will that be – your fifth shop now? Soon you'll own the whole of Boston and we won't be able to walk down any street without seeing your name in lights.'

Her face fell with Susie's second revelation of exciting news.

'You know I've been after that contract to supply the French house for the spring season?'

Ronnie groaned. 'We should do,' he said jovially. 'You've been harping on about it these past nine months! I told you then – the French have cracked it where hats and fashion arc concerned. You've no chance. Might as well forget it, sis. This time you've lost out.'

'Ah, well that's where you're wrong!' Susie took delight in telling them all, 'I sent them half a dozen samples and they've all sold. I have now secured the contract to supply for the coming two seasons. There! I told you I'd get it and I have.'

Vicky leaped out of her chair. 'Oh Susie, you clever thing.'

Glasses were raised for the second time, and everyone congratulated her.

All but Sheila, who skulked in her chair, loathing Susie as never before. She envied the girl her dogged determination to succeed in business; she resented her natural talent and skills, and the warm caring nature she had been blessed with. But mostly she envied her natural prettiness; with her gently-rounded figure, childlike features and soft shining hair, Susie was attractive in an unassuming way. Yet in spite of the fact that she was no striking beauty, Susie had caught the eye of many an admirer. As yet though, none of them had captured her heart.

To her lazy, ungrateful sister-in-law, Susie appeared to have everything, when all *she* had was a husband who lacked imagination and ambition. From the start, the loyal, hard-working and generous Thomas had never been enough for her. He knew that and because he loved her, he reluctantly accepted it.

Grudgingly accepting that for now at least, Thomas was the best meal-ticket she had, Sheila raised her glass to show willing. 'Congratulations, Susie!' she cooed. 'I'm sure we all hope your luck will continue to hold out.'

No one missed the hidden meaning of her words, least of all Vicky.

'Thank you, Sheila,' she said sweetly. 'I, too, hope *my luck* holds out.' And she did, because even though she worked hard and long, there had to be a measure of luck to bring it all together.

Her business was thriving, yes, but she was often lonely, especially at night-time when the day's work was over and she could sit for a while before starting on the neverending paperwork. It was then, when she was relaxed and alone, that she would reflect on her hard-earned achievements and wish that somewhere along the way, she could have found someone to share her success with, to share her life and be there when she needed just to talk. Someone to come home to of a night; some kind and loving man who would help plan their future together.

But as yet, there was no sign of it, and Barney's older daughter was beginning to wonder if she would ever find her soulmate.

CHAPTER TWELVE

LEONARD MAITLAND SIPPED his wine and watched the family as they chatted, and he felt like a man blessed. Since coming back to Boston with Vicky and the children, he had known happiness of a kind he had never dreamed would be his.

Years ago, against his every instinct, he had made a promise to Barney that he would never reveal the real reason why Barney had deliberately driven his beloved family away. Through all the long years, even after Barney's death released him from that promise, and in spite of many times being tempted to confide in Vicky, he had remained silent.

Now, his greatest fear had come true. A few days ago, a letter from England had arrived at his office. Deeply unnerved, he had left it unopened, his mind in turmoil as to who might have sent it. The postmark was smudged and gave him no clues. He did not recognise the handwriting.

There were only three people who might be writing to him from England. One was his solicitor. Another was Raymond Lucas, who had known the truth and with whom, over the years, Leonard had exchanged letters, which of course he had hidden away for fear that Vicky or someone else might inadvertently come across them.

The only other person who might have reason to write to

him was Lucy Baker. She had been the closest to Barney after his family left.

In the early letters exchanged between himself and Dr Lucas, there had been much mention of Lucy, of how devotedly she had cared for Barney. He knew that some time after the family's departure, Lucy had borne Barney's child; the couple had moved away soon after.

Yet Lucy had not known this address, so how could she have written to him? Lately though, she had been in touch with Dr Lucas; he knew that much because in the last letter from the doctor, he had written of her visit to Liverpool. So, had the doctor given her this address – and, if so, why? What did she want with him?

In the mist of his thoughts, Leonard could hear the family laughing and talking, and his feelings were anguished. This was *his* family now, and had been for the past twenty years. Was Barney reaching out to take them from him? No! His imagination was running riot. Barney was gone. For their future security and happiness, Barney had willingly entrusted Vicky and the children to his care. So now they were his family, but the letter had made him fearful; was something about to happen that might take his loved ones from him? It was unthinkable. He couldn't lose them. He must not!

Instinctively, his hand went to the letter in his breast pocket, and his heart pounded.

'Are you all right, my love?' Vicky's voice filtered into his mind. 'I called you twice,' she said curiously. 'You were miles away.'

Mentally shaking off his thoughts, Leonard looked up. 'Sorry, darling. I must have dozed off.'

She glanced at the tumbler in his hand. 'How many glasses of wine did you have?'

'Three, I think.' In truth he'd had only one.

Vicky was horrified. 'Oh Leonard! You know how wine affects you ... giving you such bad heartburn you can't sleep.'

Somewhere in the back of her mind she did not altogether believe him. She had not seen him take more than one glass of wine. Moreover, just now when she was calling him, he didn't appear to be asleep. Instead he seemed to be in deepest thought. 'Are you sure you're all right?' Although Barney was always with her, Leonard had earned a part of her heart, and she had come to love her second husband dearly.

'I'm fine now.' Getting out of the chair, he rested his head for a moment on her shoulder. 'Why were you calling me?'

'Susie wants to know if you would do her the honour of opening her new shop, when it's ready?'

Leonard was thrilled. 'Of course I will.' Raising his glance to the far side of the room, he saw Thomas and Ronnie talking, and over by the drinks cabinet, Sheila was helping herself to a measure of brandy. There was no sign of Susie. 'Where is she?'

'She must have gone outside,' Vicky said. Giving him a little push, she suggested, 'You'd best go and find her.'

Leonard found his stepdaughter seated on the bench by the pond. It was pitch black now, and the wind was freshening. 'Fancied a quiet spell on your own, did you?' Sitting down beside her, he took hold of her hand. 'Mom says you would like me to open your shop when it's ready.'

Susie smiled up at him. 'If you don't mind?'

Beaming from ear to ear, he said, 'Why ever would I mind? I'm flattered you've asked me, though I don't know what I've done to deserve the honour.'

'You saved me,' she murmured. 'When we came here, you saved us all.'

In the twilight Susie observed this man who had been their salvation, and a great surge of love filled her heart.

When she was just a child, frightened and confused, he had taken her under his wing, and where her beloved daddy had caused her pain, this kind and gentle man had healed the wounds, though the haunting memories could never be erased.

Leonard sensed her emotions. 'You're lonely, aren't you, sweetheart?'

She gave a wry little smile. 'Sort of. Sometimes.'

'You won't always be lonely,' he said assuredly. 'One day, sooner or later, there will be a certain someone for you, I just know it.'

She smiled at his words. 'Do you?'

He nodded. 'A bright young thing like you, I know you're not meant to live your life alone. There'll be someone some-where, just as lonely, looking for a lovely young woman like you to share his life. Fate will bring you together. You must believe that, my dear.'

They hugged for a moment, then he walked her back to the house.

One by one, the family left, until only he and Vicky remained. 'It's been a wonderful evening, don't you think?' she said dreamily.

Vicky began to clear away the dinner plates. 'And wasn't it nice to have Ronnie here? Just like old times.'

'I shouldn't pin too much on that,' her husband warned. 'Don't forget, it was Susie who dragged him here. And remember how he's twice tried to live in the family fold. It didn't work out for him then, so there's little reason to think it might work out a third time.'

'I live in hope,' Vicky answered confidently. 'I'm just relieved that Susie gets through to him, where no one else can.'

'Yes – but you mustn't be too disappointed if it doesn't happen.'

Brushing aside Vicky's protests, Leonard helped her clear away the dinner things, then helped to wash them up and put them away. Afterwards, while Vicky made him hot milk and honey to help him sleep, he sat up in the drawing room, listening to her moving around in the kitchen and pondering about the letter in his breast pocket. 'Should I open it?' he muttered. 'Or should I burn it?'

Sliding his fingers into his pocket he took out the letter and stared at it for a moment, his anxious eyes scanning the handwriting:

> *Mr Leonard Maitland,*
> *Office of Farming and Land Management*
> *Number 16, Roiter Place,*
> *Corner of Derwent and Launceston,*
> *BOSTON,*
> *U.S.A.*

Try as he might, he could not recognise the handwriting; it was not the hand of his solicitor, and certainly not the almost indecipherable scrawl of the doctor. In fact, he began to wonder whether he had got it altogether wrong in thinking it might be from Lucy.

With newfound confidence, he decided to take a peep inside. First though, he listened, making certain that Vicky was still busy at her tasks. Satisfied, he took the letter between his fingers and began to open it, almost leaping out of his skin when Vicky suddenly rushed in through the door.

'I've made a whole jug full,' she told him as he hurriedly thrust the open letter into his pocket. 'It's been such a hectic day, I thought a mug of honey and hot milk might help me sleep, too.' She placed the tray on the small table before him.

For a while they sat and talked, of Ronnie, and Thomas

and Susie. 'I'm proud of them all,' Vicky said. 'Thomas has taken to helping you manage the estate like a duck to water.' She cast her mind back, as she often did, more so as she grew older and the memories sharpened. 'Mind you, he had good training with his dad,' she said fondly. 'Though managing a small farm is different from managing a vast estate like this.'

Leonard nodded. 'It is,' he agreed. 'But when you get right down to it, the principle is the same: you plough the land, set the seeds, and reap the harvest.'

He gave a contented smile. 'I'm fortunate to have a man like Thomas working with me,' he admitted. 'I have good people in the office, but outside in the fields I can leave it all to Thomas and know everything will be taken care of. He works hand-in-hand with the office, orders the right machinery for the job, brings in the right mix of seed, and oversees the working of the land. He's good with the men, and has an instinct for the seasons. Moreover, he knows every machine inside out; there's nothing he can't fix and he's always ready to pass his knowledge on to the men. Matter of fact, I don't know what I'd do without him.'

After a while, Vicky shifted the conversation to Ronnie. 'I only wish that lad would settle down. He doesn't seem to have the heart for anything.'

Leonard was philosophical where his other stepson was concerned. 'He's still coming to terms with life's disappointments,' he said kindly. 'Give him time, he'll come round.'

'Do you really think so?'

'Yes, I do. Like Thomas, he's a good man.'

'Lonely though?'

'Well, yes, there is that. But some people like their own company.'

For different reasons, all of her children worried Vicky. There was Thomas working all hours God sent, with a wife who thought only of dressing herself up and trawling the most expensive shops. She wanted for nothing, she had a husband who doted on her, and still she wasn't satisfied and, if Vicky's instinct served her right, Sheila was in the throes of yet another affair. 'Sometimes, I wonder if Thomas ever suspects that his wife sees other men?' The words were not meant to be said out loud, but they just popped out.

Leonard was not surprised. 'So, you think the same as me, do you – that she's being unfaithful to him?'

'I'm convinced of it.' Vicky told him of her fears. 'I think she's had several affairs. If Thomas knows, he must love her so much, he can't bring himself to confront her in case he loses her – though if you ask me, that might be the best thing all round.'

'Well, I don't think she would leave him, whatever he said to her.'

'No, you're right!' she conceded angrily. 'Why *would* she leave him, when she has everything all her own way . . . a husband who adores her, money to fritter on clothes and fancy furniture, a house she helped to design. Anything she asks for she gets – holidays, jewellery – and on top of all that, whenever she fancies a fling, she just goes out and finds herself a man.'

Clenching her fists, she almost spat out the words. 'Sometimes, Leonard, I feel like pinning her against the wall and making her confess what she's been up to. I hate what she does to Thomas. I despise the way she takes advantage of him and gives so little in return!'

Seeing how upset she was becoming, Leonard reached out and closed his hand over hers. 'It's up to them,' he reminded her. 'They'll sort it out between them. One day, Thomas will wake up and realise what she is. When that happens, he'll deal with it in his own way.'

'Oh, I do hope so!'

'Trust me. For now, he's taking a beating, because he loves her. He probably knows what she's up to, but Thomas is nobody's fool. He won't put up with it forever.'

Regaining her composure, Vicky sighed. 'Susie's doing well, isn't she?'

He nodded. 'She's a born businesswoman.'

'Do you think she's lonely?'

'Maybe.'

Vicky was sad about that. 'The trouble is, she works such long hard hours, she never has time for a social life. So, she never meets anyone outside of work.'

'Well now.' Leonard had also given it a lot of thought. 'Maybe when she meets her man, it could be the very one she's been working alongside all the time. It's been known to happen.'

Vicky smiled. 'So, that could be any one of about ten.'

'There you go!' Somehow, Leonard always managed to say the right thing. 'She's got a healthy choice right there on her doorstep.'

The couple sat quiet and content for a time, their faces pink and warm in the heat from the cheery fire. In the background, the grandfather clock struck eleven, and Leonard began to nod off. 'Hey!' Vicky gave him a nudge. 'That milk and honey seems to be working well, but don't go to sleep yet,' she said. 'You lock up, and I'll put the guard in front of the fire. Then we'll away up the stairs and into bed.'

'You go,' he said. 'I'll be along shortly.' He needed to stay down for a while. He needed to think.

Vicky put the guard in front of the fire, gave him a kiss, and made her way upstairs. She thought nothing of him not going up with her. Often Leonard would work in his study long after she'd gone to sleep.

Upstairs, she made her way to the bathroom, while downstairs Leonard remained in the armchair, his hand spread over his jacket pocket where the letter was safely tucked away.

He wanted to open the letter and read it, but his every instinct once more urged him to throw it into the fire.

After a time, common sense took over. He knew he should read the letter, if only to make sure it contained nothing that could harm himself or his adopted family. And if it was a threat, he might need to deal with it as quickly as possible.

Taking out the letter he glanced towards the door; he could still hear Vicky pottering about in the bedroom upstairs. He got out of his chair and went across the room, where he quietly closed the door.

Returning to his chair, he sat a moment, the letter in his hand, his gaze mesmerised by the flames dancing in the coals. 'Come on, old man,' he chided himself. 'Open the damned thing and see who it's from!'

With trepidation he opened the letter, surprised to find another envelope inside, which was simply addressed to Vicky.

Unfolding the accompanying letter, he thought he might have recognised the sweeping scrawl, but that was not the case. Instead his fears were made tenfold by what was written there:

Dearest Leonard,

I hope you will not think badly of me for writing to you after all this time, but lately my conscience has been troubling me, so much so that I feel compelled to make contact with you.

I've spoken with Dr Lucas, who very reluctantly gave me your address in Boston, but please don't blame him for that. I can be very persuasive when needs must.

All I ask of you is that you give Vicky the enclosed letter. It tells of the tragic circumstances that made Barney send his family away. I know from Dr Lucas that you have faithfully kept the promise you made to Barney, and I respect you for that, as I realise what a heavy burden you have had to carry alone.

Now though, before the truth is lost forever, I believe it is time to tell Vicky and the family. If you give her my letter, in which I have written about Barney and the way it was, you will not be breaking your promise.

I could have addressed this letter to Vicky and sent it via your office; the doctor stopped short of giving me your home address. But I believe it is right for me to send the letter to you, and leave the choice to you and your conscience. If you decide not to give her the letter, I will of course accept your decision and I will never again contact either of you.

However, I am hoping that over the years you have been tempted to tell her, and was not able to because of your promise. This way, if you do give her the letter, it will be me who tells and your promise will remain intact.

I believe the time is right for Barney's family to learn that he never stopped loving them. For the remainder of his short life, he talked of them, and longed for them, and his heart remained broken up to the day he lost his fight to live.

I can imagine you reading this letter now, and being torn in two by it, and I am deeply sorry for that. You may pass the letter to Vicky, or you may dispose of it, and she will never know. Please, Leonard, don't be rash in your judgement.

We saw what happened, you and I, and we know what pain it caused both Barney and the family. Surely, in your heart you must accept that it is their right to be made aware of the facts.

I have enclosed my address here. Please let me know what you decide,

Yours, with fondest memories,

Lucy

Shaken by what he had just read, Leonard made no move for what seemed an age. After a while, he read the letter again, and again, until every word was burned into his mind. 'I can't tell her,' he murmured. 'How can I hurt her like that? How can I tell Barney's children that they deserted their father when he was so desperately ill?' A great burst of rage surged through him; slamming his fist on the arm of the chair he cried out, 'I CAN'T DO IT TO THEM! I WON'T! DO YOU HEAR ME, LUCY? I WON'T HURT THEM LIKE THAT!'

Taking the envelope addressed to Vicky, he crumpled it in his hand. When, emotionally broken, he bent his head and began to sob, the crumpled letter slipped from his grasp and fell to the ground, and as it did so, the door opened and there stood Vicky, alerted by his cries and looking shocked to see him so upset.

Before he could prepare himself, she had walked towards him, on the way recovering the crumpled envelope from the floor. 'What is it, Leonard?' she asked worriedly. 'I heard you cry out. What's wrong? Has something happened? Is it Ronnie?' Of all her children, it was always Ronnie she worried about the most.

Realising there was no way back, Leonard looked up with haggard eyes. 'I'm so sorry, my dear. So terribly sorry.' Holding out the letter, he pleaded forlornly, 'Read it. Read them both, and I hope you can find the generosity of heart to forgive me.'

Confused and anxious, she took the letter from him, and as she prepared to read it, he could see his whole life slipping away.

~

As Vicky read Lucy's words, a sense of horror came over her. When she had finished reading, she looked at Leonard in disbelief, her face set like stone. She said not a word, and her expression gave nothing away.

She walked to the table, where she set down the letter addressed to herself and with slow, measured movements straightened the envelope so it was readable.

Leonard watched her open it and read the letter. With a broken cry, she leaned forward, hands on the table, eyes closed and her whole body seeming to tremble in shock. Lucy's words were emblazoned on her soul . . .

> *'he never stopped loving them . . . he talked of them, and longed for them, and his heart remained broken up to the day he lost his fight to live . . .'*

Her pain was crippling. 'I didn't know,' she sobbed and gasped over and over. 'I didn't know, I didn't know. Dear God, we none of us knew!'

For one aching moment Leonard was tempted to go to her and hold her. But his instincts warned him against it. Instead he watched and prayed that she might understand the reason why he had deceived her for so long.

After a time she collected both letters and, without a glance at him, walked across the room and out of the door. Then she was gone, leaving him alone and afraid. 'What have I done?' he whispered. 'Dear God, what have I done?'

Afraid for her, afraid for the family, and for his part in their lives, he went after her.

As he came out onto the verandah, he saw her, some short distance down the garden, leaning against a tree, bent double as she sobbed his name. 'Why did you do it, Barney?' Her broken voice echoed in the still night air. 'Why did you send us away . . . why did you make us hate you, when all the time, all we ever wanted was to be with you?' The sobbing became uncontrollable. 'Oh Barney! Barney! Why didn't you tell me?'

'Vicky?' Unsure and anxious, Leonard approached her. 'Barney did it because he didn't want to hurt you. I made him a promise not to tell. I'm sorry it had to be this way. We'll get through this, you and me, and the children . . .'

He stopped in his tracks as she turned to look at him; in the light from the verandah he was shocked to see such raw anger on her face. As she spoke, slowly and with cold precision, he knew the hatred she felt for him. *You let me think bad things of him. You took me away, when he needed me most.'*

'No! Listen to me, Vicky. It wasn't what *I* wanted – it was Barney's wish. He made me promise. He did it to save you the pain of seeing him suffer. He knew what it would be like for you . . .'

Shaking her head, she gave the saddest smile. 'All that time, you knew, and you never told me, because if you had, you knew I would go back. And you didn't want that, did you?' Her damning words froze his heart. *'As long as I live, I will never forgive you.'*

Brushing by him, she returned to the house, packed an overnight bag, collected her car keys and passed him on her way out without a word or glance.

All she could see was Barney. At that moment he filled her heart and soul; there was no room for anyone else, especially the man who had kept her from him, when Barney desperately needed her.

As she drove away, Leonard called after her. She didn't hear him. Instead, all she could hear was Barney calling out to her; Barney in pain; Barney left behind, his entire family gone forever.

She needed to hold him, to tell him she was there, that

he was not alone. But it was too late. Barney was gone, and she had never had the chance to say a proper goodbye.

Another thought crossed her mind. The children! However was she to tell them this devastating news!

CHAPTER THIRTEEN

IT WAS 8.15 A.M., the morning of 4 January 1955.

The streets of Liverpool were still fairly quiet, some shops were not yet open and only the keenest of shoppers had braved the bitter cold, to catch the early sales bargains.

Warm and cosy inside the offices of Bridget's empire, Amy and Bridget had been up since the early hours. On a day when the offices were still closed and there was no one to interrupt them, this was the perfect time for the two women to go through the books and prepare them for the accountant.

Having already been ensconced in the office for almost two hours, Bridget was ready for refreshment. Stretching and groaning, she leaned away from the desk. 'I think we'll down tools for a while, Amy me darling,' she said now. 'It's been a long two hours, and the old bones are threatening to seize up.'

Pushing the ledger away, she gave Amy one of her winning smiles. 'I'm ready for a drink, so I am.'

'I couldn't agree more.' Getting out of her chair, Amy began her way across the room. 'Fancy a nice cup of tea?'

Bridget was horrified. 'Have ye lost your mind? It's not tea or coffee I'm needing. It's a drop o' the good stuff I'm after. It's in the top drawer of the filing cabinet, same as always. An' don't be sparing with it neither.'

When it came, Bridget took a tiny sip, then another longer one. 'Ah sure, there's nothing like a wee dram to warm the cockles,' she said, smacking her lips. 'Unless it's a randy man with a trim body and no clothes on.'

Grinning like the Cheshire Cat, she went on to tell the bemused Amy, 'Did I ever tell you about the time me and Oliver found a quiet spot in the countryside? Well now, he got to feeling frisky, so we climbed into the back of his car . . . and ye know there's not much room there at all.'

Amy couldn't help but chuckle. 'Honestly, when will you ever grow up? Don't you think you're too old to be rolling about in the back of a car?'

'You're right, and I won't be doing it again, I can promise ye that! Only the dear Lord knows how I ached from top to bottom for weeks after. But y'see, poor Oliver was so frustrated. He tried Gawd knows how many times to get his leg over, and well – you've never seen such a carry-on in all yer life! First off, he got his foot caught between the front seats, then he couldn't get it out . . .'

She could hardly talk for laughing. 'When I say that, I'm not just referring to his foot, though that was the divil of a problem, so it was. No, I mean he couldn't get his little pecker out neither, whichever way he turned.'

Amy tutted. 'It's a wonder you weren't arrested.'

'Ah, but that's not all.' Taking another healthy measure of her good Irish whiskey, Bridget got a fit of the giggles. 'When we realised it was no use, we got out of the car and laid on the grass. Within minutes we were fleeing for our lives, him with his trousers round his ankles, and me with me drawers in me hand.'

Amy could hardly contain her curiosity. 'What happened? Did the police come along and find you?'

'Oh no! It weren't the police. We were just getting down to business, if ye know what I mean, when we must have disturbed a nest of wasps. Sure I never ran so fast in all me life, and as for poor Oliver, he got bit twice on his dangly bits. Jaysus! They came after him like he was their next meal. And him screaming and shouting like a banshee. Never mind that I was falling behind and likely to be got any minute. As far as that bleddy coward was concerned, I could get stung to Hell and back!'

Amy almost fell off the chair laughing. 'I always knew you were mad as a hatter,' she roared. 'Whatever will you get up to next, I wonder?'

'Well, I can tell ye one thing. Next time he feels amorous, he can bugger off.'

'So, does that mean you've finished with him?'

'Oh no! Sure, I never said that. But it's the last time he manhandles me in the back seat of a car. And as for pulling up in the hedgerow and rollicking in the long grass, he can forget it.'

She took another helping of her drink. 'He can have his wicked way any time he wants, but I told him, I did. "I'm a lady with taste," I said. "From now on, it's a bed covered in silk sheets and a feather pillow under me, or it's nothing at all".'

'And what did he say?' Amy was enthralled.

'He liked the idea. Especially when he couldn't sit down for a week, seeing as his precious little bits were all full o' bumps and lumps.'

There was a flurry of laughter and more naughty talk, before the conversation ended and the two of them returned to their work.

Shortly after that, they had completed the accounts and having filed away the paperwork, began to pack up for the day.

'Isn't it tonight when Vicky arrives?' Amy recalled Bridget telling her as much earlier on.

Bridget nodded. 'Yes. She disembarked at Southampton last night, and will be in Salford by tea-time tonight.' With the effects of drink beginning to wear off, her face reflected the seriousness of Lucy's situation. 'It'll be a strange meeting, that's for sure,' she remarked thoughtfully. 'There's been a lot of water under the bridge since those two last met. Oh aye, they'll have a lot to talk about, so they will.'

'Do you think Vicky will be resentful?'

'In what way?'

'Because Lucy never told her about Barney?'

'Oh sure, there's bound to be resentment.' Of that Bridget had no doubt. 'According to what Lucy wrote me, on the night she discovered the letter to Leonard, Vicky walked out on him and she's never been back since. Cleared off for two whole months, that's what I've heard. But then she got in touch with Lucy, and today is the day they finally meet after all these years.'

She shuddered. 'I don't mind telling ye, it's thankful I am that it isn't me who has to explain why I didn't get in touch with Vicky long before now.'

Amy was torn two ways. 'Do you really think Lucy should have broken her word to Barney?'

Thinking deeply, Bridget took a moment to answer. 'For what it's worth, I believe Lucy did what she thought was right, for Barney's sake, and for the sake of the family. I mean, look now at the heartache and trouble that's been caused by the telling after all these years. Vicky's life seemingly in tatters, and Lucy riddled with guilt at having sent the letter. It's a tragedy, isn't it?'

Amy agreed wholeheartedly. 'I for one wouldn't want to be in Lucy's shoes when she meets up with Vicky.'

Bridget was momentarily preoccupied in thinking of Barney's children. 'Isn't it strange how Vicky never even mentioned the children when she contacted Lucy? She wrote of how she and Leonard had split up, but there wasn't one word on the three children.'

Amy's heart went out to Thomas, Ronnie and Susie. 'I know what it's like to see your family torn apart,' she said. 'It's a terrible thing – and those three had the added agony of being sent away believing their father was a drunk and a womaniser, a bully who thought nothing of hurting them every which way he could. And now, they discover that he was nothing of the sort, and that he loved them all along.'

'Whatever did they think when they learned how desperately ill he was?' Bridget mused. 'And that what he did, he did for the love of each and every one of them. He saved them from the pain and anguish of seeing him deteriorate with every passing day. Moreover, he secured them a decent future. If that isn't love and courage of a very special kind, I'm sure I don't know what is.'

They each reflected on that, and after a time they shut up shop and went their separate ways. 'And don't get up to any hanky-panky!' Amy quipped as she went.

'Away with ye,' Bridget replied haughtily. 'Why would I ever want to be doing that? Sure, I'm a woman in the sunset of me life, so I am.'

Amy laughed. 'Sunset nothing! You might have been around a long time, but you've not lost the come-on twinkle in the eye yet. Sixty going on sixteen, that's you.'

Bridget prided herself on keeping active and fit. 'You know what the secret is, don't you?' she said cagily.

'No, what's that?'

'When the hair goes grey and your face is so dry and wrinkled it resembles the sole of your shoe, you dip your hair in dye, pile on the make-up and go out and get your man. If ye think old and done with, you'll *be* old and done with. If ye think young and randy, you can hold off the years for as long as you like, and bugger them as thinks you're mutton dressed as lamb.'

As she got into the car she had another piece of advice for Amy. 'There's something else ye should know.'

'Oh yes, and what's that?'

'If you turn up late in the morning, you'll be sacked.'

With that daunting piece of news, she drove away, leaving Amy shaking her head. 'You should be locked up,' she muttered with a smile. 'A woman your age should be at home with her feet up and a shawl over her legs, but oh no, not our Bridget, she's got more important things to do. You defy old age, you scheme and fight and lie through your teeth to get what you want, and you show no mercy to anyone who tries to muscle in on your territory. The truth is, if you weren't running a legitimate business, you'd make a first-class villain.'

As she walked away, Amy thought to herself, I've a good mind to turn up late, just to see if you really would sack me. You're a bully and a slave-driver, and you make me tired, just watching you run around.

Bridget was like no one she had ever known. But, warts and all, she would not have her any other way.

At that moment some short distance down the street, Bridget was engaged in a heated exchange with the milkman. Having pulled up in front of her at the junction, his horse had taken the opportunity to dump a load of manure all over the road in front of her; in the process splashing the bonnet of her Hillman Minx. 'You filthy heathen!' Shaking her fist at the man, she told him in no uncertain terms, 'Look what your damned horse has done to me car. You should be put away, you and the horse along with ye!'

When the milkman took not the slightest notice, she roared off, making a most unladylike gesture as she went.

'Time was when old women stayed at home and waited on their menfolk!' shouted the milkman. 'But I don't imagine there's a fella this side of Australia that would take on a harridan like you!'

After making another rude gesture, Bridget wisely put a fair distance between herself and the milkman. She didn't want to cause too many upsets, especially with a policeman strolling nearby, and even more especially when she had never applied for a driving licence, nor ever had one granted.

Coming into the quieter part of town, her thoughts soon turned to Lucy, and the ordeal she was about to face. 'God bless you, Lucy girl,' she murmured. 'I hope it all goes well with you and Vicky.' Like Amy, she did not envy Lucy the task ahead of her.

~

Adam had been awake since the early hours.

Concerned about the arrival this evening of the woman he still looked on as Barney's wife, he decided to go across to Knudsden House and make sure Lucy was all right.

From the front window, Lucy saw him coming. She too had been awake since the early hours. 'Only a few hours to go,' she told him as he walked in the door. 'To tell you the truth, Adam, in my entire life I've never been so nervous.'

Occasionally stopping to glance at the mantel-clock, she paced up and down, back and forth, now pausing at the window and looking out on the bitter-cold January morning. 'I'm not sure if I've done the right thing. What if I've ruined all their lives?'

'You can't turn back the clock now, Lucy my dear, so don't torment yourself.' Adam had the same worries, but he did not want to convey that to Lucy. Instead he was doing his best to encourage her, because right now she was beginning to make herself ill.

'I can't help worrying,' Lucy argued. 'I've already caused a split between Vicky and Leonard. She said in her letter that I shouldn't blame myself, but if I'm not to blame, who is? After all, it was me who put the cat among the pigeons so to speak.'

'Look, Lucy, what you did was certainly not done out of malice. It was done out of concern: you thought they had a right to know. Well, I agree with that and so, it seems, does Vicky.'

Lucy was still not convinced. 'It might have been better though, if I had left well alone.'

'Ah, but in the end, my dear, the truth has a way of sneaking out. Who's to say Vicky or her children would never return home at some time in the future, even for a visit. They would find out then, wouldn't they? There can't be a single person in Liverpool who hasn't learned the sad story of Barney Davidson, and they would tell it to anyone, neighbour or stranger. No, Lucy, you did right. What happened between Vicky and Leonard is something aside, which only the two of them can sort out.'

Eager for peace of mind, Lucy nodded. 'Maybe you're right,' she conceded hesitantly. 'Maybe it would have come out sooner or later.'

'Are you ready to face her tonight?'

Lucy nodded. 'Ready as I'll ever be, I suppose.'

~

Early that evening, the car was out and Lucy was waiting at the door as he arrived, looking smart and sophisticated in her high-necked cream-coloured jumper and skirt, with a coffee-coloured winter coat and dark shoes. Her greying hair was swept up in a loop of straying curls that framed her face, and she carried her best silver-topped stick; though she half-hid it in the folds of her coat. Even now she had a reluctance to show her slight handicap.

'You look lovely as ever,' Adam commented as he held open the door for her to climb into the back. Whenever he saw her, morning noon or night, it was always the same; his old heart would leap to his throat and he had to stop himself from taking her in his arms.

As they travelled through the country roads towards Bedford town and the railway station, Lucy wondered aloud, 'What will she look like, do you think?'

Adam glanced at her in the mirror. 'I'm sure I don't know,' he answered. 'She was lovely as a young woman, but not everybody stays as handsome as you.'

Lucy laughed. 'You old flatterer,' she said. 'Truly though, Adam, do you think we'll recognise her?'

'Don't know. Can't say.'

'Do you think she'll recognise *me*?'

'I think so. Your hair's a little greyer, you're slower of foot, and we all know you're not the young thing you once were, but then none of us are – Vicky included.'

Lucy had to smile. 'Well, thank you. Is that supposed to make me feel better?'

Adam made no apology. 'All that aside,' he said, 'you're still so vibrant and your features haven't changed all that much. You have the same slim figure and those wonderful, smiling eyes. I think she would have to be looking in the opposite direction not to recognise the Lucy Baker we all know and love.'

For the remainder of the journey, Lucy fell silent, with Adam frequently glancing in his rear-view mirror to make sure she was all right.

When at last they arrived at the station, he pulled up as

near to the entrance as he could. 'Do you want me to come with you?'

Lucy thanked him. 'Yes, I'd like that, Adam. But try if you can to keep a discreet distance when the train arrives. I don't want her to think we're there in force.'

Adam understood. 'Trust me,' he said. 'You won't even know I'm around. But if you want me, I'll be only a heartbeat away.'

Lucy gave him a friendly peck on the cheek. 'What would I do without you, eh?' Adam was always there when she needed someone to share her fears and dreams. More and more she had come to rely on him. And today was particularly unnerving, for she was about to meet Vicky again for the first time in many years; Vicky, the beautiful person whom Barney adored above all others, and who had been cruelly robbed of her chance to say goodbye to him. Vicky, who had welcomed young Lucy and her little Jamie into the very heart of her family, and shown them both nothing but kindness.

Adam was still pondering on her remark. 'What would you do without me, eh?' he mused aloud. 'Let me think now.' Feigning a frown, he told her, 'You'd have to find a careful new driver for a start. Then there'd be no one to fetch and carry for you, or collect your orders from the shops when you don't feel like being in a crowd. You'd have no one to boss about or moan and grumble at, and when you feel lonely, there'll be no one there to hold your hand.'

Lucy laughed. 'I've always got Mary.'

'Ah, but it's not the same. Think about it,' he urged. 'Here you have a big handsome man ready to answer your every call; a man who's besotted with you, ready to marry you at the drop of a hat, and on top of all that, he can make the best hot cocoa that's ever passed your lovely lips.'

'You're incorrigible,' Lucy chided.

'But you love me, don't you?'

'Course I do.'

'But not enough to marry me?'

'Behave yourself. Go and park the car, and I'll get the platform tickets.'

'Only if you say you'll think about letting me put a ring on your finger.'

'Go on with you!' Dismissing him with a wave of her hand, she walked away, the merest of smiles curving her mouth at the corners. She had long thought he would make a wonderful husband, though it would never do to tell him that.

One day he'll wear me down, she thought. One fine day, he'll ask me and I just might say yes.

But she couldn't see that day in sight for a very long time. Maybe never.

Waiting for Vicky's train to arrive from London was nerve-racking. Lucy had lost count of the number of times she had walked the entire length of the platform, looking this way, looking that way, shivering in the bitter cold and beginning to despair. 'Will the blessed train ever arrive?' she asked Adam. 'Maybe Vicky's changed her mind. Maybe she's decided not to come after all.'

Adam was more concerned about Lucy. 'Don't panic. The train isn't even due to arrive for another half hour,' he reminded her. 'Look! I want you to come along to the café and get a hot drink down you. It's perishing cold out here.'

'But what if we miss the train arriving? If we're not here waiting for her, she won't know what to do.'

'Listen to yourself,' he advised. 'We won't miss the train arriving, and even if we did, she's a grown woman, intelligent enough to get a taxi. She has your telephone number and address. So come on now, Lucy.' He gently cupped the palm of his hand beneath her elbow. 'Ten minutes, that's all, to get you warmed up and comfortable. I don't want you catching pneumonia.'

'Stop fussing, Adam!' Shaking him away, Lucy was adamant. 'I'm perfectly all right. You go if you like, but I'm not moving.'

Adam knew from old that once her mind was made up, there'd be no shifting her. 'I only wish Mary was here,' he grumbled. 'She'd make you go inside, and no mistake.'

Lucy shook her head. 'I wouldn't listen to Mary, any more than I'm listening to you,' she replied haughtily. 'I'm here to meet an old friend who's travelled many miles, all the way from America. I will not have her arriving in a strange place, all alone and me not there to greet her.'

All the same, at that moment in time she wished she was any place but here. Vicky had been robbed of precious time with Barney, while she herself had earned a measure of his love, and had even borne him a child. How would Vicky react to that? What would she think? Was she bitter? Did she blame Barney? Did she blame *her*? Lucy was so frantic, it was all she could do to restrain herself from turning tail and fleeing from the station.

Adam's voice resonated in her ear. 'Lucy Baker, will you stop fretting! Lord help me, I love you more with every day that passes. You're the most caring, considerate, aggravating woman I've ever come across.'

'And you're beginning to get on my nerves.'

'Let me bring you a hot drink then, and I'll not say another word – unless, of course, you want me to?'

'I *don't* want you to. But I'd very much appreciate that hot drink. Honestly, Adam, I can't imagine why you didn't think of it before, instead of causing such an almighty fuss about me leaving the platform!'

While Adam went to get the drinks, Lucy's anxious gaze

scanned the far-off track, hoping to see the train as it appeared down the line. 'What will I say?' she fretted. 'How will I greet her? We were close at one time, but it's been so long, I don't know how it will all turn out.'

Her nerves were jangling. In her mind she could see the old Vicky, pretty as a picture and lovely in nature. But what was she like now? Had she hardened over the years? Had she turned cold and resentful because of the shocking way her idyllic marriage had come to an end?

And what of the letter that had ended her *present* marriage? It was Lucy herself who had written it, and now she was beginning to regret it deeply. Maybe Adam was right after all. Maybe she should have let sleeping dogs lie.

Suddenly the shrill tones of the announcer came out of the loudspeaker: 'The ten forty-five from London St Pancras will be arriving at Platform Two in precisely ten minutes. There are no delays.'

~

On board the approaching train, a similar announcement was given over the air.

'Ten minutes!' Vicky had grown more nervous with every passing mile. With only two other passengers in her compartment, she had found a seat next to the window, and managed to collect her thoughts.

She had never been one for travelling. In all of her life she had only ever made two long journeys; the first had taken her away from everything she had ever known. The second was bringing her back.

At least when she sailed away from Liverpool, she had believed Barney to be alive and well, although it had come as a terrible shock to learn of his death, a mere three years later. Doctor Lucas had relayed the news to Leonard, who in turn gently told her and the children. Yet part of her, a very deep part was not surprised. How could her beloved Barney survive without her love, and without the love of his children? God knew, it had nearly killed her to be without him, and look at the effect on their three children.

She glanced out of the window at the darkening rural landscape. Nothing here was familiar, though the patchwork of fields and the occasional spinney reminded her of the fields up North where she had worked alongside Barney. This area of Bedfordshire should have been meaningless to her, but it was important now, because this was where her husband had spent his last days, with Lucy, and their daughter, Mary.

She was not surprised that Barney had turned to Lucy, for the latter was not only a lovely-natured person, but she had been a close friend of the family, and like all of them, Barney had a soft spot for her. But for Lucy and Barney to become lovers and conceive a child? That would never have crossed her mind in a million years. It was a bitter pill to swallow.

Yet for all that, she looked forward to seeing her, and strangely, she also looked forward to meeting Barney's other daughter. She wondered if Mary had a look of him, and if so, she would have a look of Susie, because Barney's first daughter was more like him in appearance than any of his other children.

Thinking about her children brought a degree of pain to Vicky. When she needed them most, they had not been ready to forgive.

Unable to deal with it for now, she closed her mind to them and forced herself to remember the days when she was with Barney, happy, carefree days which would never come again. It made her heart sore to think they had gone forever, but gone they were.

Her fretful thoughts were submerged into the rhythm of

the train wheels as they hurried along the track . . . *Clackety-clack, marches the army, clackety-clack, I love you Barney.* The sound of iron against iron merged with the hiss of steam and somehow it became a song in her heart, and the song created in her a soothing sensation.

～

Lucy was grateful for the cup of tea in a thick white mug that Adam had brought. 'Did you water the plants on your way here?' she quipped, staring into the cup. 'It's half-empty.'

'An accident,' Adam told her sheepishly. 'There were people pushing and shoving at the ticket-desk. I dodged past them, trying my best to keep out of their way . . .' He rolled his eyes. 'The truth is, this infant ran in front of me and I tripped over. But I managed to keep hold of the cups.'

Lucy was at once sympathetic. 'Are you all right? Did you hurt yourself?'

'No.' Having given Lucy one cup, Adam placed his own on the bench and brushed himself down. 'There was help at hand.'

He pointed to a child now climbing onto a platform bench, and with him was a woman the size of a ten-ton truck, arms like a navvy and a turban wrapped round her hair, tied so tight her eyes seemed to pop out. 'She picked me up,' he said with some embarrassment.

Just then the woman turned round and gave him a wonky smile. Adam smiled back, his face bright red as he frantically brushed the dirt and dust from his best trousers.

'That woman there? She was the one who picked you up?' Lucy's face crumpled. 'Her unruly infant knocked you down, and *she* picked you up?' In her mind she had this hilarious image of the elegant Adam going flying across the floor, arms in the air, and that enormous person who looked more like an all-in wrestler than a woman, manhandling him as he fought to keep the cups upright.

It was all too much. The laughter sparkled in her eyes and then Adam was giggling, and now as the woman sat herself on the bench, legs apart and bloomers showing, Lucy had to quickly walk to the waiting room where she erupted in a fit of laughter, tears streaming down her cheeks.

After a time, she managed to compose herself and return to Adam. 'I would have given anything to see it,' she told him.

'You're a wicked woman,' he told her, still laughing at himself, and she gave him a kiss for being so entertaining.

Now, as the train-whistle blew, Lucy's mind was focused once more on Vicky. 'It's here,' she told Adam excitedly. 'The train's here!'

Standing their cups beside a bench, the two of them moved closer to the edge of the night-dark platform, where the train was already beginning to pull in.

As it chugged to a halt, the steam rose and all the doors opened. People spilled out and it was hard to distinguish them through the billowing clouds. 'Where is she?' Lucy strained her eyes, searching for Vicky. 'Oh Adam, what if she changed her mind at the last minute?'

Philosophical as ever, Adam calmed her fears. 'If she has, then there is nothing we can do about it.'

People thronged past and soon there was no one left. The station seemed suddenly eerie.

'Look there!' Adam pointed to the figure climbing out of the train. 'Is that her, do you think?'

They watched as the passenger stepped down to the platform. As the slim figure of a woman came out of the night, it was like watching a ghost materialising from the past.

'It must be her.' Lucy's heart was in her mouth. 'It has to be Vicky Davidson.'

CHAPTER FOURTEEN

Feeling anxious now that her journey from Boston to Salford was over, Vicky had lingered on the train a moment longer. She still harboured a measure of resentment towards Lucy, because if she had not sent the letter, then everything would have stayed the same. Now though, her life had changed and there was no going back, and it was a shattering thing.

Pulling herself together, she gathered up her suitcase and got off the train. In the chill night air she caught a glimpse of them, Adam and Lucy, waiting for her as they had promised. She could not mistake them, for those familiar features – though now older like her own – were etched in her memories of the past.

As she walked towards them it was almost as though she had turned back the years and that somewhere nearby, Barney would be waiting to take her in his arms and hold her as before. But no! That wasn't to be. Her heart was like a lead weight inside her. It was all too much . . . too much! She gave an involuntary sob. Never again would Barney embrace her, his heartbeat close to hers.

From the other end of the platform, Lucy watched her approach. Strange, she thought, how she knew it was Vicky straight off. The walk was the same, the petite figure and the way of holding herself – that was the Vicky she knew and remembered.

As Vicky came closer, she passed beneath a platform lamp, and Lucy could see the tears glinting in her old friend's eyes. Her heart leaped, and when she turned round to speak to Adam, he was gone. She glanced about, and there he was, standing over by the gate, sending her strength, sending her love, watching over her like a guardian angel.

Now Vicky was standing before her, and the emotions that ran through Lucy were overwhelming. 'I'm so glad you came,' she said, choked.

Vicky did not – could not – answer. Instead, she stood motionless, her suitcase still clutched in her hand, tears rolling freely down her face as she began to realise at last that she was here, in the company of someone who had been part of her, part of Barney and the family. 'Lucy.' Her voice broke. 'My God, it's Lucy Baker.'

The two widows fell into each other's open arms.

All those long years between, from that fateful day when Vicky and the children sailed away, to this, long-awaited moment, were as nothing now.

When the embraces were over there remained a certain awkwardness. 'There are so many questions,' Vicky said huskily. 'So much I need to know.'

Lucy nodded. 'I understand.' Of course there would be questions, about herself and Barney, about how it was between them. Questions asking why Lucy had not told her earlier; why now, after all this time?

The prospect of all those questions made Lucy deep-down nervous.

But so too was Vicky, who walked beside Lucy as they made for where Adam waited. By then, they were chatting and smiling, but he sensed the undercurrent between them, and wondered if too much had happened for them ever to be friends again.

'Hello, Vicky, my love,' he said warmly, and his arms opened and she went to him.

'It's so good to see you again,' she said, and the barriers between them were no more.

They talked for a few moments, and then they were in the car, driving back to Knudsden House. 'You might want to rest and freshen up before dinner,' Lucy offered. 'I've organised it for eight thirty. You'll meet Ben and Mary then.'

'I'm looking forward to that very much.' Vicky was anxious about the meeting with Mary, but curious all the same. However, before that, there was something else she must do. With no further ado she blurted out: 'Will you take me to see where Barney is?'

Lucy had half-expected this to be Vicky's first request. 'I've already arranged it with Adam,' she explained. 'The churchyard is too far to walk from the house, yet it's only a matter of ten minutes in the car. First though, I thought you might like to catch your breath, offload your suitcase and give us a chance to talk. I thought tomorrow morning might be a good time to go there, but we'll go straight to Barney, if that's what you prefer?'

That had been Vicky's plan, to arrive and go straight to Barney. Now though, she did feel the need to catch her breath, as Lucy suggested. She wanted to see where Barney was laid to rest, and yet she wanted to pretend it had not happened, that somewhere, somehow, he was still alive. 'You're right,' she told Lucy. 'After that long journey, a few hours here or there don't matter.'

'Good! Then that's settled.'

And the two women exchanged a deep look – of shared sorrow and an acknowledgment of the very special bond that united them.

'It will be wonderful, to meet your Mary,' Vicky told Lucy as they settled themselves into the comfortable back seat of the car. 'Although, funnily enough, I'm nervous, too. You said in your letter that she lived with you. Is that still the case?'

Lucy nodded. 'Not for much longer though. She and her fella, Ben Morris, are to be married soon. Mary's had such bad luck with men in the past, but now it seems she's found the right one.' She waved her hand, as though to bring the conversation to a halt. 'Now then, I hope you're hungry. Our Elsie has really gone to town on our supper tonight.'

'Who's your Elsie?' Vicky asked.

'Elsie Langton is the wife of our local blacksmith. She lives in the village and comes to me every day,' Lucy explained. 'It's too big a house for me to manage on my own these days and well, what with Mary's flower-shop being so successful and all, we can just about afford dear Elsie. To be honest, we'd all be lost without her.' Lucy knew she was gabbling on but Vicky seemed genuinely interested.

'She takes care of the household things – cleaning and cooking and suchlike. She's an almighty chatterbox, she's even bossier than me, and at times she can be so infuriating you could happily strangle her,' Lucy chuckled. 'But she's the salt of the earth, honest and hard-working, and totally reliable. She has a heart of gold and excels at everything she does.'

Vicky was impressed. 'She sounds wonderful.'

'Oh, she is! In fact, she's an absolute treasure. You will just love her, I know you will.'

'Does she look after the grounds as well?' Vicky was beginning to wish she had such a paragon back home in Boston.

'She would, if she could get her hands on them. But no, the grounds are Mary's domain. She grows all of our flowers, fruit and veg, plants them herself, digs and hoes, and spends hours out there, weeding and working in all weathers. The lass sells most of it in her shop or at market, and there's still enough left over for the local charities.'

Vicky was thrilled. 'She really must take after her daddy, with such love for the land. Yes, I can tell that she must have green fingers, just like Barney, because even in this wretched weather, it's easy to see how beautifully kept it all is here.'

They were pulling into the drive of Knudsden House by then.

Lucy was delighted by the compliment to her daughter. 'Mary's also got a couple of cows, which she milks by hand,' she added proudly, 'and a dozen hens that lay enough eggs to feed a whole congregation.'

'So, your Elsie is never short of milk or eggs then?'

'Not so's you'd notice, no – though if she's not complaining that she's got too many, she's moaning that she's never got enough. You can't please our Elsie no matter how hard you try.'

As it happened, the very person herself was waiting for them as Adam helped them out of the car.

'You'll be the old friend that Miss Lucy's been going on about from morning to night,' she said, rushing forward, the hand of friendship outstretched. 'I'm Elsie, general dogs-body and hard done by. How d'yer do?'

Before Vicky could get a word in, Elsie was rushing on; 'I expect that one's already blackened me name, saying as how I'm a lazy good-for-nothing who can't cook, can't make a bed without leaving lumpy bits, and doesn't know one end of a yard-broom from the other!'

'Can't keep quiet for a minute at a time, more like!' Lucy laughed. 'Behave yourself. Our guest is starving hungry and tired from the long journey, so be off and keep an eye on our dinner, please.'

Elsie tutted. 'See how she treats me?' she enquired of Vicky. 'Bossing and bullying. Do this, do that.' Rolling her eyes to the clouds, she went inside and locked herself in the kitchen.

Vicky laughed heartily. 'You were right,' she said. 'She is an absolute treasure.'

Adam went on ahead of them. 'I'll put this suitcase in your room,' he told Vicky, 'then I'll make myself scarce for an hour.'

'You don't have to,' Vicky told him.

'I think it might be best,' he answered. Knowing how these two had a lot of catching up to do, he insisted, 'I'll see you both in an hour or so.' And before they could argue, he was quickly gone.

As they walked into the hallway, Vicky looked around at the wood-panelled walls and long casement windows. 'Oh Lucy, this is so lovely!' she exclaimed. 'So full of character. Is this where you and Barney lived together?' There was a wonderfully warm, inviting atmosphere in this house, she thought.

'We lived here, yes,' Lucy replied thoughtfully, 'for the short time we had. Poor Barney was in the last stages of his illness then. I sold the cottage that Mr Maitland kindly gave to me and . . . and Jamie – thanks to you and Barney – and we managed between us to buy this place, as it was very run-down and going cheap. Dear Adam has put his back into restoring it, over the past twenty years.'

'And were you happy, the two of you?'

'As much as we could be, under the circumstances.' Lucy thought that a difficult question to answer.

Resentment rose in Vicky. 'It must have been very hard for you both.' But her voice sounded tight.

'It was. But we lived one day at a time, and somehow we managed to find a deal of joy in every moment.'

Vicky's thoughts were with Barney, and her heart ached. '*I* should have been here,' she burst out. '*I* should have been with him!'

Unsure how to deal with the situation, Lucy spoke her mind. 'I wouldn't blame you if you felt bitter . . . about me and Barney, I mean.'

Vicky's features hardened. 'I am bitter,' she replied hoarsely. 'I'm angry because you didn't think to bring me back earlier.' Her voice rose in a cry of anguish. 'You can have no idea of the heartache and regrets that haunted me . . . haunted all of us and still do!' Turning away, she began pacing the floor. 'And now when it's all too late, I discover that Barney was ill when he sent us away – that he turned to *you* instead of keeping me by his side.' Her eyes alive with suspicion, she swung round. 'It makes me wonder how long the affair had been going on. Tell me, Lucy. Were you lovers right under my nose . . . all the time making a fool of me? Is that it? He had come to need you more than he needed me . . . *even when he was dying?*' The last words came out as a howl.

Horrified, Lucy took a step forward. 'No, Vicky, you're wrong! It was never like that!'

As she reached out to touch her old friend, Vicky began sobbing, all the pent-up emotions let loose in a vehement tirade. 'How can I believe you? You! A woman who took my husband to herself and bore him a child, when all the time none of us knew why he sent us away.' She was almost screaming now. '*You* knew, though, and still you didn't think fit to bring me back. I missed him so much . . . Oh dear God! My Barney, so desperately ill, and me so far away on the other side of the world!'

Burying her face in her hands, she sobbed like a child. And when Lucy reached out, this time she did not flinch. Instead she fell into Lucy's arms and clung to her, until the sobbing eased and her pain was bearable.

Deeply saddened, Lucy continued to hold her. The tears ran freely down her own face and her heart was heavy with sadness.

Eventually, Vicky raised her head and whispered, 'Oh Lucy, I was just hitting out . . . I didn't mean it.'

Lucy nodded. 'I know.'

Vicky took a deep breath. 'It's just that . . . oh, I have so many regrets.'

After a time, when the two of them were seated and quiet, Lucy had a question. 'Did you find at least some measure of contentment with Leonard?'

Vicky did not hesitate. 'Yes, I did. But it was a strange contentment. It took a long time for me to regard him as anything other than a friend. Even then, it was as though there was something else, *someone* else, always there, between us.'

She looked away, her thoughts going deep. 'Even when I was with Leonard, laughing, working, building a home for the children, Barney was always there. Leonard knew it and I knew it, but it was all right, because Barney had sent me away, and Leonard had taken me under his wing . . . taken all of us under his wing.' She paused, her thoughts going back over the years she shared with Leonard.

'We never had a child,' she murmured softly. 'I suppose it was never meant to be.'

Sensing a deeper sadness, Lucy gently reminded her, 'Leonard was a good man and a good and loyal friend to Barney.'

'I know that. But I still can't forgive him for lying to me.'

'It isn't as if he lied outright,' Lucy suggested lamely. 'He just never told you.'

'But don't you see – it's the same thing!'

Lucy hesitated. 'Will you ever forgive him?'

Vicky shook her head. 'Never! I will never forgive or forget, until the day that I die.'

And Lucy bowed her head in shame for her part in Barney's secret sacrifice.

CHAPTER FIFTEEN

WHEN LUCY HAD shown her up to her room, Vicky rested a while, then washed and changed, ready for dinner. Somewhere in Knudsden House, a grandfather clock was striking eight. 'Got to make a good impression,' Vicky said to herself, and she did a slow, dignified twirl in front of the bedroom mirror.

The cream-coloured dress she had brought with her from Boston was well-suited to her slim, upright figure. You don't look too bad for your age, my girl, she thought approvingly. Leaning forward, she wiped the tip of her finger along her lips, evenly spreading more of the light-coloured French lipstick that brought out the colour of her slate-grey eyes. Her hair was swept back and kept in place by a sparkling diamanté clip in the shape of a curled leaf.

Vicky knew how to dress for dinner. It was one of the social niceties that were part and parcel of her marriage to Leonard. Whereas her life with Barney had been simple and easy, her position in Boston as the wife of a land baron moved her in different circles. Her values and principles had never changed, though. Forging a strong family bond and being there when needed had always been her priorities.

Down the landing, Lucy was beginning to panic. Her hair wouldn't go where it was supposed to, and the shoulder-strap on her dress had just snapped as she slipped it over her head. 'Damn and bugger it!' she cursed.

Slinging the dress over the back of a chair, she stood a moment, contemplating what to do. She could wear the white dress, but that didn't seem appropriate somehow, or she could simply put on her brown skirt and blue top . . . no, she couldn't turn up for dinner looking like a school-marm!

Flinging open the wardrobe door, she flicked through the many garments hanging there. 'Why is it I can never do anything right?' she hissed aloud. 'It's nerves,' she decided. 'It's all too much in one day and now I've got an attack of the heeby-jeebies.'

Finally, she settled on the emerald-green dress, the one with little puff sleeves and a pretty lace neckline. When she slithered into it now, she felt just right; the waist sat snugly and the skirt flounced just the teeniest bit. 'Not too frumpy, not too sassy,' she said, sliding her feet into a pair of black slip-on shoes. There was a gas fire in her bedroom, and a good coal one in the sitting room, but all the same she arranged a mohair stole around her shoulders to keep out the draughts.

With the shoes on and the dress in place, she almost tumbled over while attempting to check that the seams on her stockings were straight; next she brushed her hair and rolled it into a halo round her head, while teasing out just the tiniest curl here and there. A touch of rouge and just the smallest brush of mascara and she was ready to face the world. 'Now, if your bones don't ache too much, and you don't fall asleep at nine o'clock, you'll be all right.' Twice she had done that and never been allowed to forget it.

But that was when she had first come out of hospital so that didn't count, or so she told herself. It wasn't old age creeping up fast. It was the after-effects of lying about in a hospital bed. Well, anyway that's what she made herself believe.

At ten minutes past eight she made her way downstairs. Five minutes later, Vicky followed.

As women do, they admired each other's choice of dress, and compliments flew in all directions, all genuine and all accepted graciously. 'Is Mary here?' Vicky was on tenterhooks.

'I'm sure she'll be down in a minute,' Lucy replied. 'According to Elsie, she didn't get back from the sale until an hour ago, though I think she stayed at Ben's a while before she made her way back. She's a considerate young woman. She so wants to meet you, but I know she was thinking to give us more time together.'

Having poured two sherries, Lucy handed one to Vicky. 'She's a wonderful daughter.'

Vicky thanked her for the drink and after taking a sip she asked, 'How long has she known, about me and the family?'

'Not long. A couple of years.'

'So, Mary was kept in the dark too, was she?'

'I'm afraid so.'

'And how did she take it, knowing that she had a whole new family?'

'She welcomed it.'

'Was she bitter, that she had not been told earlier?'

'No. She understood my reasoning. As a matter of fact, it wasn't me who told her. I was ill in bed at the time. It was Adam who decided the time was right to put her in the picture.'

'Adam?' Vicky was surprised. 'Why would he do that?'

'Because he's always believed that she should be told, and as he's been with us since before Mary was born, he's almost like family. He remained Barney's best friend right up to the very end. He came with us to this part of the world. He helped me nurse Barney, and from as far back as she can remember, Mary has loved him like a second father.'

Vicky smiled. 'Adam was always a good man.'

185

Lucy wholeheartedly agreed. 'And in case you're wondering, there was never anything between us, but he was always there, always helpful and caring, taking responsibility for us. He never forgot you, or the children. In fact, it was Adam who persuaded me to contact you.'

She paused. 'I can understand why Leonard didn't tell you. It was such a hard thing for me to do, breaking my word to Barney, and even now, with you and Leonard split up, I'm not sure I did the right thing.'

Vicky disagreed. 'It *was* the right thing,' she declared. 'I'm here now, and I shall make my peace with Barney – and I can never thank you enough for that.'

'What about the children?' Lucy thought it strange that Vicky had made little mention of Tom, Ronnie and Susie.

Vicky shrugged. 'That's another story,' she muttered, and for now at least, no more was said on the subject.

At half past eight, Mary came downstairs to meet the long-awaited visitor.

Vicky caught sight of her as she came round the bend in the staircase, and her heart leaped as she looked up to see Barney's daughter; with her easy walk and smiling blue eyes, she was the very essence of her father.

And now as she spoke, even the voice had a resonance of Barney. 'Hello, I'm Mary,' she said softly.

Vicky was momentarily lost for words. She looked at this homely, pretty creature, and all she could see was her late husband. With her bobbed fair hair and those lavender-coloured eyes, the resemblance to Barney had shaken Vicky to the core.

Holding out her arms, she invited the girl into an embrace. 'You've no idea how good it is to meet you,' she said, holding Mary at arm's length and gazing into those familiar, smiling eyes. 'You have such a look of your father,' she said, 'and you're so like my Susie, it's uncanny.'

Mary told her that she, Vicky, was exactly as *she* had imagined, and that she, too, was glad that they had met at long last.

It was a warm, satisfying exchange and, as they made their way into the dining room, Vicky felt more at peace than she had done for a very long time.

'Oh, so you've decided to show your faces at the table, have you?' Elsie came out of the kitchen like a hurricane. 'There's me slaving away in that kitchen, while you lot drink the sherry and chat the chat. Well, you're here now, thank goodness, so I'll away and bring in the first course.'

'Not so fast, Elsie, my girl!' Lucy called her back. 'Are you hinting that it's all too much for you? Because if you are, I'll start the girl from the village on Monday morning. I've checked her credentials and she has excellent references. She appears to be a hard worker and an honest soul, and if you'll only give her a chance, I'm sure she'll be a godsend to you.'

Elsie was horrified. 'I never asked for no girl. Don't want her, don't need her.'

'I happen to think you do. You're not as young as you used to be. You need someone to fetch and carry. Even Charlie agrees with me.'

'Well, he's wrong, and if yer don't mind me saying, so are you. I don't want no slip of a girl in *my* kitchen.'

'Look, Elsie, you're on edge all the time, losing your temper at the drop of a hat, and you never stop work from morning till night. You've a home of your own and a husband who wants your company from time to time.'

The little woman gave a hearty guffaw. 'I've a husband who sits on his backside in front of the fire every night, and spends his days looking up the horses' rear ends. He hardly notices me unless it's to have a grumble. If I talk, he grunts from behind the newspaper, and as for a sensible conversation, I might as well go down the park and talk to the ducks. Like as not I'd get more response out of 'em.'

'Why don't you just try this girl? That's all I'm asking.'

'You can ask till the cows come home, Miss Lucy, but I'm not listening. Now, if you feel the need to send me packing, that's another thing altogether and there's nothing I can do about that. But if I'm staying, I'll not 'ave no snotty-nosed slip of a thing under my feet all hours of the day.'

To everyone's amusement, just as they thought she'd finished, Elsie got her second wind. 'You've bullied me into trying it twice now, and I've been proved right each time. They're all the same ... couldn't make a cat's bed never mind yours! They don't know how to wash a pot, ask 'em to clean the windows an' they leave smears all over the place, and as for washing the sheets, they come off the bed white and go back grey, or even bright pink as we've already seen from that first useless article you took on!'

'Oh, for goodness' sake!' Lucy feared she was already losing the argument. 'You're impossible! You wear me down, so you do.'

'Oh do I? In that case, stop interfering and we'll all be fine.'

With that she turned on her heel, marched off in a huff and a moment later from somewhere nearby, a door slammed and shook the picture on the wall. 'You've upset her now, Mum,' Mary laughed. 'I'll not get an extra share of Yorkshire pudding after all.'

Vicky thought Elsie was wonderful. 'I want to take her back to America with me,' she chuckled. 'There'd never be a dull moment.'

The meal went well; Elsie had done them proud. The cream of parsnip soup was delicious; the generous cut of best beef took up half the table; there were dishes bursting with vegetables ... chubby Brussels sprouts, winter cabbage and beetroot, sliced and diced and melting in its own juice. There was a bucket-load of misshapen but mouth-watering Yorkshire puds, and several dishes of potatoes in different forms; crispy-roasted, mashed, and the smaller ones simply left whole.

To top it all off, the meat-gravy was superb. 'The best I've ever tasted,' Vicky announced to Elsie's delight; upon which the little woman picked up the gravy-boat and promptly poured another great helping over Vicky's Brussels sprouts. 'Get that down you,' she instructed proudly. 'It'll put hairs on yer chest.'

Having witnessed Elsie's impulsive action, everyone else discreetly covered their meal before she could get to it.

Once they had reached the stage of the bread and butter pudding, the conversation recommenced on a more serious note. 'You haven't mentioned the children much,' Adam remarked, while pouring Vicky another glass of best wine. 'Put me right if I'm poking my nose in, but is there some sort of a problem?'

'Nothing I can't deal with,' she answered.

'A trouble shared is a trouble halved,' he reminded her. 'And don't forget, you're among friends.'

While Vicky was considering his remark, Lucy thought she knew what might be wrong. 'They've taken sides, is that what's troubling you?'

Vicky smiled. 'You always were able to put your finger on the spot,' she said, 'and you're right, Lucy, because that's exactly what they've done. They've ganged up against me, and sided with Leonard.'

She went on to tell them how, 'Like Leonard, Thomas and Susie believe I should let the past go. They claim there is nothing to be gained from raking it all up now. Although they are content to know their father was innocent of the things they were made to believe ... the drinking and

189

womanising, and the way he seemed hellbent on turning us all against him, and now know he was only doing that to protect us, they still think Leonard was right to keep his promise. Well, I don't! I think he should have told me years ago.'

Lucy was saddened but not surprised. 'I suppose if you think about it from their point of view, it's easy to understand why they feel the way they do.'

Vicky shook her head. 'I don't see how they can feel anger at their father; not now they know the truth.'

She looked along the row of faces and tried to explain how she felt. 'Barney did it for us! He made us hate him, but he did it for a reason. He gave up his entire family. He was prepared to live out his days in pain and alone, not for himself, but because he loved us. Whatever they say, it was *us* in the wrong, not Barney. We let our eyes deceive us, instead of realising he would never become the man he wanted us to see. WE LET HIM DOWN!' She nearly burst into tears, but by a massive effort managed to control herself.

'That's one way of looking at it,' Lucy agreed gently. 'The children obviously see it another way. Maybe he did too good a job . . . making them hate him, sending them away from everything they had ever known. Perhaps they saw themselves as the ones who were rejected! And it doesn't matter that Barney made a huge sacrifice for them, because that was his choice, it wasn't theirs. And Barney didn't ask them. He took it on himself to make that momentous decision, and maybe they resent that?' Phew! She'd never really thought that out before, but it all made sense.

Vicky nodded. 'You're right, Lucy. That's exactly how they feel. But I'll never understand their thinking, or their in-gratitude. Because of what Barney did for them, they now have a wonderful life; they want for nothing – and that's all thanks to their poor, suffering dad.'

She appealed to Mary. 'What do you think, love? Do you think I'm being unreasonable in expecting them to love him for what he did, for the life he gave them and the chance to make something of themselves? Shouldn't they be grateful? Shouldn't they feel compassion for what Barney did, out of love for them?'

'I don't know,' Mary answered truthfully. 'He was my father too, and from what I recall of him, he was a wonderful man, kind and loving. He never hurt me, but if he had, I hope it would not have stopped me from loving him. I didn't have him as long as the others; I was not there when all this happened, so I will never have to choose between the father I knew, and the father that hurt them so. If I had been a part of what happened, I can't say how I would feel.'

Vicky turned to the men. 'You've both been very quiet. Can I ask what your thoughts are?'

In his compassion for her, and his fierce loyalty to Barney, Adam graciously declined to give an opinion.

Ben, however, spoke his thoughts. 'I've tried to see it from all viewpoints,' he told her. 'I can see why you had to come here and make your peace with Barney, and I can't even imagine how you must have suffered, especially when Barney made you think he had stopped loving you.'

He paused to get his thoughts in order. 'But I can see it from your children's viewpoint as well. I think, from the minute he hurt you, they were made to grow up fast. They had to shut him out of their lives. They had to protect you, because now there was no one else to do it. It was Barney who, for all the brave reasons in the world, forced them into that position, and knowing why he did it makes them resentful and angry.'

He was loth to say it, but he had to finish. 'Maybe they will never forgive him.'

'Then I will never forgive *them*!'

191

Not wishing to end the conversation on a harsh note, Vicky changed the subject, by directing a question at Ben and Mary. 'So, there's a wedding in the air, is there?'

Mary blushed deep red. 'Ben asked me to marry him and I said yes. We're planning for it to be in early spring next year . . . maybe Easter-time.'

'Oh Mary, that's wonderful!' Vicky drank the remainder of her wine and holding up her glass for Adam to refill, she announced, 'Here's to Mary and Ben, and a wedding next spring!'

Everyone drank to that and Mary told Vicky, 'I want you all to be there, you and Susie and your sons Thomas and Ronnie.' She hesitated. 'And, of course, Mr Maitland.'

Vicky was embarrassed and it showed. 'I don't think Leonard will be there, my darling, and if my children don't have a change of heart, I can't promise they'll be there either.' She put on a bright smile. 'But I will! Hell and high water would not keep me away.'

Lucy had been recalling Vicky's previous conversation, and one thing in particular was puzzling her. 'What about Ronnie?' she asked now.

Vicky seemed puzzled. 'What about him?'

'You mentioned how Thomas and Susie had been angry at the way their father tricked them about his illness . . . making them believe he had turned bad. But you never mentioned Ronnie. You never said how *he* took the news.'

Vicky paused, her heart aching at the way her children had reacted. 'I don't know how Ronnie took the news,' she confessed. 'He simply looked shocked, then he walked out of the house and never came back.'

'What? You mean you haven't spoken to him? You don't know where he is?' Only now did Lucy realise what chaos she had caused by sending that letter. 'Dear God, I'm so sorry.'

'Don't be,' Vicky sighed. 'You have nothing whatsoever to be sorry about.' She gave Lucy an encouraging smile, but then it slipped away as she spoke of her younger son. 'Ronnie has been a bit of a loner since we left these shores. You know he adored Barney, and somehow he's never been able to come to terms with everything. But he'll come round. He'll go away and curl up in some dark corner and he'll take time out to think about it all. He'll be all right. Susie will find him. She always does.'

Adam also recalled how close Ronnie had been to his father; how the two of them would sit on the hill and talk for ages. Thomas was the worker; Ronnie was the thinker, the poet, the one who was more like Barney inside than any of them.

'Maybe, when you get back, Ronnie will be there,' he told her, 'waiting to confide in you. If I remember, he always found it hard to talk to anyone about his feelings – anyone, that is, except Barney.'

Vicky decided to reveal her intentions. 'He'll have to wait a while longer then,' she confided, 'because I'm not going home just yet. In fact, I won't be going home for quite a while. As already arranged with Lucy, I shall be leaving the day after tomorrow. But I won't be going back to South-ampton. Instead, I'll be taking the train to Liverpool. There are places I need to go, people I need to catch up with.'

Mary was curious. 'How long will you stay?'

'Weeks, months, I haven't decided yet.'

Lucy was astounded. 'Won't Leonard be worried? And what about the children? Surely they need you?'

Vicky was adamant. 'Then they will have to be dis-appointed.' Seeing how her news had shocked them all, she explained, 'Since the day they were born, I've been there for them. And so was Barney. We taught them everything, how to respect other people and have compassion. Be honest and hard-working, and always be on hand for family, because family is the most precious gift you will ever know.'

As she went on, her voice shook with emotion. 'Instead of being angry with their father, they should be grateful, but they're not. Somewhere along the way I must have gone wrong, because my children now seem to think everything revolves around *them*. But it doesn't! And now they expect me to share their anger, but I can't. They're being selfish. They aren't considering *my* feelings in this at all. They were not there for me, so I'm afraid I can't be there for them, not this time. They have each other, and I desperately need to spend time alone, to be quiet, and think about the things that were so cruelly snatched from me.'

Seeing how distressed she was becoming, Lucy reached out and laid her hand over Vicky's. 'You must follow your heart,' she said firmly '. . . and let them follow theirs.'

Vicky composed herself. Raising her glass again, she made a new toast: 'To Barney!'

Everyone chinked glasses, and the evening continued on a lighter note.

Vicky spoke of Liverpool and the old haunts, and how wonderful it would be to see Bridget and Dr Lucas, and when Lucy asked if she wanted her and Adam to accompany her, she graciously declined.

After all, she didn't want them to find out the real reason she was going to Liverpool. Dr Lucas had written and told her how the Davidsons' old home was back on the market, to be sold separately with a few acres of land.

She had an appointment to view it. And if she wanted to, she also had the money to buy it.

'Follow your heart' . . . that's what Lucy had said just now. And that was what she must do.

CHAPTER SIXTEEN

THE NEXT MORNING, Vicky awoke refreshed and feeling more like her old self. She and Lucy were waited on at breakfast by an attentive and vociferous Elsie, who proudly boasted of her 'best bacon' and new-made bread. 'You'll not find anything like that in 'Merica,' she told Vicky, who thought it might be more than her life was worth to disagree.

When left alone, the two friends enjoyed their bacon and eggs. They drank the hot tea, and talked of the old life on Overhill Farm in Comberton by Weir, just outside Liverpool. 'I've never stopped missing it,' Vicky confessed. 'Whenever I thought of Barney, I thought of us out in the field, bringing in the harvest, chasing each other in the long grass, or walking through the spinney with the dog.'

Lucy also recalled the good times – ah, there were so many of them! Before they even began on the bad things, she led the conversation away. 'Adam should be here soon.' She glanced up at the clock. She didn't doubt that he would be on time. He always was.

'Can I ask you something, Lucy?'

'Of course, anything.' Assuming it would be something personal about her and Barney, Lucy prepared herself.

'When you went back to see Doctor Lucas, did you go to

visit little Jamie . . . only you never mentioned him in your letters.'

Lucy was taken aback. 'Yes, I did.' Her voice was low.

'And how did it affect you?' Vicky needed to know. 'I'm just wondering if you were as nervous as I am now, with the thought of seeing where Barney's laid to rest. I don't know what to expect of myself. I never imagined anything like this. I never dreamed . . .' She paused. 'Oh look, Lucy, I'm sorry. Please don't be upset. You don't have to answer. It's just that – well, it makes it all so final, don't you think?'

Lucy came to sit beside her. 'It took me a long time to go back,' she confessed. 'I thought that by cutting off contact with everyone, I could fool myself that none of it ever happened. I know now, that you must never deny your past. You have to cling onto it . . . take it with you, because when it comes right down to it, *your past is who you are.* And yes, it did make it all seem so final, but I knew I had to do it, and though I never believed I would ever say this, I'm glad I went back. I'm glad I went to see Jamie. Yes, it hurt. But I feel calmer in myself for having gone through with it.'

Another question, but this time Lucy saw it coming. 'Did they ever catch that maniac, Edward Trent?'

Lucy shuddered. 'As far as I know, they never did.'

'Do you think he's dead?'

'I hope so!'

'What if he's not?'

'What do you mean?'

'I mean, if he's still around, would he ever take it into his head to come after you?'

Lucy had often wondered about that, and she said so now. 'But there is no way he can ever find me, thank God. The only people I left a forwarding address with were Bridget, Amy and the good doctor. I know they would never give out my address, especially not to him.'

'Well, I hope you're right, Lucy. I haven't forgotten how crazy he was, and how besotted with you.' She cautioned herself. 'Oh, just listen to me, frightening you like that. Of course he won't come back! Why would he, after all this time?'

Lucy laughed. 'I'm not the slip of a thing I was back then,' she pointed out. 'If he did come after me, he'd take one look and head for the hills.'

'Give over!' Vicky could still see the loveliness in Lucy; it was a timeless essence that defied age and shone through the years. 'You might have changed a little on the outside, but you're still that special person you always were.'

When she had seen Lucy waiting on the platform last night, she knew straight away that it was the same Lucy, the same good friend with whom she had shared so much. 'You've still got that everlasting twinkle in your eye,' she said with a cheeky wink. 'I'm sure Adam's told you that many a time, has he not?'

'Hmh! You don't miss much, do you? But don't get too excited, because there is nothing between us. We're both too old in the tooth to be acting like love-struck youngsters.'

'All the same, I wouldn't mind betting that he's asked you to marry him. Am I right?'

Lucy had to admit it. 'You haven't lost your nose for a bit of gossip, have you?'

'So, have you said yes?'

'No, I haven't. Nor am I likely to.'

'Why not?'

'I have my reasons.'

Vicky sensed them. 'You're still in love with Barney, aren't you?'

'If I was, would you mind very much?'

'Yes. But I would understand.' Vicky paused. 'You see, I too have never stopped loving Barney. Soon after poor Barney died, Leonard asked me time and again to marry him. My answer was always the same . . . no. But gradually I grew lonely; he wore me down, and I said yes, not because I loved Barney any less, but because I had a family to think of, and besides, Leonard had proven himself to be a caring, gentle man who had somehow wormed his way into my affections. Also, I believed in my heart that it was time to stop pining for Barney . . .' Her voice broke.

'Vicky, if I ask you something, will you promise to be honest with me?'

She promised.

'Would it have been better for all of you, if I hadn't written and told you the truth about Barney?'

Vicky took a moment to consider, but when she answered it was with conviction. 'Lucy, if you never believe anything else, you must believe me when I say this: I'll be forever grateful to you for telling me. I had *a right* to know! That's why I can never forgive Leonard.'

Lucy despaired. 'Never is a very long time.'

Vicky was adamant. 'He took us to America, away from Barney, knowing full well that what Barney was doing to us was all a desperate act, knowing full well how ill Barney was, and how nothing on God's earth would have kept me from my darling's side.'

'Don't be too hard on him, Vicky.'

Lucy too, felt a measure of guilt, for she had known the same as Leonard – more, in fact. And she had not once tried to contact Vicky, so wasn't she as much to blame as Leonard? Yet hadn't they both kept Barney's secret for the same reason? *Because Barney wanted it that way.*

Vicky's voice hardened. 'What Leonard did was wrong! He took me as his wife . . . and *still* he kept his silence, when all the time Barney had sacrificed himself for us, in order to give us good futures in America. What kind of a man could do that?'

'A man who loved you too much to see you suffer over something you could not change.'

Lucy defended Leonard, as though she might be defending herself. 'He thought he was doing the right thing, for Barney, and for you and the children. Leonard is someone who made a promise and kept it, though I'm sure there must have been times when he longed for you to know the truth . . . to be released from the promise he made in good faith to a man he admired above all others. He didn't tell, because he respected Barney's wish – *that you should never be told.*'

When Vicky would not be moved, Lucy persisted. 'You should consider yourself fortunate, Vicky . . . *we both should* . . . because with Barney we knew love of a kind that comes only once in a lifetime. And now you have Leonard, and I have Adam, both good, honest men who would do anything for us. Not many women are so blessed.'

Just then Adam himself tapped on the dining-room door. 'You'll need to wrap up warm,' he warned. 'It's biting cold outside.'

A few moments later, Lucy had collected the coats from the hallway. When the two women were ready, Adam led the way and gently ushered them into the car. 'Here,' he handed them a plaid rug. 'That should help keep you warm.'

Once they were settled, he climbed into the driver's seat, started the engine and in no time at all, was on his way. 'Don't forget we need to call in at the flower-shop,' Lucy reminded him.

'I haven't forgotten,' he replied.

They drove over to Leighton Buzzard, where Rona helped Vicky to select a huge bunch of red roses from those on offer in the family's florist's shop. 'They were always Barney's favourites,' Vicky said sadly, but Lucy already knew; in the last few years of his life, she had learned everything there was to know about Barney.

At the churchyard, Adam parked the car and Lucy led the way. 'The grave is in a beautiful spot,' she said in a hushed voice to Vicky. 'You go ahead. I'll wait in the car. Come back to the path when you're ready.' She paused, then whispered with a lump in her throat: 'I hope you like the words on his stone. Adam and I chose them to speak for all of us.'

Vicky thanked her and they parted company.

'Do you think she'll be all right?' Like Lucy, Adam was concerned.

'She's a strong woman,' Lucy assured him. 'She'll be fine. But she'll want to be on her own for a while.' Lucy knew, more than anyone else, what Vicky must be going through, and her heart went out to her.

From the car, they could see Vicky go down on her knees; they watched her set the flowers before the marble headstone, and they saw her lean forward and read the words:

BARNEY DAVIDSON

1890–1933

A MAN OF COURAGE.
HE MADE THE GREATEST
SACRIFICE OF ALL.

She seemed to be talking, then she bowed her head and clambered to her feet. For what seemed an age she stood still as a statue, her eyes downcast and her hands folded before her.

After a few more moments, she suddenly turned and walked away. She did not look back, nor did she look down. Instead she walked with her head high, dignified in her grief, and calmer of heart for having come here to speak with her beloved Barney.

As she came nearer, the two onlookers could only guess at the turmoil inside her.

'Are you all right?' Lucy hurried to meet her.

'I am now,' Vicky smiled; it was a quiet, serene smile that spoke volumes. 'When I saw the inscription on my Barney's tomb, I felt a great sense of peace and understanding come over me.'

Lucy was amazed at the change in her old friend. Where before she had been nervous and worried, Vicky now seemed to have found a degree of calm, almost as though she really had been talking with Barney, as though all these years she had wanted to tell him how much she loved him, and only now was she able to.

'Come home now,' she said. 'Let's have a nice cup of tea and some of Elsie's shortbread.'

'That would be just what the doctor ordered,' Vicky replied. She gave a long, heartfelt sigh, and told Lucy, 'I came to Bedford with a purpose: to see you and hear your story, to come here to Barney, and to meet the daughter you bore him. I've got through them all, and now I'm ready to get on with the rest of my life.'

As Adam watched them approach, arm-in-arm and talking in earnest, he thought, This is how it should be. Old friends too long parted, back together at last.

It did his heart good to see it.

~

A day later, in brilliant sunshine, Vicky set off for Liverpool. Ben and Mary said goodbye. 'Don't forget I want you all at the wedding,' Mary reminded her. And Vicky promised only that she would be there.

Lucy and Adam saw her onto the train. How different it seemed from the night when she had arrived. 'Take care of yourself,' Lucy said as they clung on to each other.

'I will,' Vicky promised.

'Let me know how you are, and when you're likely to go back to the family. And remember, you're always welcome here at any time.'

'I will.'

'And please, Vicky, will you think about Leonard? He does love you so.'

Vicky merely smiled, a dismissive smile that told Lucy she was not yet ready to forgive her husband, or her children, for siding against her.

The train arrived, and in minutes she was lost to them, her face looking sad as she waved out of the window.

'TAKE CARE OF YOURSELF!' Lucy's voice rose above the engine noise.

'You too.'

Then she was gone.

'There goes a sad and lonely woman,' Adam remarked as they walked back to the car.

Lucy made no reply. She knew how much in love Barney and Vicky had been, and she could see how that love still burned in Vicky.

It must have been hard, she thought, when instead of sharing her sorrow and compassion for Barney, the others had become angry and bitter, altogether losing sight of what he had lost and they had gained.

In the event, Vicky could not accept what she considered to be a deeply selfish attitude.

'How do you think it will all turn out, with Vicky and the family?' she asked Adam.

'I think it will turn out all right in the end,' he answered thoughtfully. 'I didn't like to say so before, but I believe they were wrong to blame Barney for doing what he did. God only knows, it was a hard enough decision for him to make!

When I remember the state he was in, poor chap. Like Vicky said, they should go down on their knees and be grateful for a man like that! And to you, for taking him in and caring for him as you did.'

Lucy glanced at the man beside her and, not for the first time, she felt the stirrings of real love. 'Let's go home,' she said, and let him escort her to the car, where she took the liberty of sitting in the front. 'What?' she demanded when he stared at her. 'What are you wearing that expression for?'

'You're sitting in the front!'

'What's wrong with that, might I ask?'

'Nothing.'

'Then will you kindly start the car and take me home?'

'Right away, madam.' In a feigned subservient gesture, he tipped his forehead. 'Whatever madam wants.'

As they drove along, the smile got wider.

And though she pretended to be looking out of the window, there was an answering twinkle in Lucy's eye.

She might be more of a tortoise than a hare these days and she had long forgotten what a kiss was. But life wasn't over yet, she thought merrily.

Not by a long chalk!

PART THREE

~

February, 1955

Old Loves and Evil

CHAPTER SEVENTEEN

T HE PRISONERS CALLED out as Edward Trent walked to
freedom. 'Have a drink on me, Carter!' shouted an old
lag in for arson. Cocking a deaf ear, the prison officer
escorted Trent along the white-washed corridor towards the
huge main gate where he had entered such a long time ago.

'Give the pretty gals a kiss from old Simon,' laughed another. 'And if yer come across Martha Clayton on yer way, tell
her she needn't wait for me, 'cause I'm on the lookout for
summat fresher and younger, who knows 'ow to treat a fella!'

Edward Trent ignored them all. He had spent years, dodg-
ing and diving to keep out of trouble in this godforsaken
place, and many was the time when he could easily have
sliced off their gormless heads, but he didn't. He had only
one thing on his mind, and that was to get out into the big
wide world, sooner rather than later.

Somewhere out there was Lucy Baker, and he had to see
her. Try as he might, he could not get her out of his mind.
As far as he knew, she could be six feet under the turf. But
assuming she was still alive, he had to look her in the eyes
and find out if he still had the same feelings for her as he
did when they were younger. After all, she had been the
mother of his only child. He drew heavily on his cigarette,
cursing savagely as it stuck to his lip.

Apart from that, he had a score to settle with her. Lucy Baker was the only woman who had ever sent him away – *him*! Edward Trent, who only had to click his fingers and the women would come running.

But then as he recalled, Lucy was different from the others. She had spirit, and wasn't afraid of anything – except maybe losing her precious kid. Oh yes! She was afraid of that; it was the one weakness in her, and like a fool he had thought he could use it against her. How was he to know she would come after him like a she-wolf after her cub; pursuing him until he went crazy.

It was *her* fault that his only son had been killed. Bitch! He gasped as a sudden pain seized his chest. Savagely stubbing out the cigarette beneath his shoe, he pushed onwards to freedom at last.

As the years went on and he grew older and more lonely, Edward Trent had begun to regret so many things. All his life he had pursued women for pleasure, nothing more. He had never experienced the urge to settle down and start a family, had never truly loved a woman – until Lucy came along.

She was the only woman he had ever warmed to; the only one to win his wicked heart, and through arrogance and spite he had foolishly lost her. Then, when he believed he had a chance to make it up and start afresh, he played it all wrong, and managed to turn her against him for good.

All these years she had haunted him, filled his dreams and beckoned to him.

He had to find her. Even if he was repulsed by how the years might have worn her. Was she haggard and bent, or was she still the same Lucy that he had carried with him all these years? He could see her now, laughing with abandon, running barefoot and free like a wild spirit . . . 'catch me if you can' – that was the Lucy he remembered. Like a butterfly on the breeze, with amazing colour and beauty. To his everlasting regret, he had caught her, had her in the brutal palm of his hand, then let her fly away.

Had time stood still for her like it had for him? Would she still hate him for what he had done? Was she even alive, and if so, how would she feel when he turned up? Was it not possible that somehow, the years had mellowed her, and that she might regret having turned him away that night?

Edward Trent raked a shaking hand through his prison haircut. After all, wasn't she as much to blame for the boy's drowning? At least, that was what he had convinced himself of over the years. Jamie . . . James Trent as should have been.

Growling under his breath, he turned to wave at the prison officers. 'Thanks for nothing,' he jeered. The loathing he felt was lit in his eyes.

'The devil go with you, Carter!' The larger of the two stared him out.

'You'll be back,' said his colleague. 'Your sort are never free for long.'

Making an obscene gesture, Trent deliberately sauntered away, and soon lost sight of them. 'Bastards!' Quickening his step he made for the bus that was pulling in at the end of the street.

As he climbed aboard, he had only one thing in mind. I'm on my way, sweetheart, he thought darkly. Who knows, she might even have been waiting for me all this time, just as I've been waiting for her. The thought was unbearably tantalising.

'Where to, mate?' The bus conductor had his hand on the ticket machine.

'The railway station.'

With a turn of the handle, the conductor rolled a ticket and tore it off. 'That'll be tuppence halfpenny.'

Fishing in his pocket, Trent found the coppers and thrust them into the man's palm.

As he walked away, the conductor stole a glimpse back at him. He observed the brooding eyes, the bull-like neck and he felt decidedly uncomfortable. Many times he had picked up ex-convicts newly released. Mostly, they were penitent and easy to talk with. You kind of got an instinct for their real character, and this one was bad. Real bad.

When they arrived at the railway station, Trent made his way straight to the ticket-desk. 'What time's the next train to Liverpool?'

The clerk checked his timetable. 'Hour and a half . . . platform four.'

'How much?'

'Single or return?'

'Single.'

The clerk checked his listings. 'Two shillings.'

Trent scowled. 'Is there nothing cheaper?'

'Nope! Not unless you want to ride in the guard's van, along with the bicycles and chickens.'

'And what will that cost me?'

The clerk patiently checked his listings. 'Sixpence half-penny should do it.'

When his place was bought and the money paid over, Trent asked, 'Where can a man get a drink round these parts?'

'Across the street, turn left . . . you'll find the George and Dragon on your right.' He glanced up at the master clock. 'Eleven thirty. You should find them open and if he isn't, you could always knock on the side door. Tell him Arthur sent you.' Thinking he deserved to be rewarded for such information, he held out his hand.

'Next time,' Trent promised. 'I'll see you right next time.' He went away grinning. The world was still full of fools, he thought.

An hour later, he left the pub and made his way back to the station, where he had to wait another half hour for his train. When it arrived, he climbed aboard and sat himself down in a second-class carriage.

Ten minutes later, the ticket inspector made his rounds. 'Tickets, please.' He tapped his fingers on the back of the seat, while his surly passenger rooted about in his pockets for the ticket.

'There you go, I knew it was there.' Trent held the grubby ticket aloft.

The inspector took one look at it and told the passenger gruffly, 'Are you trying to pull a fast one, chum, because if so, you're out of luck.' He made a gesture with his thumb. 'You'll find the guard's van back there.'

'Eh? What are you talking about?' Claiming ignorance, Trent told the inspector, 'I paid my money and there's my ticket to prove it.' He made a fairly good job of pretending not to know the value of the ticket.

'Don't give me that!' The inspector had dealt with worse passengers than this one, and he was standing for no nonsense. 'You bought a ride in the guard's van and that's where you're headed now,' he said. 'Either by the cuff of your collar, or on your own two feet – which is it to be?'

Under normal circumstances, Trent would have landed him one, but he had no intention of ending up back inside. So, rather than cause a fuss and have the police waiting for him at the other end, he went back to the guard's van, where he crouched on the floor amongst all manner of paraphernalia.

After a torrent of abuse and cursing, he laid out full stretch, and let the dulling effects of his two pints of booze take over.

If it hadn't been for the guard, who was in the process of taking out a passenger's bicycle, Trent might well have slept all the way to Scotland. 'Hey, you!' Giving Trent a gentle push, the man woke him up. 'You're getting off here, aren't you?'

'What?' Bleary-eyed and irritable, Trent glared up at him. 'What's that you say? Speak up, man!'

Instinctively backing off, the guard picked up the bicycle and hoisted it out on to the platform. 'We're at Liverpool Central, sir. If this is your stop, you'd best get yourself off the train right now!'

Panicking, Trent scrambled up. 'Liverpool, you say?' Throwing the baggage out of his way, he grabbed his kitbag and jumped off, pushing and shoving his way through, ignoring the irate passengers disembarking from the carriages around him.

It had been more years than he cared to remember since he had walked the streets of old Liverpool, but it hadn't changed much, he observed, though many of the old shops now had new frontages, and there were smart office blocks rising out of former bombsites. It was still the same old place though, he thought fondly.

Down at the Mersey, he leaned on the railings and watched the ferries coming and going. 'Just like old times,' he sighed. A feeling of contentment washed over him, although his stomach growled with hunger. At least mealtimes were regular in prison; even a plate of slop was better than sod all.

When an old man took rest on a bench nearby, Trent told him, 'I'm back, thank God! Back in Liverpool, where I belong.'

The old fella was amused. 'Been away, have you?'

'You could say that.' Trent was in a good mood. 'But now I'm back, and I've already rediscovered one old sweetheart – my home town – and now I'm off in search of another.'

'Old sweetheart, eh?'

'That's right . . . the prettiest thing you ever did see – older now, much like myself, but I don't mind betting she's still the beguiling creature that slipped through my fingers long ago.'

The old man tipped his hat. 'Age don't matter nothing,' he declared with conviction. 'It's what's inside that counts, the feelings and belonging.'

'My sentiments exactly!' Trent affirmed. 'She might have a few more wrinkles, same as me, and could be she's not as lively as she was but I'll tell you what, matey . . . I'll only have to look into them beautiful eyes and like you say, nothing else will matter.'

'Well, good luck to you.' The old chap ambled away. 'If you catch up with this sweetheart of yourn, don't let her get away this time, or like as not you'll never get another chance.'

'Oh, don't you worry.' That had been Trent's avowed intention these twenty years – to find Lucy and hold onto her, one way or another. Then, seeing the elderly man moving away, he called out: 'Hey! You there . . . Is the Prince Albert public house still open?'

'What, the one on Victoria Street?'

Trent nodded affirmatively. 'That's the one.'

'Well, you're in luck. There've been one or two old pubs closed down, but the Albert is still up and running, or at least it was when I last called in a few nights back.'

Trent gave a whoop of joy. 'Then that's where I'm headed!' He had another question. 'I don't suppose Peter Bentley is still the landlord, is he?'

The old man shook his head. 'Pete retired some years back,' he answered. 'His missus took bad and the work got too much for them, so they retired and bought one of them terraced houses on Gas Street. His eldest son Mike is the land-lord now.' He frowned. 'Though I must say he's not a patch on his father . . . stays out most nights gambling. His wife works hard though, bless her heart. They've got a woman living in

213

and helping behind the bar. Between them, the girls manage to make up for Mike's shortcomings. You'll find Pete calls into the pub most days, but he never interferes. He just sits at the bar chatting and lets them get on with it.'

It was enough for Trent to know that the pub was still up and running. 'I might just look him up,' he said. 'Me and Pete Bentley supped many a pint together in the old days.' Patting the old man on the back, he told him, 'Nice meeting you, matey. It's a change to speak to somebody who isn't looking for a fight!'

As the elderly man set off again, he mumbled under his breath: 'Rough sort. I wouldn't mind betting he's just out of gaol. He'll probably get drunk as a skunk and won't be able to find his way to bed, let alone go after an old sweetheart!'

When he got to the Albert, Trent stood for a moment, just soaking in the familiar things; that same worn dip in the pavement outside the door, where the feet of many a thirsty traveller had walked. The street-lamp which still leaned slightly to the left, and the name-sign over the pub door, cracked down one side, and creaking as it swung in the breeze.

Licking his lips at the prospect of that smooth dark liquid running down his throat, he pushed at the door, growing impatient when it remained fast. 'Damn and bugger it!' He pushed again, and when it still wouldn't budge, he banged his two fists on it. 'Come on, open up!'

'Hey!' a voice called from a window above. 'What the devil d'you think yer playing at?'

On looking up, Trent could see a shadowy face behind a fluttering lace curtain. 'I'm a customer,' he yelled. 'Open the blasted door.'

'You're too early – can't you see we're closed? Go on, bugger off!'

Something about the tone of the woman's voice evoked a memory. 'Lizzie? Good God, is that you, Lizzie?' Stepping back to get a better view, he tried to focus on the face behind the glass. 'LIZZIE MONK, IS THAT YOU HIDING BEHIND THE CURTAINS?'

'Who's asking?' The voice sailed out, the face remained hidden.

'It's *me*, you fool! Edward Trent as was.'

'You lying bugger, Eddie were hanged years back . . . an' if he weren't, then he should've been.'

'Look at me, you silly mare!'

Standing well back, he threw out his arms. 'I'm not a ghost. I'm all flesh and blood, you can bet on that!'

Suddenly the window slid up and a woman's face appeared; in her early forties, without lipstick and her long brown hair wild and dishevelled, she made an awesome sight.

Trent was astonished. Some long time back, he and this woman had enjoyed a brief fling, but she had been a young girl then of barely sixteen, while he was over twice her age.

Nothing ever came of it, mainly because her elder sister Patsy took charge and drove a wedge between them. She tried every which way to drive him out of town and even informed their father of the affair. After that there was no real sense in having the girl anyway; her virginity was gone, and so was the fun. So he left.

Besides, by that time, he had already met Lucy.

Lizzie Monk was eager fodder, while Lucy was elusive and unwilling. That only made him more determined to have her; which he did in the end. And he would have her now, just as before, once he had tracked her down. But there was time enough yet. Meanwhile, he would catch his breath and enjoy whatever came his way, including Lizzie.

'Well, as I live and breathe, it really is Lizzie Monk.' He

beckoned to her. 'Come down 'ere, you little darling! I'm gasping for a pint.' With the memories now stirring deep in his groin, he was gasping for something else too, but first he had to see the lay of the land.

Patsy was a loud-mouthed, formidable type – not that Trent was worried about her in particular, but if she was still around, the bitch, she just might cause enough of an uproar to get him sent back inside, and that was not a risk he was prepared to take for any woman, let alone the likes of Lizzie Monk.

The latter appeared downstairs a good ten minutes later, looking more human with her hair brushed loose and her make-up impeccably applied; in fact, she almost looked inviting. 'I honestly thought they'd hanged you long since,' she said, her brown eyes ogling the sight of him. 'My God, but you've kept well.'

She noted the strong arms and the thick muscular neck, and his long coarse hair gave him a youthful look. 'What are you now, Edward Trent? You must be getting on for sixty, but you still have the body of a younger man.'

'Never mind all that, me beauty.' Grabbing hold of her, he swung her round, eagerly anticipating the fun they might have in store. 'You're the first familiar face I've seen in a long time,' he told her, 'and, if you don't mind me saying, Lizzie my darling, you look as lovely as ever.'

Setting her on her feet he took stock of this buxom brown-eyed woman who, despite being in her forties, was only lightly worn round the edges, and still somewhat of a looker.

Laughing, she shook her head in disbelief. 'Eddie Trent, of all people! Where in God's name have you been all these years?' But before he could answer, she put her fingers to her lips, saying, 'No! Don't tell me. You've been locked up, haven't you? My sister Patsy said that's where you'd be – "locked up till he rots away", that's what *she* said.'

His grin became a frown. 'As I recall, your sister never did have a good word to say about me.'

'You can't blame her though, can you? I mean, I was still wet behind the ears when you took advantage of me. For some reason, from the first time she clapped eyes on you, she said you were no good.' Lizzie scowled. 'Come to think of it, she was right too, wasn't she, eh? Once you'd had your fun, you were away like your heels were on fire!'

'Ha! You can thank your sister for that – and your father. Jesus! He was a crazy man.'

'Crazy like you, you mean?' It was all coming back now, how she had suffered at his hands, and still bore the scars to this day.

'What! I'm nothing like him. He were a damned lunatic!' Trent glanced about, wondering if they were being watched.

She answered the question that was crossing his mind. 'No need to be nervous.'

He took umbrage at that. 'You'll never see the day when Edward Trent is nervous. But I have good reason not to get involved in skirmishes and the like.'

'Really? It's never bothered you before.'

'So, why isn't he around?' Lizzie's father was the only person whose strength and temper matched his own. Because of that, Trent held a slight but grudging regard for him. 'Moved out the area, has he?'

'You could say that,' she replied. 'Four years ago, our mammy took ill and didn't get better, and he followed her soon after.'

He was pleased at that. 'Oh. So you're an orphan then?'

She laughed. 'A bit old to be called an orphan, but yes, I suppose that's what I am all right.'

'And your sister?' His intense dislike for Patsy had never gone away. 'Did she leave the same way as the other two?' He wished.

'That's a cruel thing to say!'

He asked again. 'Is she still around?'

'Would it bother you if I said yes?'

'Not particularly, no.'

'Don't give me that,' she teased. 'I know you, and I know you're after bedding me, and you're worried she'll make life difficult for you. That's the truth, isn't it?'

'What makes you think I still fancy you?'

She glanced down. 'Because I can see the bulge in your trousers.'

He laughed out loud. 'How do you know that's not my baccy tin?'

'Hmh! Funny shape for a baccy tin.' She nudged him playfully. 'Come on, then – do you fancy me or what?'

'Mebbe. Mebbe not.' He fancied her like he might fancy a cut of beef. At the moment, *any* warm, red-blooded woman would do, just for the night, until he was satisfied, rested and cleaned up, and ready to face the one real love of his life.

'There's no need to hide and pretend,' she promised. 'I'm a grown woman now, or haven't you noticed?'

'Oh, yes, I've noticed all right.' In fact, all he could see was the considerable size of her firm breast and the bold way she stood, legs astride, as though inviting him inside.

'You never married then?' he smirked. 'Never got over me, eh?'

'Don't kid yourself! I got married a year after you left.'

'Did you now?' Damn and bugger it, he thought. On the one hand there was her sister Patsy, and now a husband to contend with. Bedding Lizzie Monk might not be as straightforward as he would have liked. 'So, you're happily wed then, eh?'

'We might have been, if the bastard hadn't gone off with some tart from Ackeroyd Street!'

That was more like it, he thought. 'Oh, I'm sorry to hear that.'

'Liar!'

'No, I am really.' He always prided himself on being as good a liar as the next bloke. 'Bet you weren't on your own for long though, eh? A good-looker like yourself?'

'I was for a while,' she answered soulfully. 'Then I hitched up with the landlord from Daisy Street, and life didn't seem so bad after all.'

'Oh, I see.' Disappointment betrayed itself. 'You're not one to waste time, are you?'

'It didn't last long though,' she grumbled. 'All he wanted was a good time. He didn't want to go serious, so I dumped him.'

'So now you're on your own again?' he probed. 'Or is there another man in tow?'

'Well, kinda.'

He cursed under his breath. 'Someone I know, is it?'

She grinned wickedly. 'His name's Edward Trent . . . the only man I ever really loved, but he went away and broke my heart.' She gave him a come-on wink. 'I'm wondering whether he might stay this time?'

Secretly thrilled and giving little away, he answered quietly, 'I'm sure he'll stay, if you was to ask him nicely.' The most satisfying thing in the world was making a woman grovel.

'All right then, will you stay?'

'Only if you keep your sister at bay. I can't be doing with nagging women.' His smile slipped and his eyes grew darker. 'Women like her send me crazy. They make me liable to turn nasty.'

'She won't nag you. If anything, it'll be *me* she has a go at. But don't worry, I'm not that foolish young girl any more. I'm all grown up, and able to take care of myself.' Lizzie looked him in the eye. 'You would do well to remember that.'

Ignoring the hint, he asked guardedly, 'So where does she live, this Harpy of a sister?' He glanced up at the window. 'Not here with you, I hope?'

'Nope.' She leaned closer. 'As you can see, I work here.' Her fingers stroked the back of his neck, making the hair stand on end. 'Mike, the landlord, is away with his wife. They asked me to stay the night to keep an eye on things. I do stay over on the occasional night, and up until recently, I used to live over. But I got taken advantage of, getting caught for extra hours at the bar and nothing in return. So, I took a little house on Dock Lane. It's not much, but my name's on the rent book.'

Dropping her hand to his nether regions she squeezed up to him. 'We could go there later, if you want?' she said, nibbling his ear. 'Mike and his wife are due back about eleven. I can ask the barman to shut the pub, and there'll be no need for me to stay tonight.'

Trent gave her a smile that melted her at the knees. 'You little hussy,' he teased, and thought he might give her a kiss, but decided not to rush things. Make her wait, he thought, make her hungry for it. She's not Lucy, but she'll do for a couple of nights, until I've got my bearings.

Taking hold of her hands he pushed her away. 'Your offer is real tempting and I dare say I'll take you up on it later. But right now, believe it or not, all I want is a long cold drink.'

'A drink it is then.' Surprised and disappointed, she led the way inside to the bar. 'You still haven't told me where you've been all this time.'

'I've been away at sea. That's all you need to know.' The fewer people who knew where he'd been the better, he thought cagily.

'Hmh! I might believe that, but my Patsy wouldn't.'

Her remark made him curious. ' "My Patsy", is it? So, you two get on all right, do you – even after she made it her goal in life to split us up?'

'She looks after me. She always has.'

'Bosses you about, more like!' But Patsy was a stupid cow who didn't deserve a minute more of his time. 'Stop the gabbing, Liz, and get me a drink, will you?'

Hoisting himself onto the stool, Trent watched her moving about behind the bar. 'I'm in no mood for questions, so leave it be, because I'm back now and raring to go,' he said. 'First a few pints, then a hot bath, and after that I wouldn't mind wrapping my arms . . . and legs . . . round a warm female. If you know what I mean.'

He winked meaningfully. 'You don't happen to know of a sexy woman who might be looking for a randy fella to keep her occupied, do you?'

'I expect that has to be me,' she laughed. 'No one else would want a ruffian like you.' Taking down a pint glass from above the bar, she slid it under the beer tap, to release a torrent of froth and ale. 'One pint coming up.'

Making his mouth water, she leaned forward, just far enough for him to see the rise of her voluptuous breasts inside the open neck of her shirt.

She slid the pint of beer towards him, pointing to the crooked bend in her elbow. 'That's thanks to you,' she said, not smiling this time.

'What d'you mean?'

'That day when you ran for it – remember you and Dad got into a terrible fight? I tried to stop you, and got a broken arm for my trouble.'

'I didn't know that.'

'That's because you didn't stop to find out. But I'm not blaming you. All's fair in love and war, isn't that what they say?'

Edward Trent recalled the fight in detail; him and her father, and that witch of a sister who started it all by opening her big mouth. He pushed it to the back of his mind, preferring instead to remember the fun he'd had while he and Lizzie were on the rampage. 'We had a good time though, didn't we, you and me?'

'The best!'

'After all the disappointments you've had with lesser men than me, I hope you haven't forgotten how to please a fella.'

'That's for me to know and you to find out,' she murmured coyly.

When other drinkers started arriving, Trent retired to the corner table. 'Keep the pints coming,' he told her. And she told him he'd be no good to her with Brewer's Droop.

'You've no need to worry on that score,' he promised. 'I have been known to cover three women in one night of non-stop boozing.'

'That I'd like to see.'

'Well, you won't, because I've got eyes only for you,' he lied.

'That's all I need to hear,' and she told him how she couldn't wait to have him all to herself.

In fact, after the bar was closed and he had downed some five pints, Trent was not even halfway drunk. He waited for the bar to close, and he watched while Lizzie helped the portly barman shut up shop, and afterwards he walked her to Dock Lane and took her inside. 'You've been teasing me all night,' he said hoarsely, 'so now let's see what you've really got.'

No sooner were they in the door than he was tearing at her clothes. 'Hey! Watch the new blouse!' Pushing him off, she made him wait while she peeled off the blouse and the skirt, and then her frilly undergarments one after the other, each strip more tantalising than the last.

'My God!' It had been too long since he'd seen a woman stripped to the bone. 'I could eat you,' he growled. 'Every last ounce of you.'

She laughed nervously. 'Then there'd be nothing left for you to love.'

And love her he did, wild and wanton, with the appetite of a man condemned. In the first hour he took her once on the floor and twice in the bed, and then again when he woke from a slightly drunken stupor.

'Ssh! Who's that?' On hearing a noise downstairs, he sat up to listen. 'I could swear I heard a door go . . . listen!' There was another clatter, followed by a mouthful of abuse.

Fearful, Lizzie leaped out of bed. Throwing him a dressing-gown, she hissed instructions. 'Get in the back room – quick, dammit!'

He hesitated. 'Who is it? What's wrong?'

'It's Patsy. She has a key. Sometimes she calls round on her way home from the club. She's a cloakroom attendant in a nightclub – works evenings and weekends.'

He couldn't believe his ears. 'What! You mean to tell me that big-mouth sister of yours is downstairs right now? Gawd Almighty, woman, what the devil are you playing at?'

She began to panic. 'Quick! It's best if she doesn't catch us together.' While she talked she quickly dressed. 'You know how she feels about you. She's never forgotten how you used me.'

Suddenly the door burst open and there she was, a wizened figure with small sharp eyes and an even sharper tongue. 'What's all this?' From the slur in her voice it was obvious she was the worse for drink.

Her quick eyes went to Trent, who made no move; instead he stared back defiantly. 'Hello, Patsy, my love,' he growled. 'I'd like to say you've aged well, but you haven't – not like your baby sister here. You see, I've just been admiring her figure – plumper than the last time I saw her, though a pleasant handful all the same. More filled out and soft to the touch,' he gave a nauseating wink, 'if you know what I mean?'

For what seemed an age she looked at him, eyes widening as she began to recognise who he was. 'Edward Trent . . . the baby-snatcher!' The blood drained from her face. 'You bastard! What are *you* doing here?'

Smiling and arrogant, he pointed to their half-naked bodies, 'I should have thought that was obvious.'

Taking him by surprise, she launched herself at him. 'Get out of here! Go on, get out of here now, you no-good filth.' Drawing blood, her nails caught him across the cheekbones. 'It was your fault we lost our dad. You worried him sick with the way you carried on – bedding a girl half your age and laughing in his face when he begged you to leave her alone. And as if that wasn't enough, you beat him half to death before you ran off like the coward you are. Go on! Get away from her, you dirty bastard! She doesn't need your sort.'

'You're drunk as usual.' Lizzie took hold of her. 'Leave him alone! I want him here – I invited him.' Lizzie tried to pull her away but she was no match for her sister's bull-like strength.

Suddenly it was uproar, with Patsy hell-bent on gouging out his eyes, and Trent fighting to get his clothes back on.

'What the devil's going on in there?' From downstairs the front door rattled under a barrage of thumps. 'I'm calling the police! D'you hear me up there? If the noise doesn't stop right now, I'm fetching the bizzies!'

Fearing the police more than anything else, Trent threw Patsy off. 'I'll be back,' he told Lizzie. 'I promise I'll be back.' No drunken slag was running his life, that was for sure.

Outside, he airily told the neighbours who had gathered there, 'It was a row that got out of hand. No need for the police to get involved.' With that, he sauntered off, leaving them nattering amongst themselves. 'Nosy rats!' he muttered angrily. But his anger became uncontrolled rage when he thought of what Patsy had said . . . called him 'filth'. Nobody did that to him, let alone a woman.

Fingering the scratches on his face, he licked the blood from his finger. 'Want to kill me, do you?' he smiled. 'Well, I'm sorry to disappoint you, Patsy my love, but you will never see the day.'

At the end of the street he waited until the neighbours had gone back to their holes, then retraced his steps as far as the shop doorway, where he slid inside and stayed hidden in the shadows for what seemed hours. He grew cold and began to shiver, but his determination kept his angry blood warm.

It was two hours later when she came out; he heard her loud, aggressive voice: 'You're not to let him through that door, d'you hear me? He's no good and never will be. If you ask me, he's spent the last twenty years in prison. Pity they didn't hang the no-good layabout! If he comes back, I'll do for him, and then it won't matter any more, because he'll be out of your life for good and all.'

Then she lowered her voice and it was all he could do to hear her. He shifted closer, cringing as she issued instructions.

'Remember how he treated you last time. For pity's sake, our kid, stay away from him. Think what he did – beat our dad senseless, broke your arm, and left not an inch of flesh on your bones that wasn't bruised or bleeding.'

Her voice shook with rage. 'He'd better not come back, that's all I'm saying, or I won't be responsible for my actions.'

As she came up the street it was easy to see from her unsteady gait that she had consumed even more booze while under her sister's roof.

When she passed within inches of him, Trent pressed back into the darkness. He saw her mean profile and the hard set of her mouth. Her shoulders were stooped as though she carried the weight of the world on them, and he hated her with every fibre of his being.

A few minutes later, she was almost run over when a lone taxi driver had to slam on his brakes in order to avoid her swaying figure. 'You silly mare! I nearly ran into you! Stay on the path, why don't you!' He went away, shaking his fist out the window, while she made a rude gesture and told him to, 'Sod off, you useless git!'

All fired up, Trent followed, keeping enough distance between them so she was not able to detect his presence.

As they neared the river, the street-lamps became further apart and the streets grew darker, until now they were so close to the water he could reach down and touch it. The walkways were deserted at this time of night, which suited his plan.

When they descended towards the railings, he got so excited he let his concentration lapse and didn't take enough care where he was walking; the loose stone bounced from under his foot and hit the side of the railings. Startled, Patsy turned round, peering into the darkness. 'Who's there?'

He gave no reply. Instead he remained still as a statue, not daring to move, thankful for the shadows that were thrown in his direction from an isolated nearby street-light.

She stood quite still for a while, her small sharp eyes cutting through the night air, but not seeing him at all.

Muttering under her breath, she went on.

At the end of the walkway, the railings broke where the steps led down. There she stumbled, leaning on the railings before spewing her heart out all down the steps.

Delighted, he took his opportunity.

As he dashed forward, she heard him and turned round, her face open with surprise. 'You!' Wiping the vomit from her mouth she demanded to know what he was doing, sneaking about in the middle of the night. 'If you think you can make me change my mind about you and my sister, you can think again', she slurred, 'because if it's the last thing I do, I'll turn her against you. I won't be satisfied until she hates you as much as I do!'

Her tirade ended in a gasp as he lunged at her with both arms outstretched. One vicious push and her unsteady legs couldn't hold her.

As she went tumbling down the stairs, her head hit the steps, dulling her senses and making her lose all sense of direction. When she ended up in the river, he laughed out loud. 'Not so clever now, are you, eh? Met your match, haven't you?'

He watched as she floundered in the murky waters, her head appearing then disappearing, her eyes staring at him in disbelief each time she surfaced. 'Help!' She found the strength to scream out. 'Somebody help me!'

He looked round. There was nothing to hand, save for a wooden bench nearby. When she wouldn't stop screaming, he wrenched a plank of wood from the seat, waited until she surfaced again and threw it like a spear at her head. There was a muffled thud, a frantic splashing of hands, then silence. Wonderful, calming silence.

He stared into the water, making sure. But no! There was no sign of her at all. However, in the flickering light there appeared to be a patch of darker water on the surface. In the back of his mind he thought it might be her life's blood. Serve her damned well right. The bitch had had it coming.

Christ, he had a headache! Trent took a deep breath, then, smiling to himself, and satisfied with a job well done, he walked away, a lazy, swaggering walk.

As though he had all the time in the world.

CHAPTER EIGHTEEN

SPRING IN Boston, Massachusetts, could be chilly, but today the weather was so exceptionally cold that even the workmen kept stopping in their labours to rub their hands together in an effort to get the blood flowing.

'I reckon all my toes have dropped off.' Born in the far reaches of Scotland, and used to weather extremes, the truck-driver was frantically stamping his feet in order to revive them. 'How much longer before I can be away?'

'Last panel coming down now.'

Having spent these many years working on the spread for Leonard Maitland, the burly foreman was accustomed to being outdoors in all weathers; summer, winter – it made no difference to him. If a job needed doing, it had to be done properly, and dismantling this huge grain-barn was just another task.

'CLEAR AWAY!' When the cry went up, the workmen ran to safety while the mighty crane toppled the one remaining fifty-foot-high panel. The jaws of the crane wrenched the heavy timber from its roots and with the sound of creaks and groans, the timber lurched sideways before falling to the ground, broken and buckled as it dug itself into the soil.

It was then just a matter of sawing the pieces into smaller, more manageable sizes, which were then hoisted onto the back of the truck to be taken away. 'I'm not sorry to see the back of that.' As the dismantled grain-barn was driven away, the foreman stood back to survey the damage. 'I'm surprised it hasn't fallen down before now.'

The old barn had covered a huge area of prime farming land, which was now scarred and torn by the immense weight of falling timber.

'The soil will find its own level in a week or so,' the foreman told his men. 'Meantime, we've a few miles of ditch-dredging to get on with, before the better weather returns.' When that happened, the land would keep them toiling non-stop, until the last harvest was taken.

From the top of the mound, Leonard felt a surge of sadness when he saw the grain-barn topple. 'That barn has been standing longer than I've been alive,' he told his faithful old mongrel, Chappie. 'But it's a fact of life – we all grow old and outlive our usefulness.' That's how he felt now, useless and old.

He was especially vulnerable these days, what with Vicky gone from his life, and the children torn two ways over the recent revelations regarding their father and the sacrifice he made for them. 'Will she ever come back?' he murmured. 'My life is so meaningless, so empty without her.' Not a minute went by when he wasn't thinking of her. He was desperate to go to England and find her, yet afraid in case he only made a bad situation much worse. He hoped and prayed she would come home soon, of her own volition. Because, God help him, he couldn't live without her.

He walked on. Following the bridleway which ran along the perimeter of the fields, he paused a while and raised his gaze to the far-off horizon. 'See that?' he asked the old dog. 'Every square inch of land as far as you can see belongs to me. But it means nothing, not without Vicky by my side.'

'Morning, Mr Maitland!' The young woman on the bicycle

gave him a cheery wave. She passed him every morning on her way to help milk the cows and pack the eggs, and turn her hand to anything else that came along.

'Morning, Jeanie, how's your mom?'

'Better by the day,' she said merrily. 'She said to thank you for the eggs you sent her.'

'You're very welcome, I'm sure.' He gave her a wave and went on his way.

Entering through the stable-yard, he stopped to talk with the groom while Chappie trotted off to meet the other couple of dogs there. 'How's the gelding coming along?' he asked.

'Raring to go,' the young man replied with a grin. 'Come and see for yourself.'

The gelding, Jack, was a favourite of Leonard's; big and strong, it took his weight without hesitation. 'What did the vet say?'

Strolling along beside the boss, the groom told him excitedly, 'Well, as you know, he feared Jack might have to be put down, but this morning, he was really pleased with the way the wound is healing. The swelling has gone down, and the bone is intact. Jack's still limping slightly, but he doesn't seem bothered when he puts his weight forward.'

'Well, that's a blessing, at least.' Leonard was relieved. 'He's a fine horse. It would be a sin and a shame to have had him put down.'

When they got to the stable, the horse heard Leonard's voice and came to look over the door. 'See what I mean?' The groom was thrilled. 'All fired up and ready for action.'

Letting himself into the stable, Leonard asked the gelding to lift its hoof and it did so without fuss. But the minute Leonard bent to examine the wound, it shuffled nervously. 'Woah, boy, I'm not here to hurt you.'

With soothing words he calmed the animal before taking

a good look at the six-inch wound which, as the groom had already explained, was healing nicely. 'Wonderful!' Leonard gently released the limb. 'Good fella,' he said, stroking the softness of the horse's neck. 'You'll soon be out on the bridleways. But you're one lucky Jack! A kick like that would have finished any other horse, but you've come through and I'm proud of you.' He laughed as the horse nuzzled up to him, tickling his hand with the fine hairs around his big, soft nostrils. 'All right, all right. No need to keep thanking me.'

Outside, he discussed the future of the bad-tempered stallion, Duke, that had kicked the younger horse. 'I've never known a horse to go for another one, like he went for Jack. A vicious kick like that could have snapped his leg clean in two!'

'Have you decided what to do with him?' asked the groom.

'I'm thinking of selling him on. I've had two good offers, but the money isn't the priority. It's knowing he'll go to a good home. Duke's been a faithful old fella. It wouldn't be fair to let him go to just anybody because of one jealous moment.'

'So, that's what you think it was, that he was jealous of the young gelding?' The groom wasn't so sure.

Leonard nodded. 'I do think that, yes – mainly because he's never done anything like it before, and it happened only weeks after we brought the gelding in. Besides, Jack did escape into Duke's field, and you know how territorial he can be.'

For some time, the groom had not been happy with the older horse, and he said so now. 'You know, Mr Maitland, how some stallions can turn rogue without warning, and when they do, it's a bad thing.'

'Well, he won't be doing it again, not on this yard,' Leonard declared. 'We've got eight horses here, all of them good, honest animals, and I'm not willing to take risks with any of them.'

He glanced towards the stallion who was at the field gate.

'At the same time, I want the best for him. We've had him a long time and he's never put a foot wrong until now. I'm determined to find him a good home, where he'll be treated properly.'

'So, who have you got in mind?'

'I've arranged for Georgie O'Sullivan, who runs the stables for Abe Devine, to come down and look at Duke later this afternoon.'

The groom was impressed. 'O'Sullivan, eh? If anybody knows a thing or two about horses, it's the Irishman.'

'Right!' Leonard wholeheartedly agreed. 'I have urgent business in Boston, but I've explained everything to Georgie. He knows what he's getting, and he knows I'll stand for no nonsense. So will you be all right to deal with him in my absence?'

'I'll be fine.'

'Good. Then we'll talk later.'

Bidding the groom good day, Leonard strode off, his mind now filled with an idea which, once planted, would not go away.

Inside the house, he fed the dog and while the elderly animal worked its way through a bowl of leftovers, Leonard came to a decision. 'If I can't go and find your mistress, I'll get a private detective in to do the job for me,' he told Chappie. 'I need to know that she's safe and well. If I can satisfy myself on that, at least I won't have to worry quite so much, and I can keep an eye on her from a distance.'

Vicky was the love of Leonard Maitland's life. She meant more to him than anyone or anything. She might not approve of what he was doing, and he hoped she would never find out; but either way, he knew it was the right thing to do, for his peace of mind, and for Vicky's own good.

~

That same evening, Thomas and his wife Sheila dropped in. 'You wanted to talk about that new combine-harvester,' Thomas reminded Leonard. 'Is now a good time?'

As always, his stepfather was pleased to see him. 'Couldn't be better,' he confirmed. 'As you know, I've just acquired another eight hundred acres, so I'm thinking we should trade in the old machine against one of the larger John Deere models.'

Thomas was pleased. 'So you've come round to my way of thinking at last!' he said triumphantly. 'That's good. You won't regret it, Leonard.'

'I'm sure I won't,' Leonard answered. 'But if we're now agreed on going ahead with it, I reckon we should do it now. We've a way to go before harvest, but it'll be here before we know it, so we need to get the deal done before everybody else begins to think along the same lines of trading up to these new, larger combines.'

'I'm all for getting the deal done,' Thomas nodded. 'And while we're on the subject of machinery, we need to rent another grain-wagon, and hire a driver to work it.'

'It that's what we need, then go to it,' Leonard told him. 'Discuss it with the foreman first. But you're right – we don't want to be halfway through harvest and discover that all the good drivers have been snapped up.'

Wearied by all this farming talk, Sheila wandered across the room, where she lingered by Vicky's photograph. 'Have you heard from *her* yet?' she asked casually, a knowing smirk on her face.

Leonard took offence at the tone of her remark. 'Heard from whom?' He knew who she meant all right, but he wanted some measure of respect when she mentioned his wife's name.

Sheila feigned surprise at his question. 'Well, Vicky, of course.'

He stared her out. 'For all I knew, you could have been talking about the cat.'

Shrugging her shoulders, she smiled sweetly. 'I'm sorry, Lenny. I didn't realise you would be so sensitive.'

Sensing an atmosphere building, Thomas intervened. 'Have you heard from Mother?' he asked worriedly. 'Has she been in touch?'

Composing himself, the man took a deep breath. 'No. Not a word, I'm afraid.'

'Hmh!' Sheila made a snorting noise. 'You shouldn't be too surprised,' she said peevishly. '*I'm* not. I mean, when all's said and done, she did leave you high and dry. In fact, she left all of you high and dry. What decent wife or mother would do such a thing? If I were you I wouldn't even *want* to hear from her.'

Leonard retaliated angrily. 'It's just as well that you're not me, then, isn't it?'

With an exaggerated tut, and a sharp click of her heels, his daughter-in-law slammed out of the room. 'She didn't mean all that,' Thomas said wearily but he was beginning to tire of defending her, especially when she seemed to take pleasure in hurting people, himself included.

Leonard was no fool. 'Oh, she meant it,' he assured the younger man. 'But it doesn't matter, because I know your mother will contact me when she's cooled her heels for a while longer.'

'Do you really think so?' If Sheila hadn't been constantly goading him about how shocking it was for a mother to walk out on her family and not even tell them where she was, he might have started wondering whether he and his brother and Susie had been too harsh on her. As it was, he held fast to his belief that Vicky had let them all down badly.

'If you really want the truth', Leonard said quietly, 'I can't say for certain that she *will* ever come back. All I know is that life is unbearable without her. I miss her dreadfully, and I want her home again the sooner the better.'

'So you don't know where she is?'

'Not yet, no,' Leonard said woefully. But he intended to, he thought. However, he wasn't certain whether Thomas would approve of him hiring a detective to find his mother.

'Can I ask you something, Tom?'

'Ask away.'

'Do *you* think I was wrong in not telling her about your father?'

'I honestly don't know.' Thomas had asked himself that same question many times, but as yet he had found no answer. 'I'm not sure about anything any more,' he confided. 'You have always been a man of your word, and you gave your word to our father when he asked you to promise never to tell Mother, or any of us. You kept that promise. How can a man be blamed for that?'

'But that isn't the only reason why you sided with me, is it?' Leonard could understand their bitterness, but he wanted it to end. 'Oh, Tom, how I wish you could forgive your father for not confiding in all of you! He was a very ill man, desperate to ensure you had the chance that was taken from him. You must believe that he loved you all above anything. He wanted his family to embark on a new life; he wanted to be with you all every step of the way but he couldn't – and that was not his fault.'

It all came back to Leonard, the night he found Barney in the woods, curled up in pain, not knowing which way to turn. He was a special man, a special father and husband, and Leonard wanted his family to appreciate that. 'Please, you must try to understand his motives. Don't belittle the awesome sacrifice he made. Make Susie and Ronnie understand why he did what he did. Barney did not tell you about his illness, because he knew you would never leave him. The last thing he wanted was for you all to stay and watch him fade away, in pain, filled with regret because he had stolen your only chance of starting a new life.'

Thomas considered his words, and they made some sense. But the anger in his heart was strong as ever. 'Susie and Ronnie feel the same way I do. We're angry and bitter. We feel we were tricked into letting him down, when all we wanted was the right to be there for him, just as we've always been there for each other.'

His voice trembled with emotion. 'Dad should have told us! We had a right to know . . . to make the sacrifice for him, just as he made it for us. He was dying, and we should have been with him. But he took away that right, and I don't know if I can ever forgive him!'

Leonard despaired. 'If you can't forgive Barney, then how is your mother ever going to forgive *you*?'

'At least she has a choice.'

Thomas's jaw was clenched hard. He looked at Leonard a moment longer, before in a harsh voice he told him, 'I miss her, of course I do. We all love her and want her back. But she has to accept the way we feel. She's already forgiven Father. We probably never will and, like I say, we were robbed of the chance to look after him to the end, to show him how much we loved him and always would. But all that's gone forever – just like him!'

He squared his shoulders. 'So, we've chosen to side with what you did in not telling Mother, because it was all too late by then. But as to forgiving and forgetting how Dad lied and deceived us, sending us away hating him, sick with pain and disgust at what he had done to us . . . to Mum, not knowing how ill he was, that it was only a year or two before he would be gone . . .' The big man was crying now, unashamedly.

As he turned to leave, Leonard asked, 'Have you seen Susie?'

237

Thomas shook his head. 'She's not back from the fashion show in Paris.'

'And Ronnie?'

'I don't know where he is – off gallivanting somewhere, I expect, as usual. You never know with him, but he'll turn up. He always does.'

'I worry about him,' Leonard admitted. 'He seems to have no purpose in life.'

Thomas gave a wry little smile. 'There you go,' he said. 'What Dad did has affected us all in different ways. I don't sleep well and I'm riddled with guilt at the terrible things I said to my father; Susie throws herself heart and soul into building the business, so she can't remember how it was, and Ronnie . . . !' He rolled his eyes to the ceiling. 'Poor old Ron is so mixed up, I wouldn't know where to start unravelling him!'

Leonard bade him goodnight. 'Think about what I said,' he pleaded. 'Talk with the others. See if you can bring them, and yourself . . . some kind of peace.'

'Goodnight, Leonard. I'll get the ball rolling on that combiner,' Tom sighed. As far as he was concerned, there was nothing for him to talk about with the others.

And so the two men parted company, firm friends, each hurting in different ways, because of one man, and the bitter-sweet legacy he had left behind.

CHAPTER NINETEEN

THOUGH SHE HAD come up in the world and was now
Bridget's right-hand woman in business, Amy's modest
home on Penny Lane reflected her true personality.

Bright and cheerful, with the firegrate burning merrily on
a winter's night and filled with flowers in the summertime,
the house was a cosy little place. There were pretty pictures
hanging on the wall, chubby armchairs and flowery curtains,
and a rag rug all colours of the rainbow set in front of the
hearth. A gleaming coal-scuttle sat next to a companion set
of tongs, poker and a little brush to sweep the fireplace free
of ash.

When on this drizzly February morning, Bridget rapped
on the door and walked in, it was as if she had strayed into
the most glorious summer's day. The warm colours and
smell of new-made bread filled her senses. 'Amy? Are you
there?' she called.

Following her nose through to the kitchen, she found
Amy in her cosy old candlewick dressing-gown holding a
toasting-fork to the range fire.

'Would you like some toast?' Amy asked, removing the
slice and dropping it on a plate.

Bridget shook her head, then she licked her lips. 'Oh, go
on then. Just the one piece.'

Cutting another chunky slice off the loaf, Amy placed that on the fork and held it up to the flames. 'You can make a pot of tea while you're waiting,' she told Bridget. 'And don't make it too strong . . . remember, it's two level spoons of tea-leaves to the pot.'

Bridget pointed to the loaf. 'The smell hit me as soon as I came in,' she said happily. 'That can't be above a few hours old.'

Amy chuckled. 'You're right! Madge next door used to be a baker. Since she gave up work a few weeks back, she bakes every day . . . scones, muffins, bread and cakes of all kind. She gives the stuff away to anybody who wants it; the baker ran out on his rounds a few weeks back, so he bought half a dozen barm-cakes from Madge. Folks liked them so much, the baker and Madge came to an agreement, so now she's baking, and earning as well.'

When the tea was made and four slices of toast cooked to perfection, they sat down to enjoy it. 'What do you want anyway?' Spreading her butter over the toast, Amy licked her fingers when it leaked through the bread and melted all over her plate. She dug into the pot of Gale's runny honey and drizzled it over the butter.

'Well now!' Bridget had taken a bite of her toast and little bits of bread flew out of her mouth as she spoke. 'Sure, that's a nice way to welcome an old friend, I must say.'

Amy chided her. 'Don't talk with your mouth full.' She took a sip of her tea. 'I can't believe it!' she cried. 'You've actually made a decent pot of tea.'

'Of course, and why wouldn't I?'

'You still haven't answered my question.'

Selecting a cheese triangle from the round cardboard box on the table, Bridget spread it on her toast and with a sigh of satisfaction, took another huge bite of her bread. 'Mmm – delicious. What question was that, then?'

Amy groaned. 'You're a mucky heathen, aren't you? Just look at you . . . spitting bread all over the place and butter running down your chin. You're worse than a bairn. I'm thinking I should have got you a bib!'

Bridget snorted. 'Away with ye! I'm really enjoying this. You tell Madge from me, she bakes the best bread I've ever tasted.' She looked at Amy with a frown. 'What's the matter now?'

'There's nothing at all the matter with *me*. All I want to know is, why are you here? It's Saturday, my day off, and you're supposed to be going to the races with your precious Oliver. So, what's gone wrong this time? Fallen out again, have you?'

Bridget rolled her eyes to the ceiling. 'Sure the man will never learn! I don't mind having it off in the back of a cramped car, and I don't even mind rolling about in the long grass with the ants biting my arse. But I told him, I draw the line at being fondled when there's a thousand eyes all looking at us, instead of watching the horses.'

She tutted. 'I might not be the world's most dignified person, but I have not made, and never will make, a spectacle of meself!'

Amy tried hard not to giggle but the laughter broke through and she was obliged to apologise. 'Are you telling me he tried it on at the races, in front of everyone?'

'Bold as ye like, so he was!'

'And you walked out on him?'

'I did, yes.'

'And that's why you're here?'

'It is.'

'So, what do you expect *me* to do about it?'

'I expect you to finish your breakfast and we'll go shopping.' Bridget glanced at the mantelpiece clock. 'You'll have to be quick or the shops will be shut. It's already

241

half past twelve, and you just out of bed, you lazy article!'

They wolfed down their toast and tea, then Bridget put the guard round the fire, and washed the crockery in the sink while Amy went away upstairs to get ready.

An hour later, the two women got off the bus in the centre of Liverpool, with an appetite to shop and purses at the ready.

Two hours after that, weary and spent out, they made their way to Kenyon's, a delightful café which served hot pies, toasted muffins, and lots of other tasty snacks.

'Jaysus, Mary and Joseph!' Dropping her shopping-bags to the floor, Bridget fell into a seat. 'I'm that parched, my tongue is stuck to the roof of me mouth.'

'I don't see how it can be stuck,' Amy quipped. 'It hasn't stopped you from grumbling, has it? You moaned and groaned all the way through town, and you're still at it now.'

Bridget wagged a finger. 'Don't you get clever with me, my girl,' she chided. 'Just be a darlin', why don't ye, and fetch that lazy idle waitress over here . . . Will ye look at what she's up to, the dirty wee devil!'

She drew Amy's attention to the girl behind the counter. 'Filing her nails, so she is . . . and all the food lying uncovered.'

While Bridget ranted on about health and hygiene and 'bone-idle eejits who've forgotten what it's like to do a day's honest work', Amy went to order. 'A pot of tea for two, if you please, nice and hot?' she said politely.

'Do you want anything to eat?' The girl carried on doing her nails. 'We've some teacakes just in, nice and fresh they are.' Having filed her nail sharp enough, she then blew away the residue.

'HEY!' Bridget's voice sailed across the room. 'Don't fetch me none of them iced buns!' she told Amy. 'Sure, the dirty little bugger's just covered them with nail filings.'

The girl looked up, her face contorted in a frown. 'What's she say?'

Preferring a peaceful life, Amy didn't want to get involved, so she smiled sweetly and explained, 'She said she'd love one of your nice fresh teacakes. Me too, if you don't mind.'

The girl put her file in her pocket. 'A pot of tea for two, two teacakes – with butter and jam?'

Amy had visions of the jam clotted with nail-filings. 'No, thank you. Just plain teacakes, and we'll put our own butter on if that's all right.' She intended to examine the butter before it got spread over the teacakes, just in case the girl had been plucking her eyebrows in the kitchen.

When they arrived, the teacakes were fresh as the girl promised, the tea was piping hot, and the butter was clear right through. 'Thank you, that all looks very nice,' Amy told her.

Bridget glared at her, and said nothing.

'That one's a miserable git,' the waitress told her young assistant, scratching her bottom as she spoke. 'What d'you reckon . . . she's lost a pound and found a penny?'

The other girl shook her head. 'Don't know, I'm sure.' Her eyes shifted to the iced buns, all covered in nail filings, and she made a mental note never to eat anything here that wasn't covered or fresh in.

The café soon began to fill up. 'There must be a train just in,' Amy remarked as the customers entered carrying suit-cases and bags, and rolled-up newspapers under their arms.

Two loud, painted dolls who couldn't stop giggling placed their order. 'Two coffees and two o' them iced buns, and be quick about it, 'cause we've a train to catch,' said the taller of the two.

'Pink icing or white?' The waitress had taken an instant dislike to this arrogant pair.

'Pink . . . no, white. No, hang on!' She called to her friend

who had sat herself at the table. 'Joyce, what'll you have –
pink or white icing?'

'One of each, Sandra, and have you told 'em we've a train
to catch?'

'I've told 'em, but they don't seem to be shifting themselves.' Turning to the assistant who was making the tea, the
girl snapped, 'Are you deaf or what? I told you we were in a
hurry. Get a move on, will you?'

'We're going as fast as we can!' The waitress was losing
her temper now.

'Pair of bloody slowcoaches, that's what you are.' Turning
to her friend, the one called Sandra sniffed, 'I could bake
the cakes and a tray of loaves as well, in the time it's taking
this lot to serve us!'

When the assistant saw how her boss was ready to explode,
she stepped forward and, placing a large teapot and two
cups on a tray on the counter, she reached into the cake
section and took out one pink and one white iced bun.
'There you go,' she said. 'That'll be ninepence for the two
teas. The iced buns are on the house.'

The girl thought she'd won the day. 'That's more like
it,' she declared, fishing ninepence out of her purse and
dropping it onto the counter. 'Took your time though,
didn't you?'

Taking a huge bite out of the pink iced bun, she put it
back on the tray, and carried the whole lot over to where
her friend Joyce was sitting. 'You have to put them in their
place straight off,' she told her loudly. 'Else the buggers'll
walk all over you.'

Behind the counter, the waitress was threatening to take
the cost of the buns out of her assistant's wages. 'What on
earth did you go and do a thing like that for?' she asked
crossly. 'I was just about ready to throw that pair out onto
the street.'

'Ah, you don't want to go doing that,' came the sly answer. 'Look how much they're enjoying their buns.' She watched them licking the icing off the buns before greedily wolfing them down. It did her heart good to see it; especially when she had chosen the ones that were positively littered with nail filings.

A few minutes later, the two girls left after swigging down their tea. As they rushed out, a tall, well-built man in his forties stepped aside to let them by. *It was Barney's younger son, Ronnie, looking well and more confident than he had done in a very long time.*

He didn't speak. Instead he merely nodded to the girls as they looked him up and down; a good-looking man was always an attraction to these two, never mind if he was older than themselves.

Having arrived in Liverpool a few weeks back, Ronnie had trudged the streets daily, hoping he might see his mother walking about, or in a shop, or even getting on a bus. So far, he had seen neither hide nor hair of her. But he wasn't about to give up just yet. He had come here with the intention of finding her, and find her he would. And it didn't matter to him how long it took, or whether she would not be too pleased at him coming all this way. None of that mattered. He just needed to know that she was all right. He felt he had treated her badly, but he still believed his father had done wrong in not letting them take care of him in his final illness.

He went straight to the counter. 'I'll have a coffee, please, black and strong,' he said. 'Oh, and could I get a doughnut?'

The waitress served him quickly and when he sauntered over to a table, she ran to the back of the shop where the assistant waitress was washing up. 'There's a Yank come in,' she said, all big-eyed and wondrous. 'Well, he sounded like one of them GIs, but now I come to think, it was a funny kind of accent.'

'Maybe he's Canadian,' the other girl ventured. 'They do sound a lot like each other.'

Having witnessed his entrance and heard him speak, Amy and Bridget had also noticed his accent. 'It doesn't sound like he was born in America,' Amy said, 'but he must have lived there a long time.'

Like the others, she couldn't take her eyes off him, and just then, as though he could sense her looking at him, he turned and smiled pleasantly at her and her heart flipped over. 'Oh dear!' She felt flustered. 'He saw me looking.'

Bridget had never seen Amy blush as bright red as she did now and she said so. 'Fancy him, do you?' she teased. 'Well now, I can't say I blame you. He's a fine-looking fella, so he is. D'you know, darlin', if he wasn't from overseas, I'd say I'd seen him somewhere before. Oh well – I'm getting daft in me old age. Look, why don't you go and ask him to sit over here with us?' There was a twinkle of mischief in her eyes. 'I'm sure he'd jump at the chance.'

In terror of what the Irishwoman would do next, Amy collected her shopping together. 'It's time we left,' she said firmly. 'We've been out too long already.'

'Hey now! Hold your horses.' Bridget picked up her cup and took a sip of her tea, which by now was stone cold. 'Sure I haven't finished my tea yet.'

Taking off his overcoat, Ronnie draped it over the back of the chair. Drinking his coffee in one go, he went up for another. He was in no hurry to leave. He needed to think, to decide what to do. He had borrowed money in Boston and sold what few possessions he had, in order to pay his passage out here, and now there were only a few pounds left. So what he had must be made to last.

On his way back with his coffee, he tripped over Amy's shopping bag, horrified when his coffee spilled all down her coat, 'Aw, gee, I'm sorry!' Grabbing a serviette, he began frantically dabbing at the stain. 'It doesn't look good.'

'It's all right.' Amy gently pushed him off. 'It'll come out at the cleaners – things usually do. And besides, it was my fault. I left my shopping bags right across your path. It's me that should be sorry.'

'No, no!' He wouldn't hear of it, and besides he liked the look of this darling woman, who made little fuss about what to him was a terrible accident that might well cost her a new coat. 'Let me make amends. I'll buy you a coffee, will that do?' He crossed his fingers in front of her. 'And I promise, I won't throw it all over you.'

'No, it's all right, honestly.' In all her life she had never taken to any man the way she had taken to him. It was as though she had known him all her life. It was the eyes, she thought; warm and smiling they were, though he looked kind of sad, as if he had been through some awful trauma.

'Well, if you won't let me buy you coffee today, how about I buy you one Monday? I'll see you here, same time?'

Smiling reassuringly, Amy graciously refused. 'I don't think so, but thank you all the same.' She so much wanted to accept his invitation, but she was unsure. She didn't know him. She didn't know anything about him.

'I understand,' he said, and as the two women were about to leave, he asked, 'You wouldn't know a clean, reasonable place where I could board for a while, would you? Only I'm not long in from the States, and the place I've been staying at is far too expensive. You see, I'll be in Liverpool for some time yet, so I'm thinking, a more modest lodging would suit me better, and perhaps even the chance to do some honest work.'

Bridget interrupted. 'What kind of work?'

'Farmwork would be ideal,' he answered. 'It's what I do best, but I'll turn my hand to anything if needs be.'

Bridget had an idea. 'I'll keep it in mind,' she promised.

'If anything comes up, I'll leave a note with the girl at the counter; providing you ask her whenever you come in.'

'Oh, I will!' Any chance of earning an honest dollar was fine by Ronnie. 'That's very good of you, thank you.'

'I'm not promising anything, mind.'

Meanwhile, Amy had been searching her brain as to where he could stay that would not cripple him financially.

'There's a small, family-run place along Preston New Road,' she told him now. 'It's nothing fancy, but it's clean and reasonable, and they do a great breakfast. There's a sign up: *Belmont's Boarding House.*'

'That sounds just the ticket.' He smiled cheekily. 'And now do I get to know your name? After all, I did spill hot coffee all over you, and ruined your coat into the bargain.'

Not for the first time that day, Amy blushed hotly. 'You didn't ruin my coat,' she protested. 'It really will be fine.' Though she wasn't altogether certain. She smiled shyly. 'Got to go now.'

Ronnie was disappointed. 'Goodbye, ladies – my name is Ronnie, by the way.'

'Mine's Amy,' she answered softly. 'And this is Bridget.'

'How do you do, Bridget and Amy.' As Amy turned to leave, he bent his head to look her in the face; whichever way she turned she could not escape his smiling, searching eyes – nor did she want to. 'Will I see you again then?' he asked hopefully. 'Monday – here, same time?'

Amy hesitated. Oh, she did so want to see him again. But she felt awkward; if she was on her own with him, she wouldn't know what to say, so she chose to refuse. 'Sorry, I can't,' she lied. 'But I hope you get on all right with the lodgings.'

Outside, Amy glanced back into Kenyon's, to see Ronnie looking at her, the disappointment written on his face. She shrugged her shoulders by way of an apology, and when he smiled sadly, she felt a rush of regret. She had not meant to make him sad, for she had already sensed his loneliness.

'Don't you like him?' Bridget demanded.

'Well, yes I do, but –'

'You're a fool, so ye are!' Bridget had seen the magic between Amy and Ron, and she spoke her mind. 'When two people, strangers, spark it off like you two did in there, it is something very special and precious. It only happens once in a lifetime, and you just threw it away, like it was nothing. Tell me, what harm would it have done to see him again? A chat over a cup of tea in a public place! He's hardly likely to murder you in front of that nosy pair of articles, is he now?'

'No. Don't suppose so.' The very same thoughts had been running through Amy's mind.

'So what in God's name are you afraid of?'

'It isn't that I'm afraid,' Amy assured her, 'it's just that, well, you know how tongue-tied I get with strange men. I wouldn't know what to say. I might open my mouth and he'd run out of the door as if his pants were on fire.'

'He didn't run just now.'

'Forget it, Bridget. I'm just not easy around men. I never have been.'

'Ah, sure, that's only because ye don't give yourself time to get to know them.'

They walked on for a while, when suddenly Bridget gave a shout. 'Jaysus! Now look what you've made me do!' she exclaimed. 'I was so enchanted with the pair of youse, I've left my purse on the table, so I have.'

Amy was horrified. 'Wait here. I'll run back and get it for you.'

'No. You watch the shopping bags. It won't take me but a minute or two.'

When Bridget came in the door, Ronnie was just leaving. 'Hello again.' Looking over her shoulder he searched the street for Amy.

'She's not with me,' Bridget explained. 'Look, I'll have to

be quick. I came back to tell you something.' Seeing the two waitresses stretching their necks, she kept her voice to a whisper. 'It's about Amy.'

'What about her?'

'She'll see you, like you said – Monday afternoon, same time.'

His face beamed with delight. 'Is that so?'

'Yes, but not here. There's a tearooms on the corner of George Street. That's where she'll be.'

She made a quick exit, with some parting advice. 'Be gentle with her. She's always been a bit on the shy side where men are concerned.'

'She'll be safe enough with me. Oh, and thank you . . .' He only now realised that he had been so intent on discovering Amy's name, he had completely forgotten that of her companion.

'Bridget,' she prompted, not at all offended, but secretly amused.

'Well, thank you, Bridget.'

Making her way back to Amy, who was sitting on a shop wall, Bridget suddenly remembered. Fumbling about in her coat pocket, she took out her purse and holding it up, feigned a gasp of relief. 'Got it!' she cried. 'Sure the little divil was right where I left it.'

'Did you see him?' Amy asked.

'I did.'

'And did he mention me?'

'Ah sure, why on earth should he mention you, after you turned him down the way ye did?'

Amy didn't answer. Glancing back, she saw the American leaving the café and was already regretting her hasty decision not to see him again.

As they clambered onto the bus, Bridget said, 'What an eejit I am.'

'What's wrong?'

'The two-piece.'

'What two-piece?'

'The one we saw in Able's window. I meant to go back for it, but I forgot. Never mind, there'll be another time, and when I get to try it on, ye can tell me what you think.'

Amy nodded, not really listening because her mind was back there, with *him*.

'That's settled then.' Bridget congratulated herself. 'We'll pop back on Monday. We'll get the appointments all set up in the morning, and leave instructions with Jackie. Then we'll take a few hours off in the afternoon. Is that all right, Amy? Does that suit you?'

Still not altogether listening, Amy nodded. 'Whatever you say, Bridget,' she answered irritably. 'Whatever you say.'

~

On Monday morning, Bridget had everything organised in half the time it normally took. 'Right then, Jackie.' She presented the woman with a wad of paperwork. 'It's all in there, everything in order. All you have to do is make sure it all goes as written. Oh, and tell Maureen to wear her business suit for the convention. We can't have her attending a formal function in the low-cut dress she wore last time.' She frowned. 'I put her on a warning, so she should know the score. Make sure anyway . . . check her out. I'm beginning to doubt her judgement of late.'

She had a few more instructions before she left. 'Tell Annie to wear her new dress for tonight's Law Society dinner. It's likely there will be people there who attended the previous one last month, and they might notice if she wears the black one again.'

With everything taken care of, she marched into Amy's office. 'Time to go,' she said.

251

Amy groaned. 'Can't we go tomorrow or Wednesday? I've all these to take care of yet.' She pointed to the thick leather ledger on her desk. 'There are calls coming in left right and centre, and I'm still only halfway through next week's appointments.'

'Leave it to Jackie. I've just briefed her. She knows what's urgent, and what can be dealt with another day.' Bridget gave her a nudge. 'Come on. Time we were out of here.'

'Oh Bridget, must I?'

Ten minutes later, the two of them were in a taxi, headed for town.

They went straight to Able's shop on the High Street, where Bridget made a show of trying on the two-piece. 'Well, what do you think?' She did a few twirls for Amy's benefit.

'It looks good on you.' Amy thought the dark green fitted jacket and long fussy skirt sat well on her employer's curvaceous figure.

'Can I return it if I change my mind?' Bridget asked the shop-assistant.

'Of course.'

So she bought it. Forty-five bob – not too bad. It was well cut and fully lined. 'Maybe I can buy some shoes to go with it,' she suggested, and she and Amy set off for another tour round the shops.

Keeping an eye on the time, Bridget steered Amy down George Street. When they drew alongside the tearooms, she suddenly developed a thirst. 'Shall we take time out for a cuppa?' she asked.

'All right, but then we'll get your shoes. I need to get back,' Amy fretted. 'I've got piles of work waiting.'

Bridget led the way in. She looked around, but *he* wasn't there.

'Just a cuppa is it, Bridget?' Amy asked.

'Thanks, love – yes, just a cuppa.' She checked her watch.

Five minutes to go. Hurry up, Ron! she thought. I won't be able to fool her for much longer.

Amy had just brought the tea over and they were sitting talking when Bridget saw him come in. 'Well, I never!' Feigning astonishment, she leaped out of her chair and called him over. 'Ron! How lovely to see you again.'

He came over, his eyes glued to Amy. 'Hello again, Amy.'

Amazed that he remembered her name, she nodded. 'Hello,' she said shyly. When he looked at her like that, the hairs on the back of her neck tingled, and she could hardly breathe.

'Is it all right if I sit with you?' He sensed her nervousness and thought it best to take things slowly. He liked her so much, the last thing he wanted was to frighten her off.

'I'll get you a black coffee,' Bridget recalled he was drinking before. 'You sit down.'

At the counter she turned round to see the two of them quietly talking; Amy was obviously nervous, but seeming to warm to his natural and easy manner. 'Oh Amy, me darlin' . . . I do hope he's the one,' she murmured.

It would do her old heart good, to see Amy settled with someone who would look after her and love her the way she deserved to be loved.

Placing the coffee cup on the table, she looked out of the window and exclaimed, 'Good grief! Look there, it's Robert Clark. I've been trying to get hold of him for ages.' Apologising, she told Amy and Ronnie, 'I'll have to go. Sure, I don't want to lose sight of him.'

When Amy started to get up, Bridget pushed her down. 'No! You stay me darlin'. I'll have a quick word with Robert, then I'll get back. Enjoy your drinks, the both of you, there's no rush.'

With that, she hurried away. After hiding round the corner for a few minutes, she sneaked back to peer through the window; delighted to see the two of them still talking, and Amy seeming much easier in his company.

She went away, well pleased with herself. 'Oh Amy, my darlin',' she gave a merry little skip. 'Sure, I've a feeling this is the start of something good.'

~

It was two hours later and growing dark, when Ronnie walked Amy to the nearest taxi-rank. On the way, they heard the street-vendor calling out the headlines in the evening paper: 'Woman fished out of the river . . . police suspect foul play.'

Amy commented, 'Murdered! God, that's awful.'

Ronnie told her not to worry. 'Because from now on, I'll be looking after you . . . that is, if you'll let me?'

'I can look after myself,' Amy answered.

'So you don't need me, is that what you're saying?'

She looked up, a smile of contentment on her face. 'No, that is not what I'm saying. Actually, it would be really nice to have someone who cares about me.' All the same, she cautioned him, 'But we hardly know each other, so let's just take it as it comes, eh?'

'Okay. If that's what you want.'

After a while he felt her hand slide into his, and he was thrilled. His every instinct told him that Amy was the woman he had been waiting for, and suddenly, his life had a purpose.

When they got to the first taxi, the driver was reading the *Echo* by the light of a flickering street-lamp. 'Nasty business,' he said, holding up the newspaper. 'Some poor woman was pushed into the Mersey and drowned. According to this, she had been well and truly battered into the bargain. They don't say exactly, but there's a lunatic out there on the loose, that's for sure.'

Ronnie reprimanded him. 'I'm not sure the lady needs to hear all that,' he said.

'Oh sorry, mate.' Folding the newspaper, the driver turned the key in the ignition. 'Where to, miss?' he asked.

Ron saw Amy safely inside the cab. 'I'd feel much better if you'd let me see you all the way home,' he suggested worriedly.

Amy gave no answer, but when she patted the seat beside her, he lost no time climbing in. Amy gave her home address in Penny Lane, and the taxi set off. 'If you don't mind me saying, I think you're doing the right thing in seeing your lady home,' the driver offered. 'I mean, for all we know, the murderer might be on the lookout for his next victim.'

'That's enough!' Ronnie leaned forward. 'I'll thank you not to alarm the good lady here. Wherever your lunatic is, and whatever he's about to do next, I don't imagine he's likely to ever touch *our* lives, do you?'

'You never know,' came the wry answer. 'You never know.'

~

As it happened, he was right, and Ronnie was wrong.

Because at that very moment, the 'lunatic' who had drowned Patsy Monk was lurking not too far away, more determined than ever to track down and find Lucy Baker.

CHAPTER TWENTY

BY LATE EVENING, the news of Patsy Monk's murder was being discussed all over Liverpool.

In her home, not too far from where Ronnie and Amy had got into the taxi, Lizzie Monk was like a caged animal, pacing up and down, afraid and distressed. She thought of Edward Trent, but no, he might have a wicked mouth on him, and he didn't like Patsy, but he would never have murdered her.

Calling her to sit down, the Inspector asked more questions: When had Lizzie last seen Patsy? Was there anybody who bore her sister a grudge?

'Think carefully,' he urged. 'We're looking for a vicious killer. Is there anything you can recall about her friends . . . any small, seemingly insignificant thing?'

'No!' Patsy took to pacing the floor again. 'I've already answered all your questions. For God's sake, why don't you leave me alone?'

The Inspector observed how exhausted and distressed she was; he glanced at his young colleague who shook his head, and he decided enough was enough, at least for now.

So far, he had no reason to believe that Lizzie was involved in any way with the tragedy of her sister, Patsy.

'Very well, that should do for now. We'll leave you in

peace,' he told Lizzie. 'But I might have to call in again, so don't go too far away. Meantime, if you can think of anything, anything at all . . .'

'I don't know anything,' she answered wearily. 'I've told you all I know.'

'Would you like a WPC to stay with you for a while?' he asked. 'I can arrange that if needed.'

'No. I'll be all right. I'm better on my own.'

After they were gone, she watched out the window while they climbed into the Black Maria and drove off, the headlights making weird moving circles on the road ahead. 'Good shuts to you!' They wouldn't leave her alone. Why did they keep coming back? It was all too much.

Yanking the curtains together, she went to the cabinet and took out a bottle of whisky and a glass. She poured herself a tot and carried it to the fireplace, her sorry gaze following the leaping flames as they vaporised up the chimney. 'Trent, you bastard! If it was you who hurt her, I swear to God, I'll swing for you!'

Taking a gulp of the spirit, she coughed and cursed and took another sip, which she then spat into the fire – jerking backwards when the alcohol sent the flames into a flurry.

She thought of her sister, floundering in the water, maybe even calling for her, and her heart broke. She took to pacing again, then poured herself another drop of whisky and carefully drank of it; somehow the pain seeming to ease. But not the reality. Somebody had murdered Patsy. Was it somebody she had known and fallen out with? After all, it had to be said, Patsy had a spiteful tongue at times. Who could have killed her? And why?

'Did you do it, Eddie?' She pressed her face through the curtains and looked down at the street. 'Did you kill my sister?'

She took another swig of the drink. 'Where are you? Out with some other poor unsuspecting woman?'

In a wild fit she threw the glass across the room. It smashed into the wall, then lay in shards on the floor, the liquid seeping into the carpet.

Sobbing, poor Lizzie fell into the chair and covered her face with her trembling hands. 'I'm sorry, Patsy,' she cried out. 'God help me, I'm so, so sorry.'

~

The news had spread far and wide; people talked of it in the streets, in their homes huddled round the wireless, and in the pubs across Liverpool. But some people had still not heard about the woman who had been fished out of the river. These included workers on night-shift, who were only now getting out of their beds, the desperately ill, or the drunks who had been womanising since earlier that day. Among the latter group was Edward Trent. After picking a couple of pockets he had a few quid stashed in his wallet and was feeling on top of the world.

'See you another time, sweetie.' He stumbled out of the terraced house, gave the woman inside one last, slobbery kiss and a quick fumble, then made his way along the darkened streets, chuckling and congratulating himself. You've still got it, matey! he thought proudly. Ain't nothing in a skirt can resist *you*.

He came to a sudden halt. Narrowing his bloodshot eyes, he peered at the headlines on the paper-stand:

LOCAL WOMAN FOUND DROWNED.
POLICE CONFIRM MURDERER
STILL AT LARGE.

Horrified, his mind filled with the sequence of events that night. He saw Patsy struggling in the water, pleading for him to help her. He recalled the way he had wrenched the plank from the seat and smashed it into her head in a drunken frenzy of rage.

And he was terrified.

Making straight for Dock Lane, he constantly glanced about, more nervous than he had ever been in his life.

Lizzie saw him coming, that burly familiar figure, swaggering and stumbling as he headed for safety. Taking him by surprise, she flung open the door and lunged at him.

'Did you do it?' she screamed. 'Did you kill her, you bastard?' Sobbing and broken, she clawed at his face until, grabbing her by the wrists, he thrust her backwards into the room.

'Shut your mouth, you stupid cow!' He kicked the door shut. 'Want to get me hanged, do you, yelling that sort of stuff to all and sundry?' Sobered by the reality of it all, he pushed her against the wall. 'You don't really believe I killed her, do you?'

'I don't know what to believe,' she choked. 'The police won't leave me alone.' She gabbled on, 'I told them I don't know anything, but they keep coming back . . .'

He threw her into the chair. 'Stop your whining, woman. Tell me exactly what they said.'

She told him how the Inspector had asked her to report anything she might think of that would help track down the killer. 'You didn't hurt Patsy, did you?' she begged. 'Tell me it wasn't you.'

He turned on the charm. 'Of course I didn't hurt her.' Taking Lizzie into his arms, he rocked her backwards and forwards. 'I didn't like her, you know that much . . .' An awful thought struck him. 'You didn't tell the police that we fought, me and your sister – you didn't tell them that, did you?'

'No.' She hadn't said anything because, whatever he was, she still loved him, God help her. But if he *had* murdered Patsy, then that would be a different tale. 'I don't want to believe it was you,' she confessed tearfully, 'but I know how much you hated her. Eddie, I don't know who or what to believe. My head is pounding so hard, I feel I'm going insane.'

'Ssh.' He kissed the top of her head. 'Like I said, I didn't care much for Patsy, no use pretending I did, but what in God's name makes you think I could do a thing like that to her? Drowning her like you would a diseased rat . . . smashing her head in when she was pleading for help. What kind of a monster would I be if I'd done a terrible thing like that, eh?'

He felt her stiffen in his arms, and knew straight away what he had done. 'Slipped up there, didn't I?' he asked cunningly. 'So, you didn't know that part of it, eh?'

When she tried to loosen herself from his hold, he held on even tighter. 'Silly me!' he laughed. 'Letting my tongue run away with me.'

'YOU!' From somewhere she found the strength to free herself. 'YOU KILLED HER . . . *like that?*'

His words made a picture in her mind, and it drove her crazy. Sorrow became rage; she started battering at him with her fists, screaming at him, wanting to hurt him like he had hurt Patsy.

Like a mad thing he turned on her, hitting out with bunched fists, sending her crashing into furniture, snatching her up and knocking her down again, until bloodied and battered, she lay on the floor, her nose split, her front teeth gone and her eyes swelling out of her head.

He looked down on her and laughed contemptuously. And when the laughter stopped, he issued a grim warning. 'If I find you've opened your trap to the police or anyone else – *ever* – I'll be back to finish you off . . . just like I finished your sister.' He had no pity or compassion. *'Do you hear me?'*

Her hands up as though to protect herself, she moved her head in acknowledgement. Blood trickled out of her mouth.

'Good girl.' He grabbed her purse and emptied it, leaving a few shillings. 'There's enough there to get you right away from here – the sooner the better, if you know what I mean?'

He next went to the kitchen, where he stuffed his face with food before leaving. 'Don't forget what I said, Lizzie girl,' he said chillingly. 'One word, and you know what will happen.'

Fearing for her life, she lay still as he went out the door, remaining that way for what seemed an age; she heard the clock chime the passing hours. Drifting in and out of consciousness, she wasn't sure of time or place, or even if she was still alive.

After a time she crawled to the chair and pulled herself up. Going on unsteady legs to the bathroom, she washed and changed and patched herself up the best she could.

Returning to the bedroom, she took the small suitcase out of the wardrobe, packed a few things and left.

She didn't know where she might go, or how she would manage once she got there. All she knew was, if she stayed he would be back. If she talked he would find her and kill her, just as he had killed her sister, Patsy.

And so she left, as silently and quickly as her injuries would allow.

Because just as Patsy predicted, Edward Trent had ruined her life, yet again.

CHAPTER TWENTY-ONE

'CLEAR OFF, YOU filthy devil!' The burly proprietor of a butcher's shop in a little parade a few streets away from Dock Lane, opened his door to find Edward Trent sprawled across the porch and lying in his own vomit. 'Go on, get off with you. I don't want the likes of you on my premises!'

When Trent made no movement, the butcher gave him a vicious prod with the brush-end of his broom. 'Go on, you drunken bugger . . . GERROUT OF 'ERE!'

Opening one eye, Trent rolled over in his vomit and clambered up. 'What the 'ell's wrong with *you?*' His bloodshot eyes met the look of disgust on the other man's face. 'Can't a poor bloke lie his head down for the night, without being poked and prodded awake?'

The big man gave him another shove with his broom. 'Bugger off . . . or you'll feel the sharp end where the sun don't shine.'

'Who the devil d'you think you're talking to, eh?' Trent squared up to retaliate, until he saw the other man's massive, muscular neck. On better days he would not have thought twice about going for the throat, but feeling drained by a night of booze, violence and fornication, he had neither wish nor energy to tangle fists, especially with a man the size of an ox. 'All right, all right! Hold your horses.' He coughed and spat. 'Give me a minute to pull meself together.'

'Pull yourself together somewheres else.' With a mighty shove, the butcher sent him flying backwards, where he fell in a heap on the pavement. 'If I see you round these parts again, it'll be more than a broom-end that comes at you! It'll be a bloody great meat-cleaver!'

Still grumbling and cursing, he went back inside, returning a moment later with a bucket of water, which he slung over the vomit and Trent as well. 'That should wash the stink off you!'

Laughing, he went back inside and slammed the door, leaving Trent hobbling down the street, with water dripping from his every angle.

Heading for a public convenience, he relieved himself and afterwards swilled his hands and face at the sink. He flattened his hair with the palms of his hands, straightened the collar of his shirt and tidied himself up for his next port of call. 'It's your long-lost lover-boy, Lucy darlin',' he crooned to himself in the mirror. 'Up to now I ain't been able to pin you down, but I will, my pretty. Come rain or shine, I'll not give up till I find you.'

Trent had made a trip out to Overhill Farm the day before, to check out the lie of the land. It had been a blow to hear from the village tobacconist that Lucy had moved south many years ago; the man who sold him his packet of baccy seemed to imply there'd been some scandal, but Trent couldn't take it in. One of his headaches was starting up, and the proximity of the river where his son had drowned made a rushing noise go through his head, like the sound of the water on that terrible night. He had had to leave the shop in a hurry.

Maybe Lucy had come back, he thought. Back to Liverpool where she belonged. But where would she go? The thought struck him like a flash of lightning. *To the Irish-woman's house, that's where.*

His next stop was Bridget's old house, the brothel at 23, Viaduct Street.

He banged on the door, until a young girl emerged.

'Can I help you?' she asked politely.

'I want to speak with Bridget,' he growled. 'Tell her I'm looking to find an old friend, and I reckon she's the one to help me.'

Frowning, the girl began to close the door. 'No one called Bridget lives here.'

Trent thrust his foot forward and jammed the door. 'I don't believe you.' He bent his head to her. 'You'd best go and get her,' he threatened. ''Cause if you don't, I might just force my way in. So you'd best shift yerself and do what I say.'

Growing afraid, the girl continued to argue. 'I told you there's no one here of that name. Now please go away!' Again she tried to close the door and again he stopped her, until she called out for help. 'Daddy!' Her voice sailed through the house. 'Dad, it's a man and he won't go away.'

On hearing heavy footsteps come down the stairs, Trent decided to leg it. The man might report him to the police and have him arrested – and then who knew what might happen.

Snatching the girl by the lapels, he told her gruffly, 'If I find out you've been lying to me, I swear I'll be back to punish you.' Although from her demeanour he had a sneaking suspicion she might be telling the truth and if so, that was a real setback in his search for Lucy.

As he ran away, he could hear the girl sobbing, then the man shouting as he ran in full pursuit, 'HEY YOU! COME BACK HERE!'

At the bottom of the street, Trent turned to see the man

gaining ground, so he darted into the ironmonger's and when he saw his pursuer run past the shop, he made a cautious exit, afterwards cutting down an alley and getting away, out of sight.

A short time later, having retreated to a public house in search of ale, he was seated by the window downing pint after pint. 'I'll find her, you see if I don't!' he told anyone who would listen. 'She'll not get away from me this time.'

Bleary-eyed and incoherent, with no one taking any notice of his ramblings, he took to gazing out the window. *And that was when he saw her walk by, a tall woman with a bold step and a pretty face. A woman who stirred a memory deep down inside him.*

She was older than he remembered, but there was something about her – the walk, the profile – something that he recognised from years gone by.

Then it came to him: she bore a distinct resemblance to Vicky Davidson, the wife of Barney and a dear friend to Lucy. He had been told in the village that Vicky and her family had left England and emigrated to America – so what could she be doing here?

Growing excited, he followed the woman, becoming more and more convinced that she was Vicky Davidson.

Unaware that she was being watched, Vicky went into the estate agent's office down the road and seated herself on a chair set before a desk. 'Is it all ready?' she asked the young man seated opposite.

He greeted her with a smile. 'It's all done,' he informed her. 'The house is yours, for twelve hundred pounds.' He handed her the key, together with an envelope. 'Congratulations, Mrs Maitland.'

With his hands in his pockets, and his cap pulled down well over his eyes, Edward Trent strolled into the shop and meandered about as though he was in no particular hurry, examining the For Sale details pinned up on the wall. And when the young man promised to be with him shortly, he merely nodded and looked away, and no one was any the wiser about his true intentions, though he had been slightly thrown to hear the woman being addressed as Mrs Maitland.

'You're the first person I've ever had who's come in to buy back a house they lived in many years ago,' the young man was saying to Vicky. 'You must have loved it very much.'

'Oh we did.' Vicky cast her mind back over the years to those happy days in the little farmhouse, when her three bairns were born, and her beloved Barney had been with her. They had not had a care in the world. Paradise lost, indeed.

None of this felt real to her. It was as though she had stepped back into a time that was so long gone, it might never have existed. And yet it had, for it was stored right there – in her heart, her mind and in her soul. Secure in her deepest memories.

From that first moment when she had returned to this part of her world, she instinctively felt as though she belonged. The poor, war-damaged streets of Liverpool had welcomed her like an old friend. Despite the passage of the years, its character had not changed all that much, and even the very air smelled the same – thick and salty from the Mersey, alive with the essence of people and life. This was her world, this had been the true magic in her life; Liverpool, Overhill Farm, and her precious family.

'How long did you live at the farmhouse?' The young man sensed how she had slipped into her memories and he was intrigued.

Vicky smiled apologetically. 'Sorry, I was miles away. It seems a lifetime ago that we lived there,' she answered. 'My husband Barney and I had our three children in that same house. We lived in it, worked the land around it and were very content.' She said wistfully, 'In fact, the years in that lovely place were the happiest of my entire life.'

'And now you're moving back in?'

Taking the envelope, she stood up. 'That's the idea, yes.'

'With your husband, Barney?'

Deeply moved, she merely shook her head, then said quietly, 'I really must be going now.'

'You do know the house needs a deal of work?' The young agent wanted to sound businesslike.

'Yes, I'm aware of that,' she answered confidently. 'I've already arranged for a builder to renovate some of the original features that have fallen into disrepair, and I've spoken with a decorator and such. I'm assured they can complete the work within a month. Meantime, I intend to stay at the hotel, though very soon, I shall be going down south for at least a week, as the daughter of my old friend Lucy is getting married.'

'Something else to look forward to then?'

'It certainly is. We go back a lot of years, me and Lucy Baker.' She held out her hand to him. 'Thank you so much for all your hard work.'

Before she left, Edward Trent sneaked out of the shop, moving quickly to where he could easily follow her while she could not see him. So! His eyes darkened. Lucy had a daughter, did she? Didn't take her long to get over the death of their own bairn, did it, before she was opening her legs to some other man!

A wedding? He spat on the ground. 'We shall have to see about that, won't we?'

He followed Vicky out of the town centre and on towards the boulevard, where she appeared to be heading for a bus. Suddenly, taking him by surprise, she hailed a passing taxi and was quickly driven away.

'Damn and bugger it!' Trent cursed. Quickly, he made his way back to the estate agent.

The young man was busy with some paperwork when

Trent entered. He looked up and recognised the unsavoury character who'd been hanging around before. His heart sank; he had a bad feeling about this one. 'How can I help?' he asked politely.

Trent lost no time. 'The woman who was in here just now, the one who bought back her old house. Which hotel is she staying in?'

'I beg your pardon?' The young man's initial suspicion strengthened. 'I'm afraid I can't give out confidential information.' Snatching up Vicky's case-file, he slipped it into the filing cabinet and locked it, placing the key into the top drawer of his desk. 'Now, if you have no other business, I'd very much like to get on with my work.' He gestured to his overcrowded desk.

For a moment the two men eyed each other, until Trent wisely decided to leave. However, he had a plan, which he fully intended carrying out sooner the coast was clear.

Later that evening, after forcing an easy entry from the back of the shop, he went straight for the desk drawer, took out the key and opened the cabinet. Skimming through the file, he found everything he needed to know.

Carefully he replaced the file, returned the key to the drawer, and left the shop the same way he had arrived, leaving everything as he found it. After all, the last thing he wanted was for the police to be alerted; particularly since they were still actively searching for the 'monster' who had murdered Patsy Monk. Trent wished now that he'd finished off that stupid bitch Lizzie, too. She'd better keep her trap shut or he'd be along to shut it for her . . .

A wave of giddiness swept over him and he clung to the doorframe for a long moment. Then it passed. Making good his escape, he smiled to himself. 'Handy place, prison,' he chuckled. 'Full of men who know every trick of the trade.'

Not too far away, seated in his car outside Vicky's hotel,

the American private detective was still keeping watch over her.

Taking the opportunity to fill out his surveillance notes for Leonard Maitland, he wrote down his report, at the same time deciding to send a cable to warn him about the other man who watched her.

Your wife paid a further visit to the land agent that I mentioned in my recent despatch. I'm not certain as to what transpired there, but as you know from my previous reports, she had paid numerous visits to a farmhouse at Comberton-by-Weir, both in the presence of the agent and on her own. She also consulted builders and other tradesmen, who consequently joined her on her visits to the house.

Most days she either goes out to the farmhouse or walks the shops in Liverpool; some days she stands by the docks, just watching. She then makes her way back to the hotel, where she remains until emerging the next day, sometimes early, sometimes later, but always on her own.

Before ending this report, I think I should draw your attention to the fact that today, a certain rough-looking man showed a decidedly unhealthy interest in Mrs Maitland. He appeared to follow her to the agent's office, and afterwards he trailed her to the boulevard where she took a taxi back to the hotel.

Would you like me to find out more about this man, should he show his face again? I am sending you a cable that will arrive before this letter, and will await your instructions.

Meantime, rest assured I will be diligent in my discreet observation of your good wife.

There! This report would be on its way to his client in no time at all. And if he wasn't very much mistaken, Mr Maitland would want him to watch that ruffian. Calling up Edward Trent's image, the detective shook his head woefully. 'The guy was up to no good – that much was obvious.'

~

When the cable was delivered to Leonard's office, he tore it open, fearing the worst.

'Are you ready for coffee now, Mr Maitland?' Marybelle, his typist, inched open his office door, visibly surprised when Leonard dismissed her instantly. 'Leave me be, girl!' he snapped. 'I'll let you know when I'm ready to be disturbed!'

Po-faced, the girl returned to her desk outside his office. 'Whatever's wrong with him? He's real grumpy this morning,' she told the woman at the other typewriter.

The woman looked up knowingly. 'Did the mailman bring him a letter from England?'

'No, but he got a cable. Why?'

'That's the reason why he is so touchy, then. I don't know anything about the cable, but he has the letters regularly, as you'd know if you'd been here longer. When he reads them he likes to be alone, with no interruption.'

'Who are they from?' the junior asked curiously.

'If I knew that, I might tell you.'

'Is it to do with his wife, only I heard someone saying how she'd gone off to England and nobody knew if she was ever coming back.'

'If you want to keep your job, honey, you'd best shut your ears to idle gossip.'

'Hmh!' The girl shrugged impatiently. 'I only asked.'

'And I'm only saying, the least you know the better.'

A short time later Leonard rushed out of his office. 'I won't be back today,' he told the woman. 'Call the house tonight if there are any urgent matters to be dealt with.

Meantime, inform Taylor Crompton that the price of grain remains the same; and that if he wants a delivery, he pays top dollar for top-class harvest. If he dithers, call Bambridge and offer it to him. At least he's a regular customer who knows a good crop when he sees it.'

The woman saw how flushed he was, and her concern was genuine. 'Are you feeling okay, sir?'

'No, I'm not.' He took a deep, invigorating breath. 'I have just received a cable that might mean me going to England. I have urgent calls to make, which will be best served in the privacy of my home.'

He issued a few more instructions before enquiring where his son Thomas might be at that moment in time.

'I believe he went to the Southlands,' the stenographer said. 'There seems to be a problem there.'

'Contact him, will you,' he said. 'Get him to come out to the house straight away. Tell him it's urgent!' With that he made a hasty departure.

'The poor guy looks flustered.' Marybelle was intrigued. 'Do you think the cable carried bad news?'

The older woman pointed to the girl's ledger. 'You just get on with the orders, young lady, and leave Mr Maitland's business to Mr Maitland.' She got out of her seat. 'I'll be a few minutes,' she advised. 'I need to catch Jim. He's taking out a few samples of that new seed for Thomas to look at. If I hurry, I might just catch him before he leaves.'

As it happened, she did catch him in time. 'You're to ask Thomas to make his way immediately to the house,' she informed him. 'His pa needs to see him straight away. It's very urgent.'

Jim told her he would deliver the message, and he did.

～

'What's it about?' Deep inside the workings of a massive truck, sleeves rolled up and covered in oil, Thomas was none too pleased to be summoned away. 'I'm in the middle of trying to get this darned machine to work. It cost the company an arm and a leg, and now it's given up the ghost for the third time. I've got a man from the manufacturer on the way, so I can't leave right now.'

'I'm only passing on a message,' Jim protested. 'The boss wants you up at the house and it's urgent. That's all I know.'

Thomas gave a long, weary sigh. 'Jacob!' Calling his right-hand man over, he said, 'It looks like I'll have to leave this to you. When the engineer comes, don't let him swan off without taking a proper look, and don't let him sweet-talk you, either. Like I said, this machine is a rogue. No ifs or buts, Jake. They're to take it back today if possible or tomorrow at the latest, and supply us with a full refund. I want it replaced with one that actually works.'

'They won't agree to a full refund,' Jacob argued. 'You know how tough they are.'

'Not half as tough as I can be! If they won't cooperate, you can tell him from me, their name will stink throughout the farming community, and their business will fall through the floor overnight. Okay?'

Jacob grinned. 'Okay, boss. You got it!'

Wiping away as much of the grease and muck as he could, Thomas leaped onto his motorbike and was away across the fields like the wind. 'He'll never get this machine replaced, not with a full refund!' one of the men exclaimed. 'Not when he already squeezed them down to their knees on the price.'

'Oh, they'll replace it all right, *and* with a full refund.' Jacob was confident. 'They know when he says he'll make their name stink, that's exactly what he'll do.'

'What d'yer reckon the old man wants?'

'Search me.' Like his workmate, he glanced towards

Thomas's speeding vehicle. 'There seems to be some sort of panic on, that's for sure.'

~

Kicking his boots off at the door, Thomas found his stepfather in the drawing room, pacing back and forth like a caged lion. 'What's wrong? What's the urgency?' he asked.

Leonard looked at him for a brief moment, at this big, hardworking man who had grown to be like his own son. 'We need to talk,' he said quietly. 'It's about your mother.'

Thomas stepped forward. 'What about her?'

His face drained of colour. 'Has something happened? She's not hurt, is she?'

Leonard shook his head. 'No, no, son. She's not hurt.' He paused before adding, 'At least, I hope not.'

'What's that supposed to mean?' Thomas stared at him. 'I think you'd best explain. Why am I here? What is it that you so desperately needed to tell me, that you had to drag me away from my work?'

Leonard took a deep breath. 'As you know, your mother went to England, to your father's –'

'I know why she went,' Thomas interrupted, 'and I think there have been enough discussions on that particular issue. I happen to believe Dad was wrong not to tell us how ill he was.'

'I understand,' Leonard answered quietly. 'I know how you feel, and I have to respect that.'

'No, you *don't* know how I feel ... how we *all* feel! We should have seen him through what must have been the worst, loneliest time of his life, and he sent us away. Did he think we were so selfish that we'd resent having to stay by his side and help him? Did he really think we weren't strong enough to cope with it all?'

His voice began to shake with emotion. 'No, Leonard! We all believe he should have given us the choice of leaving or staying. He took that choice away, and we can't forgive him for it. Mother doesn't agree – she never will. So, if she prefers to be with him now, when it's too late and there is nothing we can do, then so be it. That's her choice.'

'Listen to me!' Squaring himself, Leonard stopped Thomas in full, vehement flow. 'Your mother is hurting too. Look, I felt the same, all those years ago. I tried hard to persuade your father that he was doing wrong in sending you all away. But now I think I understand, and maybe I was wrong in condemning his actions. I can't imagine how he must have felt, watching his entire family sail away from him, after he had put himself through what must have been torment . . . drinking himself stupid, fighting and cavorting with street-women, all to make you think he was not worth the saving. When all the while, he was so desperately ill. He did that, yes, and there are those who will always blame him for it.'

He had never lost the image of Barney curled up under the tree, a sorry, broken man. 'In all honesty, could any one of us do what he did? Could we torture ourselves like he did, and all for the ones we love? Look, Tom, maybe it isn't for us to judge his actions, brave or foolish though they might have been. What he did, he did for you – *all* of you. And for the rest of your life, you must never forget that!'

Thomas was taken aback. 'But you sided with us! You said we should try to forget, and carry on with our lives. You did your best to stop Mother returning to England. You said there was nothing to be gained from it, that it would only cause more pain.'

'You're right, I did,' Leonard admitted. 'But only because I didn't want her hurt any more. But now, I'm afraid I may have lost your mother forever, and all because I promised

275

Barney that I would never tell her the truth. I kept my word, but she found out anyway, through Lucy. Now your mother has turned away from me, Thomas. All I hope is that she can find it in her heart to forgive me, the same way I hope you, your brother, and Susie can find it in your heart to forgive your father.'

'Never!' Thomas was adamant.

'Don't say that,' Leonard implored him. 'We can't change the way things were, all those years ago. We did what we thought was for the best; maybe it was, maybe it wasn't. And maybe we will never know.'

He paused. 'There's something else you need to know,' he revealed. 'I've booked a flight to London. I must go to your mother straight away. I'm afraid she might be in danger.'

Thomas was visibly startled. 'What do you mean, in danger?'

Leonard explained. 'Do you recall how we told you of a man by the name of Edward Trent, the same man who came to Lucy's cottage at Overhill Farm and caused the death of little Jamie?'

'Yes, but didn't Edward Trent disappear without trace? Wasn't it rumoured that he'd been hanged for some other crime?' Tom well remembered little Jamie; he and the others had loved playing with the little lad. He had been like a part of their own family, and dark days had followed his death by drowning.

'Nobody ever knew for sure. But now, there appears to be some ruffian following your mother when she goes about her business. From the description, I suspect it might be him.'

Thomas was surprised. 'How do you know all this?'

'Your mother is hurting badly, Thomas. I've been so worried about her that I hired a private detective to keep a watchful eye on her. I receive a report twice a week.' Taking the cable from his pocket he handed it to Thomas. 'This arrived earlier today.'

Thomas read it through quickly. When he had finished, he handed it back to Leonard and in a quiet voice, asked, 'When do you leave?'

'I have booked a flight to London with a private airline; the plane leaves this afternoon at four.'

'Book another seat. I'm coming with you.'

Smiling with relief, Leonard patted him on the back. 'Good man. I was hoping you might say that.' God willing, this could be the first step towards reuniting his family.

Before Tom went off to arrange things, Leonard asked him, 'Is there any word from Susie?'

Thomas shook his head. 'Not recently. Since Mother left, she's thrown herself into her work. The last letter I had from her, she was in New York drumming up business.'

'And Ronnie – have you heard from him?'

Thomas shook his head. 'Nope.'

'I've been wondering . . .'

'What?'

'Well, since no one seems to know of his whereabouts, do you think he might have gone to England, to look for his mother?'

'It wouldn't surprise me.' Thomas grinned suddenly. 'In fact, he might be the ruffian that's following her.'

That brought an answering smile to Leonard's face. 'Could be.' The smile slipped away. 'But somehow I don't think so.'

With that disturbing thought in mind, the two men prepared for their journey.

Leonard fearing for Vicky's safety.

Thomas wondering who the ruffian was that showed such an interest in his mother.

PART FOUR

~

March, 1955

The Wedding

CHAPTER TWENTY-TWO

I N SALFORD, ELSIE Langton watched her grandson from the kitchen window. 'Just look at him,' she tutted, hands on hips. 'Anybody would think he was a child of ten, instead of a man of twenty-two.'

Charlie was of the same mind. 'Gawd Almighty!' He shook his head, rolled his eyes and sighed. 'It's no wonder his mum's chucked him out on his ear. What I want to know is, why should we offer him a roof over his head? He won't work, he lolls around in the garden kicking that damned football about, and if you so much as ask him to help dig the allotment, he carries on alarming. I thought his National Service would have sorted him out, but no. He's about as much use as Andy flippin' Pandy, or Looby Loo, come to that.'

A third voice intervened. 'He's not really lazy. He's bored, that's all.' Ben's daughter Abbie was staying with her father until after the wedding. Having taken to Elsie and Charlie, and having made acquaintance with their grandson Stuart, she often called round to say hello.

'What d'yer mean, he's bored?' Elsie demanded. 'There's enough work round here to keep him occupied. He's not bored, he's downright idle, and if he doesn't buck his ideas up, he'll find himself out on his ear.'

'That's right!' Charlie could never abide with time-wasters, and said so. 'I've worked all my life, man and boy, and even now when I should have my feet up and resting, I'm breaking my back down at the smithy.'

Elsie smiled fondly. 'You love it,' she reminded him. 'You wouldn't be doing it if you didn't.'

'That's not the point, is it?' he commented with a grunt. 'All I'm saying is this: every man has to work for a living, or he's not worth salt.'

'And what about every *woman*?' his wife demanded.

'What's that ye say?' He cupped his earlobe.

Elsie raised her voice. 'YOU SAID EVERY MAN HAS TO WORK FOR A LIVING, AND I ASKED, "WHAT ABOUT EVERY WOMAN?" OR IS IT NOT WORK, WHAT I DO UP AT THE HOUSE?'

Charlie laughed. 'Oh, it's looking for a fight now, is it?'

'If you want one, yes.'

'Oh love, I'm sorry. O' course you work hard, I know you do. It was a slip o' the tongue, that's all.'

'Well, you'd best not let it happen again, or I'll not bother cooking you a meal for a while. Soon teach you a lesson, that would.'

Having got used to their banter, Abbie offered to have a word with Stuart. 'He's not happy doing nothing,' she said in his defence. 'It's just that he doesn't yet know what to do with his life. He's . . . well, he's still contemplating.'

Charlie raised his eyebrows. 'Well, I'll be blowed! Contemplating, is it? If he doesn't soon get off his backside and pay his way here, he can bugger off and contemplate somewhere else, where they'll feed and lodge him for nothing.'

Elsie was not quite so harsh. 'Oh, give over, Charlie, the girl is right. Anyway, I thought you were off to pull up a few o' them cabbages for me? And don't worry about Stuart. Once he's made up his mind as to what he really wants out of life, he'll be right as rain.'

Charlie cupped his earlobe. 'Gonna rain, you say?' He glanced out the window. 'Best get yer washing in then, hadn't yer?'

'YES, AN' YOU'D BEST GET YOUR HEARING AID IN, YOU SILLY OLD SOD!'

Whereupon Charlie scurried out of the room. 'Why didn't yer tell me afore?' he groaned. 'I left the blessed thing out on the garden bench. If it rains as you say, it'll be ruined and no mistake.'

When he left the room, Elsie told Abbie softly, 'He's dead crafty, you know. He doesn't want to pull up the cabbages, so he pretends not to hear.' She put her finger to her lips, and winked. 'Just listen.'

She raised her voice very slightly. 'Good grief, is that a ten-bob note on Charlie's chair? It can't belong to him as he said he were broke, so it must be mine.'

'It's *mine*, yer thieving old divil!' Rushing into the room, Charlie looked shame-faced on finding he'd been tricked and rushed out again. 'Steal the fillings out of a man's teeth, she would,' he grumbled. 'I've always said it: yer can't trust no woman, not even yer own wife.'

While Charlie was outside, Elsie took a moment to speak with Abbie. She had come to like her a lot, as Abbie was a sensible young woman. 'Are you all set for being bridesmaid to your daddy and Mary?' she asked. 'Have you got your dress all ready and waiting?'

She thought Abbie would make a lovely bridesmaid. With her long dark hair and big black eyes, she was a striking little thing.

'Not yet, no.' Abbie was a trifle nervous. 'I'm going out with Lucy and Vicky this afternoon. They're taking me shopping for my dress, and all the bits and pieces.'

'Leaving it late, aren't you?' Elsie was the type who liked everything to be in place weeks before an event. 'I mean, if the dress needs altering, they'll not have much time. It's only four days to the wedding. Before you know it, Easter Saturday will be on us and it'll be too late to start worrying about dresses and such then, won't it, eh?'

Abbie was convinced everything would be all right. 'We visited so many shops in Bedford, I've lost count,' she said. 'There's only two more to visit now, so I've got to get it today, or you're right. It will be too late.'

Elsie sighed. 'It's already too late for Stuart,' she worried. 'Rona and I have nagged at him, threatened him and pleaded till we're blue in the face, and *still* he's made no effort to get himself a decent suit and shirt. If he doesn't get it soon, I've told him, he won't be welcome at the church.' She set her mouth hard. 'I'm not having him show us all up, and that's that!'

Abbie got to thinking. 'Has he got any money?'

'Enough. You know that his dad died a few year ago, and Rona, poor lass, has always given him as much as she could. We help out, too. His grandad might grumble and argue, but he thinks a lot of the lad. He had him helping out at the smithy and gave him a few pounds so he could get some clothes for the wedding, but he still hasn't been anywhere to find any – not that I know of anyway.'

'Would you like me to have a word with him?' Like Charlie, Abbie too had a soft spot for Stuart. 'He might listen to me where he won't listen to you.'

'Yes, why not give it a go. If you think you can make him smarten up, nobody would be more grateful than me and Charlie.'

'Right then!'

A few minutes later, Abbie had run out to where Stuart was kicking the ball. She chased after it and snatching it up, held it tight. 'I want you to come out with me tomorrow morning – will you do that?' she asked.

Stuart launched himself at her, trying to grab the ball though not very successfully. 'Grandma's been on at you, has she?' he asked with a cheeky grin. 'Don't tell me . . . if I don't get myself some decent clothes I'll not be allowed in the church, and I'll shame them by not being there. Am I right?'

'Yes, so will you let me take you shopping tomorrow morning?'

'No. Whatever would folks think if I turned up at some poncey shop with you telling me what to buy?'

Abbie observed this fair-haired young man, with his sky-blue eyes and physique to be proud of. 'They'd think you were a lucky man, to have me looking after you.'

He smiled. 'Thank you, but I'll get my own clothes.'

'I bet you've spent the money and daren't tell your grandad.'

'Then you'd lose your bet!' Digging into his pocket, he took out the money Charlie had paid him. 'It's all here, every penny.'

'So why haven't you bought some decent clothes for the wedding then?' When he didn't answer, she guessed, 'You don't know what to buy, do you?'

'Not really, no,' he confessed. 'I'm not used to getting all trussed up like a joint ready for the oven.'

'I could help, if you'll let me?'

'No!'

'Aw, go on. I promise it won't be too painful.'

'I said NO!'

'No shopping, no ball.' With that she ran off, the ball under her arm and Stuart in full pursuit.

Going at a run he threw himself at her in a tackle, bringing her down. Laughing, she threw the ball into the lake. 'You'll have to swim for it now,' she said, smiling up into his eyes and thinking what a handsome bloke he was.

He made no reply. Instead, he looked into those big dark eyes and he was lost. 'You're a devil-woman,' he teased.

'And you're a coward . . . won't even come shopping to please Elsie and Charlie.' She felt the warmth of his smile and when he kissed her, it took her by surprise. At first she lay there, arms wide, then she wrapped them round his neck and right there, in that wonderful moment, she fell hopelessly in love.

Some time later, Elsie saw them approach, hand-in-hand, talking and laughing. With the ball under his arm, Stuart was dripping wet, and shivering in the cold March air. 'Look at that!' Coming up behind his wife, Charlie was open-mouthed. 'Well, I never!'

Elsie stared at him. 'What are you on about?'

'The lad . . . look at him.' He pointed to Stuart. 'Can't y'see he's soaked to the skin? That little bugger . . . she's only gone an' pushed him in the lake. Well, I never!'

Shaking her head, Elsie walked away. 'Roll on Saturday,' she groaned. 'Let's get this wedding over and done with, afore somebody else gets pushed in the lake!'

'Does that mean me?' Charlie thought he wouldn't put it past her.

'If yer like,' she laughed.

'I should hope you'll have a word with that young madam . . . pushing our grandson into the lake, indeed!'

'Oh I will,' she replied. 'I most definitely will.' She had seen the way they gazed into each other's eyes, and she was thrilled.

'I wouldn't mind betting she's talked him into going shopping with her,' she remarked.

'Never!' Charlie thought it most unlikely.

'Trust me,' Elsie said. 'I might be a bit old in the tooth, but I still know a thing or two, Charlie, me darlin'.'

And what she thought she knew, was that their grandson and Ben's daughter were attracted to each other.

And she was proud as punch.

Charlie, however, had no idea of what was going on. Rummaging in the dresser-drawer, he asked, 'Where did you put my best tie?'

'Well, you'll not find it screwed up in the drawer, that's for sure! I've ironed it.'

'Oh yes, and where is it then?'

'Upstairs, hanging in the wardrobe.'

'An' where've you put me best shirt?'

'Hanging in the wardrobe with your tie.'

He would have gone on, but Elsie intervened. 'Your tie is with your shirt and your shirt is with your Sunday suit. Your shoes are all polished and shining. They're in the wardrobe, all together, and I don't want you moving them. I know what you're like, and I will not have you panicking on the morning. You already know they all fit, and so all you have to do on the morning is to get washed, shave off your whiskers, and get dressed like the handsome fella I wed . . . Gawd help me!'

Charlie wagged a finger. 'It'll not be me panicking on the morning, you'll see.'

'Oh yes, an' who will it be then, eh?' Going into the kitchen, Elsie took a tray out of the oven, filling the house with the warm smell of fresh-baked bread.

Charlie followed her. 'In my experience, something always goes wrong with weddings.'

'Not this time,' his wife assured him. 'It's been planned right down to the last tiny detail. Ben and Mary's wedding will go like a dream.'

'Yes, well – that remains to be seen.'

Many miles north, up in Liverpool, things were already start-ing to go wrong.

Edward Trent had waited and watched while Vicky went about her business. He followed her to the solicitor's office; he trailed her when she was shopping for hats, and he had gone back and forth to the farmhouse when she met with builders and the like. And on every occasion he was both discreet and cunning, invisible as the wind, but present all the same.

Today, wearied with the waiting and eager for her to make her way to Lucy, he took up his position in the public house opposite the hotel where she was staying. He ordered what he considered to be a well-earned pint, and settled back to enjoy it.

Today he had a feeling in his gut that she would be making her way to Lucy. He mustn't lose her. Not now. Not when he had resisted the temptation to waylay the woman and knock Lucy's address out of her by brute force.

So far, he had avoided any direct confrontation with Vicky – not because he didn't want to hurt or frighten her, but because if he caused a furore, she or someone else was bound to call the police.

So he wisely decided to play a waiting game, and today when he was almost at his wits' end, he was certain his patience was about to pay off.

Across the street and out of sight, Leonard was talking with the private detective. 'He's in there.' Pointing to the public house, the detective explained, 'I arrived here about seven, and he was already here, walking up and down the street until the pub opened.'

'And have you managed to find out anything about him?'

The other man shook his head. 'Not much, I'm afraid. He covers his tracks well. All I know is that he's some kind of vagabond. He never gives his name and never gets into trouble. He's a dark horse, that's for sure.' He issued a warning. 'If I were you, I wouldn't approach him on your own. Matter of fact, with him having followed your good wife and all, I think you should call the cops.'

'There's time enough for that,' Leonard replied thought-fully. 'Once the police get involved, he'll clam up. His sort always do. I need to know what he wants with my Vicky.'

With his jaw set hard and his stepson by his side, Leonard made his way towards the public house. 'Leave it to me,' he told Thomas. 'We're just two men looking to quench our thirst, okay?'

Thomas nodded. 'What I'd like to do is take him by the scruff of his filthy neck and shake the truth out of him.'

'Not yet. We don't want to frighten him off.'

Inside the pub, Trent was downing his third pint when they came up behind him. 'I'd like a word with you.' Closing him in on one side, Leonard gestured for Thomas to keep close to the left, effectively blocking any escape route.

'Who the hell are you?' Wide-eyed with fear, Trent looked from one to the other. 'What d'yer want from me? I ain't got no money, if that's what yer after!' Scrambling from the stool, he found himself hemmed in.

'What can I get you gents?' The landlord was a weasel type, with sharp beady eyes. 'Two pints, is it?'

Thomas was about to refuse, but Leonard replied with a smile, 'That'll be fine, yes. Two pints of best bitter, if you please.'

'Coming right up, sir!' He went away to the other end of the bar.

'You!' Taking hold of Trent's arm, Leonard gestured to the far table in the corner. 'Over there . . . NOW!'

'What's yer game, eh? Who are you?' Discreetly escorted across the room, Trent was scared out of his wits; it was one thing beating up a helpless woman, but being faced with two big blokes like this was an unnerving experience.

'Shut up, and keep walking!' Thomas wanted only half an excuse to lay him flat. 'We've a few questions to ask, and if you know what's good for you, you'd better have the answers!'

'Sit down.' Leonard approached the table. 'We won't be disturbed here, so now you can tell me why you've been following my wife all over Liverpool.'

'Your wife?' Trent was filled with dread. 'You must be crazy!' Realising he was in deep trouble, he began struggling. 'You've got the wrong bloke,' he protested. 'I know nothing about your wife.'

As they began shuffling him into the chair, he shouted out, 'Landlord! Hey, landlord, these thugs mean to do me over!'

Already on his way with the beers, the little weasel stopped in his tracks. Looking suspiciously from one to the other, he sensed there might be trouble. 'What the devil's going on here?'

While Leonard was assuring the little man that he had no need to worry, Trent took the moment to break loose.

Thomas went after him, but was stopped in his tracks when Trent picked up a chair and smashed it over his head.

'Hey! I want you out of here – all of you. NOW!' Slamming the beer down on the table, the landlord threatened to dial 999 unless they cleared out.

With Trent already away down the street and Thomas reeling from the blow, there was little choice.

From his safe vantage point in the hired car, the private detective had seen it all. 'Get in!' he shouted as they emerged from the pub. 'We'd best get after him.'

They drove in the direction Trent had fled, but there was no sign of him. They scoured the area relentlessly, but in the end had to give up. 'Like I said, he's a real cunning guy,' remarked the detective. 'It's no use looking any more. We won't find him, not now.'

Disheartened, the two men made their way back to their hotel.

Later, when they were washed and changed, with Thomas having bathed and treated the gash across his forehead, Leonard told him how the next phase of their journey, to visit Vicky at her own hotel, was going to be the most formidable for him. 'I don't know how your mother will react when she sees us,' he remarked nervously as they climbed into a taxi. 'I hope she's had time to reflect on things. My one desire is to put things right between the family.'

Thomas shook his head. 'I wouldn't count on it,' he said heavily. 'You know how stubborn Mom can be.'

He was right, because when Vicky opened her hotel-room door to them, her face fell. 'If you've come to try and make me change my mind, you've wasted your time, the pair of you.' But she let them in all the same. 'How did you know where I was?' she asked, hugging Thomas but keeping her distance from Leonard.

Leonard had only ever kept a truth from her once, and that was when he had given his word to Barney. This time he thought it best to tell the truth. 'I had you watched.'

'You did *what?*' She never imagined he would do such a thing.

'I had to,' he confessed. 'I was going crazy, not knowing where you were or whether you were all right. When you still didn't get in touch, I called in a private detective, just to keep a watchful eye on you, that's all. Just so I knew you were safe.'

Vicky was none too pleased. 'Did you think I wasn't capable of taking care of myself?' she snapped. 'I came here to be among friends, and I'm perfectly safe, thank you!'

'No. It wasn't like that at all,' he replied. 'I ... we ... needed to know that you were safe.' He had missed her so much, he had nearly gone mad. He wondered whether he would ever get her back: it seemed to him that, here in Liverpool, she was reunited with her beloved Barney, even more strongly than before.

'Oh, did you now?' she said crossly. 'So you sent a dirty, scruffy-looking detective to follow me every step I took. Oh, he was clever, or he thought he was, but I saw him, always a step behind, watching every move I made. I thought it was some old tramp after money.'

Shocked at her description, Leonard thought it safer to tell her. 'That was not the private detective,' he told her. 'He is a smart-looking professional.'

'What do you mean? If it wasn't him, who was it then?'

Thomas answered. 'We don't really know. The detective wrote to Leonard to warn him about that particular fella, and that's why we're here, Mom, to try and find out who he is, and why he's following you. We're worried about your safety.'

Vicky was suspicious. 'Really? Are you sure about that, or is this all a devious plan to make me come home? Because if it is, you're in for a disappointment.' She looked angrily from one to the other. 'You, Thomas, because you turned against your own father. Poor Barney! Not one of you children could see the enormity of the sacrifice he made for you – for all of us!'

Her voice shook with emotion as she turned her attention to the older man. 'As for you, Leonard, how can I forgive you? I will never understand how you could have been with me all those years, sharing my life, my days and nights, with the knowledge that you had taken me from Barney. You should be ashamed. You saw how ill he was; you knew he was putting on an act, draining his energy in doing things

292

to turn us against him, when all the time he must have been crying out for us to help him, to be with him.'

When suddenly she was crying bitter tears, Leonard took a step forward. 'Please don't torture yourself,' he pleaded. 'It was what he wanted, you have to believe that.'

'Please, Mother.' Thomas intervened with his own plea. 'Can't we resolve our differences? Don't let it split the family forever.'

Looking up with tear-filled eyes, Vicky asked softly, 'Will you forgive your father for turning us away?'

Thomas shook his head. 'I can't. I just can't. I'm so sorry.'

Looking from one to the other, she said calmly, 'I'd like you to go now. I'm here for Barney, and I'm here for Lucy. You don't need me, any of you. You must all take comfort from each other.'

Leonard could not believe she was turning them away, but as Thomas had already pointed out, his mother had a strong stubborn streak, and besides, she was still deeply shaken by what had happened to Barney. It would take a long time for her to come to terms with that, if she ever did.

'All right, my dear, we'll leave you now,' he said gently, his love for her evident in every word and gesture. 'But we won't be too far away.' Slipping his fingers into the breast pocket of his jacket, he took out a card and laid it on the sideboard. 'That's the name of the hotel where we're staying. Please, Vicky, think about what's happening here. Think about the family. This isn't what Barney intended, you must realise that.'

He looked her in the eye. 'And you're wrong in what you said just now,' he promised in a low voice. 'Because we all love, and need you.'

There was a moment, one brief heartbeat, when her resolve almost melted. Then she thought of Barney and her heart hardened. 'Please go now,' she repeated, and then she turned away.

After she had closed the door against them, she stood with her back to it for what seemed an age, questioning herself. Was she being selfish? Her head told her yes, her heart told her different.

For now though, all she could think of was Barney, that small solitary figure, left alone and terminally ill as they went out of his life forever. Dear God, how lonely and desolate he must have felt. She and the children had gone away, confused and hurt, despising him. But he never stopped loving them. Lucy had told her, 'Barney talked about you, right up to the day he lost his fight to live.'

Falling onto the sofa, she closed her eyes and let the tears flow. 'You were my first love,' she said brokenly. 'My first and last.' Though she had been with Leonard for an age, and she had deep feelings for him, it was never the same passionate, all-consuming love she had felt with Barney. Leonard knew that. And of course, he understood.

CHAPTER TWENTY-THREE

'OH MUM, DON'T fuss so much!' Mary had stood until her legs ached and now she was ready to sit down. 'What on earth are you doing?' she asked Lucy. 'All I asked you to do was snip off a wayward thread.'

'Stand still, child!' Lucy waved her scissors about. 'If you keep fidgeting, you'll make me cut a chunk out of your dress, never mind the thread!' She snipped once, then twice and now she was satisfied.

'There were tag-ends hanging all round the hem,' she explained. 'I shall have words with that dressmaker when I next see her. I shouldn't be getting down on my old knees, not at my age,' she added. 'They're already creaking and groaning as it is.'

Elsie tutted. 'It's your own fault,' she said. 'I did offer to do it, but oh no! You had to do the job yourself, so if yer don't mind me saying, it serves you right if yer old bones ache.'

From the far end of the room came an offer none of them could refuse. 'It's a tipple of the good stuff ye need,' Bridget informed them merrily. 'That'll stop the old bones aching, so it will.'

'Good idea!' Scrambling up with a groan or two, Lucy stepped back to see her handiwork. 'That's better,' she told Mary. 'A job well done, though I say so myself.'

They each had a glass of 'what the doctor ordered', and taking another long look at her daughter in her wedding gown, Lucy was close to tears. 'You look so beautiful,' she said brokenly.

'Aye, so she does!' Bridget nodded. 'And when the groom claps eyes on her he'll be knocked out, so he will.'

Mary's dress was simple but lovely. Straight and slim, with pretty puffed sleeves and a sweetheart neckline, it suited her beautifully. The veil was figured in delicate lace, with a deep scalloped train that fell to just below the hem of the dress. Her hair was caught up in a mother-of-pearl comb which belonged to Lucy, and altogether she made a stunning figure.

Proud Amy was maid of honour, and Abbie was brides-maid; both dressed in long flowing dresses of blue, with posies of pink silk roses and matching silk roses in their hair. 'Youse look a picture, so you do!' Bridget was already three sheets to the wind.

'Stay off the booze, now, Bridget,' Lucy warned. 'Or we'll be carrying you down the aisle.'

Looking proud and glamorous, all the women had turned out in their new outfits: Lucy, Vicky, Elsie, Bridget – all the good women, except for Vicky's daughter, Susie. Her absence on such a day had been a huge disappointment to Lucy and Vicky, though they made little of it, because this was Mary's day.

Vicky had joined in the excited preparations and no one knew how bittersweet were her thoughts. Her own children were not here. The bride was Barney's other daughter, borne by Lucy out of a union with her husband. Had they loved as she and Barney had done? And when Mary was born, small and helpless, did Lucy and Barney feel the same way she and Barney did when their own daughter was born?

Envy and regret tinged her thoughts, and she was ashamed.

Barney had turned to Lucy for comfort, and a kind of love had grown between them. For that she should be thankful. Mary was a lovely girl, Barney's flesh and blood, and today, the biggest day of her life, she was getting wed to Ben. For the moment, little else mattered.

'I hope Charlie is taking good care of the bridegroom,' Elsie declared. '"Go straight to the church", I told him. I hope he was listening, 'cause he's a silly old bugger at times. One time, he lost our old dog on the way to the vet's; he slipped his lead, ran off, and didn't come home for days.'

Bridget sniggered. 'And what happened to the dog?'

Along with the others, Elsie squealed with laughter. 'He found Charlie an' brought him home, o' course!' she said, and the place was in uproar.

'Where's Adam?' Frantic, Lucy looked about. 'I hope he hasn't forgotten he's walking Mary down the aisle.'

'I'm here.' Appearing at the door, Adam looked the part in his dark suit and white shirt dressed with a smart tie. 'Are we ready then?'

Lucy had it all organised. 'The rest of us are all ready to leave, so we'll be away now and will be waiting for you at the church. Give it ten minutes and then you and Mary will follow in the front car. Bridesmaids go in the second car.'

And so they set off as planned.

Having kept herself busy since early light, Lucy suddenly found the occasion overwhelming. Making her excuses, she hurried away upstairs. 'You all go ahead,' she told the others. 'I'll be down in a minute. I've forgotten to collect a hankie.' She smiled tearfully. 'You know how mothers cry at weddings,' she joked.

Her eyes met those of Vicky, who was looking at her with a sincere gaze, as if to say, 'It's all right, Lucy, I understand.' Because didn't she also have those very same feelings, about

Mary, and Barney, and hadn't she come to love Lucy all over again?

Lucy nodded, and made her escape. She was glad Vicky was here, so very glad.

Upstairs, she watched through the window as the others made their way down the path, Elsie organising them all in her inimitable manner, and the others looking up to her, following every instruction. 'Oh Barney, my precious darling . . .' Lucy glanced up at a shifting sky. 'Can you see what's happening? Vicky is here to see your daughter marry. We're friends, Barney, just like always.'

Gulping back the threatening tears, she made her way out to the others. 'Here I am,' she announced with a grin. 'Now let's be off, before we're all late for the big event.'

And so they set off as planned.

~

When Lucy and the women arrived at the church, everyone was there, all gathered outside waiting for the bride. 'Oh Lucy! I'm nervous as a kitten.' Stuart had made his grandparents so proud when he agreed to be best man. 'I keep thinking I've lost the ring and everything.'

'Nonsense!' Lucy was having none of that. 'You'll be fine. Just keep a clear head, that's all you need to do.'

Already the church was close to full with neighbours and well-wishers, as well as those who loved a wedding regardless of whose it was.

Now, at the sound of the organ music striking up, Charlie suggested they should all get inside. 'Else the bride will be in there afore we are.' Feeling important because, after all, he'd been put in charge of the groom, he led the way inside.

As Vicky and Lucy settled themselves in place, Lucy saw

Ben turn to glance at the door. She caught his gaze and smiled encouragingly, and he smiled back, albeit nervously.

Vicky turned to see her son, Ronnie, just a short distance behind, and her heart jumped with surprise – and a deep maternal affection. 'I hope you'll go to him afterwards,' Lucy whispered. 'Oh Vicky, I do so wish you could make your peace with them.'

Suddenly there were others making their way into the church.

'It's Leonard!' Vicky leaned towards Lucy. 'They're all here . . . Leonard's brought Susie and Thomas. Look!' Tears poured down her face as her beloved family trooped into the church, proving their love, and their solidarity. Never had her heart felt fuller. Nor Barney so close to them all. Light poured through the stained-glass windows, and a huge burden rolled from Vicky's shoulders.

As Lucy turned to look, the organ thundered into life, and the majestic chords of The Wedding March rolled out . . . Everyone stood and as the bride went down the aisle, there were gasps of delight and admiration from all sides.

Ben turned and his soft shy smile said it all. Here was his love coming to wed him, his life and his joy.

And, as the service got underway and eventually the rings were exchanged, that love and joy was written on both their faces.

Lucy and Vicky had opted to stand together, and for a moment there were no words whispered between them, though their hearts spoke volumes. At one point, when Ben placed the ring on Mary's finger, Vicky took hold of Lucy's hand and the smile they exchanged said it all.

In that special moment, when Mary and Ben returned down the aisle as man and wife, it was as though Barney walked beside his daughter. With soft, tearful eyes, Mary glanced to Lucy and Lucy smiled encouragingly. They both felt his presence and were comforted. Old sorrows had been put to rest now, and the years between were as nothing.

Outside, the photographs were taken and everyone clapped, and then it was time to leave for the wedding reception.

~

Having driven the long journey down to South Bedfordshire in a stolen car, Edward Trent left the churchyard after the guests, following the wedding party from a discreet distance.

He had recognised Lucy straight away: the eyes, the way she held herself when she walked, the voice, the laughter. Through the greying hair and the laugh-lines, she was still the same woman. The mother of his son. The virgin whom he had deflowered. The woman he should have married. The light, to his darkness.

He wanted her. He needed her.

He glanced at the hand-gun beside him.

A lightning flash seared his brain, and he gasped with the pain of it but the thought drumming through his mind kept him going.

One way or another, he meant to have her.

~

He chose his moment well.

The guests were all inside the hotel, drinks in hand and waiting to be called take their seats at the tables.

Lucy was walking alone in the garden, deep in thought as she strolled the walkways. She was thinking of Mary and Barney, and how proud of their daughter he would have been.

Sitting on the swing, she gave vent to her emotion as the tears ran silently down her face.

That was the moment he decided to intrude.

Having parked the car round the corner and out of sight, he had been lurking behind the fountain. Now, though, seeing Lucy alone, he could not believe his good fortune.

'Well, isn't this cosy, eh?' Taking Lucy by surprise, he stepped forward from his hiding-place. 'Just the two of us.'

Lucy was shocked to the roots. 'YOU!' Clambering to her feet, she looked at Trent in disbelief. Her heart was hammering with shock, and with revulsion. 'I thought you'd be long dead by now,' she whispered. 'I hoped you were. I prayed you were.'

He laughed. 'Sorry to disappoint you. As you can see, my lovely, I'm very much alive.'

Catching sight of the gun in his hand, Lucy instinctively stepped back. 'What do you want? Why are you here?'

'I'm here for you, Lucy.' Darting forward, he grabbed hold of her. 'Oh no, my darling.' Pressing the gun into her side, he whispered in her ear, 'You mustn't scream. I don't want to have to shoot you. Not when I've been through so much trouble to find you.'

Keeping a tight hold on her, he began dragging her towards the car.

'Just keep quiet and do as you're told, and there'll be no trouble. I mean, you wouldn't want anyone to get hurt, would you? Not today of all days. Barney's daughter getting wed, eh?' Jabbing her with the gun, he made her wince. 'I can't believe you let him give you a child. It turns my stomach!' The pain was drumming again, maddening him. Then it was gone.

Suddenly he was quietly charming. 'We'll go somewhere quiet, you and me . . . talk about old times. Make plans. Oh Lucy, my lovely, I can't tell you how many times I thought of this day when I was locked away. Y'see, I've never stopped wanting you. Oh, I've had other women, young and not so young, but they've never made me feel the way you do. I'm worried, because I have to make sure you never get too close to this Adam. He seems to have your favour, and we can't allow that, can we now? Oh no! No, my lovely, you and me belong together . . . for always. But we need to talk first. To decide what to do.'

Lucy kept her silence, because she now realised that he was totally insane. Any minute now, he might burst in on the wedding party and shoot everyone in sight. She was mortally afraid. It was cold, so cold in the garden, and she began to shiver.

Having come out to look for her, Adam saw her in the distance, and was puzzled. Who was she with? Certainly, it was not one of the wedding party. 'Lucy!' he called out, surprised when she did not turn.

Behind him, Leonard sauntered up with a glass of champagne in his hand. 'Is something wrong?' he asked.

Adam shook his head. 'I think there might be.' He began to walk down towards the edge of the gardens.

Concerned, Leonard went with him.

'Lucy, are you all right?' Adam called.

With her arm twisted behind her back and Trent trying to keep the gun on her and open the car door at the same time, Lucy began struggling to escape.

Seeing this, and with Leonard shouting that it was the man who had been following Vicky, the two older men made a lunge for Trent. In the ensuing confusion, Edward Trent pointed the gun at them, Lucy was thrown aside, and as she went down she managed to pull on his leg, enough to unbalance him.

That was when the two men darted forward. Caught in this trap, Trent was like a madman. While Adam tried to get the gun from him, Trent smacked him with a vicious blow on the side of his head. As he fell, Leonard went for Trent, the gun discharged itself and Leonard fell to the ground, where he lay still and silent, seemingly lifeless.

'Jaysus, Mary and Joseph! They've killed him!' Bridget had appeared, and her appalling cry rang through the air. Scurrying into his car, Trent made a dash for it.

He was heading for the open road when two police cars rammed him. Blinded by the persistent pain in his temples, he felt so terribly weary, he tried to reach for his gun but his strength was ebbing fast. Quickly now the police moved in.

'You left a trail of unhappy people behind you,' the officer said as he handcuffed him. 'Stealing cars, breaking into offices and causing trouble in the public house. We have a lot of questions needing answers – and so do our friends in Liverpool,' he stated. 'There's the woman who says you beat her up. She also says you killed her sister. And now we've got attempted murder. Well now, that should be enough to be going on with, don't you think? It'll be the gallows for you this time, chummy.' Snapping shut the handcuffs, he threw Trent unceremoniously into one of the police cars.

~'

Behind them, the ambulance took Leonard away, with Vicky beside him and his family following.

'Don't you die on me, Leonard Maitland.' Vicky's tears fell on his quiet face.

He didn't hear her.

He had no sense of her nearness.

The guests watched him being taken away. 'Dear God, let him be all right.' Lucy was still shaking, her mind in turmoil. 'Edward Trent said we had things to talk about, and then we'd be together forever.'

She felt desperately afraid for Leonard. Poor Vicky was in a terrible state. 'We must go to the hospital,' she said to Adam.

Then, with Adam's arms around her, she felt safer and more at peace than she had been for a long time. 'I'm sorry,' she whispered. 'Sorry for everything. It's all my fault.' It frightened her to realise how any one of them might have been killed.

'No, Mother, it isn't.' Mary too, was shaken, but deeply thankful that Lucy was safe.

'Leonard . . . and Vicky,' Lucy murmured again. 'We must go to them.'

Adam looked at Mary, as though seeking her approval. 'Please take her,' the new bride told him. 'We'll wait for news.' There was little else they could do.

~

It had been touch and go.

With the bullet lodged in his chest, Leonard had undergone dangerous surgery to remove it.

A fortnight later, Vicky having spent every possible moment at his bedside, Leonard finally turned the corner to recovery.

'I love you,' Vicky told him on this bright April morning.

'And are we forgiven?' he asked weakly.

Vicky nodded. 'You were right and I was wrong. It was what Barney wanted. I understand that now.'

~

On a glorious day in mid summer, Lucy made her usual visit to St Andrew's churchyard. She knelt by Barney's little cross and she told him everything that had happened.

'At last, our hearts are settled and we're able to get on with our lives,' she said. 'Abbie and Stuart are already planning a future together, as are Ronnie and Amy. Vicky and the rest of the family have resolved their differences and have returned to America, though of course we'll always keep in touch and hope to see each other again before too long.'

She laid her posy of flowers on the grave and as she arranged them she carried on talking, though somewhat shyly. 'Adam has asked me again to marry him, and this time, I've said yes. We're getting old now, Barney, and we need each other. He's a good man, as you know. I do love him, but not in the same way I loved you. I will always love you, deep in my soul. That's where you will always be, my Barney. I can never change that, nor would I want to. Vicky and I have reached our journey's end now, and we are reconciled. We both love you, oh so much, and we will never forget you. Our four children will love and honour you always. Goodbye, my darling. Goodbye.'

Suddenly a small voice spoke from beside her. 'Is your Barney in Heaven?' The little girl was blonde-haired and blue-eyed, with the look of an angel.

Lucy smiled. 'I hope so, yes.'

'That's where my grandad is,' came the reply. 'He was very special, my grandad. Was your Barney very special too?'

Lucy took the girl by the hand and walked her back to where her mother was waiting. 'Yes,' she whispered. 'My Barney was very special.'

With a smile, she handed her back to her mother, and walked on.

Mary met her, and escorting her to the gate she said, 'I've got something to tell you, Mother.'

'Have you, dear? And what's that then?'

'Ben and I . . . we're having a baby.'

Filled with emotion, Lucy turned to look at her. 'A baby!' The tears fell and suddenly the two of them were embracing. 'Oh Mary, my love, congratulations!' She glanced back at Barney. 'Did you hear that, my darling?' she asked him silently. 'Your daughter is going to make you a grandad.'

They strolled on, talking and laughing, and feeling so incredibly happy. 'A grandchild,' Lucy sang. 'Oh Mary, your daddy would have been so happy.'

'He is,' Mary said. 'Look!' She pointed to the skies. 'Do you think he's given his approval?'

Filled with wonder, Lucy looked up to see the most beautiful rainbow!

~

Six months later, Mary gave birth to a sturdy little boy. They named him after his grandad, for he was strong in character, brave in heart. He was a fine boy, with his grandfather's blood flowing through him. In the years that followed, Barney would have been proud of his grandson.

Here was a special man in the making.

Another Barney.

CHATTERBOX
The Josephine Cox Newsletter

If you would like to know more about Josephine Cox, and receive regular updates, just send a postcard to the address below and automatically register to receive Chatterbox, Josephine's free newsletter. The newsletter is packed with competitions and exclusive Josephine Cox gifts, plus news and views from other fans.

Chatterbox
Freepost
PAM 6429
HarperCollins Publishers
77–85 Fulham Palace Road
Hammersmith
London
W6 8BR

Alternatively, you can e-mail chatterbox@harpercollins. co.uk to register for the newsletter.

Also visit Josephine's website – www.josephinecox.co.uk – for more news.